The Debutante Murder

by

Robin Jansen

The Denton Series

This is a work of fiction. Names, characters, places, and incidents are either the product of the author's imagination or are used fictitiously, and any resemblance to actual persons living or dead, business establishments, events, or locales, is entirely coincidental.

The Debutante Murder

Contact Information: info@thewildrosepress.com

Cover Art by *Debbie Taylor*

The Wild Rose Press, Inc.
PO Box 708
Adams Basin, NY 14410-0708
Visit us at www.thewildrosepress.com

Publishing History
First Crimson Rose Edition, 2016
Print ISBN 978-1-5092-0715-2
Digital ISBN 978-1-5092-0716-9

The Denton Series
Published in the United States of America

"Yesterday, there was a body face down in your flowerbed?"

"It was awful, Yulan. I cannot begin to tell you."

"Try."

Talia touched her forehead as though she had a headache. "I don't even want to think about it."

"A dead body was feet away from you, and you didn't call me?" the American Asian woman wanted to know. "I watch Nancy Place criminality show all the time on TV. This is just the kind of murder she loves to analyze. We both ask tough hitting questions, pay attention to small details, so you can understand we have much in common, but she'll never know about me—her greatest fan. I feel a sense of disappointment."

"Sorry, but you weren't my first thought." Dressed in white cropped pants and a simple navy cotton T-shirt, Talia fastened her vintage state fair bracelet around her wrist.

"Who was the dead person?"

"No introductions were made." For her sanity, Talia tried to make light of a horrific situation.

"Not what I meant." Yulan crossed her arms.

"The media hasn't released the name yet. A body in my yard is hard to think about."

Praise for Robin Jansen

Robin Jansen, at the time writing as Robin Shope, optioned her first book as a major motion film.

Writing under the same name, her book *The Christmas Edition, Journey to Paradise* was made into a film by a Wisconsin Indie company, Salty Earth Pictures. It is now on DVD and also runs on UPLIFT TV.

Robin Jansen is a popular speaker on faith, writing, and books.

Dedication

To my Beloveds
Kimberly,
Matthew,
Wild Boys,
and Lance

~*~

I offer my heart to the love which surrounds me.

~*~

Special thanks to my editor Lori Graham, whose tenacity and vision brought this book together. And who also freed me to write under Robin Jansen.

Chapter One

Her purse was bubble gum pink.

Talia Bonilla swung the bright bag back and forth as she walked the leafy, tree-lined street. The purse held a secret that might reverberate like D-Day on the shores of Omaha Beach, but this time, it would happen in Denton, Texas. Accepted at the Sorbonne to be disciplined in the art of painting, Talia was on her way to share the news with her fiancé, Luis Arroyo.

Her body moved with sultry purpose and a long-legged gait; she crossed Hickory Street pausing just long enough to check her reflection in a store window. Her long, thick, black hair held its spot neatly, kept in place by two antique Mexican sterling clips. Only a few wisps floated down around her pouty lips painted cinnamon red. She straightened her shoulders and gazed at her slim five-foot, seven-inch frame, feeling apprehensive.

Would it come down to choosing between Luis and the Sorbonne? The answer weighed in the balance. Breaking up with Luis wasn't what she wanted but was acutely aware it was a possibility. She knew it wasn't fair to expect him to wait a year, but neither was she ready to remain here and be married. Not yet. Not today. Not next month. Not this year. To become an artist in her own rite was important; there had to be more to her life than being the wife of the county's district attorney.

Then again, with a bit of good luck, he would congratulate her, wish her well, and promise he'd wait. She'd eventually have her two loves—art and Luis.

She sighed thinking about him. Luis's dry sense of humor, his urbane charm, and that smile of his were positively lethal in making women swoon. What if he swooned back? What was that expression? *Out of sight, out of mind.* The ache caused at the thought of him possibly finding someone else nipped at her high heels with each step.

The pedestrian crossing light turned red. Jittery with nerves, she tapped the sole of her shoe on the pavement. Next to her stood a cement-block, sort-of-a man wearing a baseball cap and carrying a newspaper under his arm. The headlines read, *Six Denton County Women Missing*.

In spite of this jolting information, which was new to her, pressing matters of the heart needed her full attention. She'd put the grim headline right out of her mind because Luis waited and she didn't want to be late. He'd be watching the door and his wristwatch at the same time. But the moment she walked through the door, his face would light up as though she were the loveliest woman on earth. Yes, this certainly was D-Day in Denton—decision making time—worthy of being circled on the calendar because the next twenty-four hours would forever change the direction of her life.

Nearly blinded by sunlight glaring off the building, Talia cupped her hand above her brow to see the fifteen-story condo a few blocks east of I-35—her wedding gift from Luis. A generous gift, that is, for anyone else. The problem was the condos faced one another, seeing cement and aquarium-like windows, instead of the sky, trees, and clouds. Luis loved the concierge perk and a building filled with amenities such as a workout room and swimming pool, while she loved the quiet small town streets of cracked sidewalks, arthritic tree limbs, and flowers spilling over the lips of glazed pots.

A cottage house with a garden suited her just fine. Though small, she'd be pleased if they settled in her place. *Why haven't I told him? Where is my voice?* It was probably hidden beneath her lack of courage. Her mama always taught her to please the man which was in direct opposition to how she wanted to live her life. It seemed they should please one another.

Hiding her feelings was the polite thing to do, according to her mama, and she became quite adept at it. On the other side of the Pecos was Luis—charging ahead, making unilateral decisions for both of them, all the while thinking he was taking good care of her. She forgave him for that since it was done out of love, but didn't she deserve more happiness than pretense?

There was no way she could stand beside him in church and say the words *forever, until death do us part. Will love be enough? Will it ever be enough if I'm not fulfilled? Will I come to resent Luis for holding me back?* She was an artist and needed to express herself, not only on canvas but also in her environment.

The light turned green. She pinned her dark eyes on the restaurant, Mellow Mushroom Pizza. Only steps away from the inevitable. Her stomach lurched.

An immediate blast of cool air engulfed Talia as she swung open the restaurant door. Her eyes took a moment to readjust in the dim ambiance of the room. Noticing a tray of Greek pastries, she wondered if the news should be broken to Luis before lunch or after dessert. Ah, there he sat, in the back corner, smiling. Her heart tugged with love for him. Her hands shook. *Am I about to make a mistake*?

Talia walked across the busy room, trying to avoid the servers with heavy trays of pizza. Piped country music played from well-hidden speakers. Pieces of framed artwork, painted by local artisans, hung from the brick walls. A few of them bore her signature in the bottom right-hand corner. She straightened her back proudly as she passed them—desiring her artwork to hang in a famous gallery, like in Dallas, Chicago, New York, or even Paris.

Luis's thick mop of black hair was brushed back, causing a few maverick curls to turn up at the top of his ears. He smoothed them out with his hands, stood, and then pulled out her chair. Just as predicted, Luis's smile came out bright and sunny, just for her.

"Thanks, Luis." She set her purse under the table, lifting her cheek for his kiss as she straightened her cotton dress before sitting.

"Hi, guys, my name is Remi and I'm your server today. May I bring you something to drink?" The server resembled a pixie with her freckled snub-nose and red, curly hair.

"Remi, I'll take your raspberry iced tea with tons of ice."

"Water is still fine for me." By now, Luis was seated and drumming the lip of his glass seemingly distracted.

"I'll be right back with your drink, miss, and take

both your orders."

Luis loosened the tie on his shirt and then undid the top button while he looked at his menu. "What looks good to you today?"

She glanced around to see what everyone else was having while simultaneously realizing the stress of the moment had stolen her appetite. "It's so hot I may just go with a salad."

"Good choice. That's what I'll have, too."

"What happened to your predictable, mid-day protein choice?"

"I feel like something different for today." He closed his menu and looked into her face. She cast her eyes away not wanting him to read her thoughts. He bristled but quickly recovered. As Chief District Attorney for Denton County, he was a master at changing tactics. At times, it made her wonder which Luis Arroyo she loved the most—the no-nonsense District Attorney, or the man who was down to earth and open.

"Talia, how's enrollment in your classes at North Texas shaping up for the fall semester?"

"Great news." Eager to fill the air with words in hopes of relieving the discomfort she felt, Talia put down her menu. "Dr. Hancock, head of the art department, was about to cancel one of my classes due to low enrollment, but five more people registered this morning."

"If these students hadn't enrolled, you'd be part-time, correct?"

"Yes, but I'm not. So, it's a non-issue. Wait until I tell you who I am teaching this semester in my En Plein Air Drawing class…Amanda Pudding."

"You say her name as if I should know her, do I?"

Talia moved her head, blocking his view, so he was forced to look at her and not at the man seated at the table near them. "She's an amazing young talent who's already had her own art show. We went to it together last year on campus, don't you remember?"

Luis didn't respond, so she continued, "I guess not. Anyway, she's had a private art tutor since the age of six, so her gift is highly evolved."

Wherever Luis had mentally gone for those few nanoseconds, he came back. "Since the age of six, huh? That must have been some teacher she had."

"Correct. He's fabulous and pricey."

"But now she has a greater teacher who also inspires…you."

"Thank you, Luis." She laughed, and he did, too. His words did such things to her, like play an invisible violin to her heart, her mind, and her soul. She noticed the tiny crinkles form around his eyes, and when they unfolded, his face was softer.

"Tell me again. What class of yours is she taking?"

"En Plein Air Drawing, French. It's about observing and studying landscape details and drawing compositions of trees, plants, water, and flowers. We also study and draw clouds and ground shadows. Using charcoal, I teach shading techniques and show contrast of light, medium, and dark shades."

"You got me to thinking." He grinned into his water glass.

"What about?" She suddenly wanted to kiss him.

"I worry about you. The economy is bad and seems to be getting worse. Budget cuts happen all over the place, including my office. The fine arts are especially risky and one of the first to go. Have you thought about returning to teaching art in elementary school, Talia? Get a contract with some school district. It's great security. No matter what happens, I want you to be well taken care of."

"What an odd thing to say, Luis. What could happen?" Talia tipped her head in thought. Luis had seriousness, a reserve, unlike anyone she had ever known. He always looked at things more closely, thought more carefully about the worst-case scenario, kept himself a half step apart from others as though to keep from being contaminated by their opinions while forming his own.

"What could happen?" he repeated before displaying a shrug. "Life."

Talia pulled her purse onto her lap, opened it, and looked down at her acceptance letter. *Should I show him now while there seems to be an opening*? *No*, she'd wait just a bit longer. She shut her purse and set it back on the floor. Her creativity was her wings while he was practical. He held her feet to the earth when all she wanted to do was fly far away and paint the sky in newly discovered colors as she went.

"Backup plan. Always good to have one." He drained his water glass.

Talia covered her face with both hands and, peeking out between her fingers, answered, "Stop trying to talk me into going back to public education."

"You love children."

"I do. Very much."

"Without dedicated, talented teachers like you, there may be no more little artists who will grow up to become great Latino artists like del Corazon. Teach them while they are young."

"What is your back-up plan? I bet you don't have one."

"As a matter of fact, I do." Luis matched the corners of his napkin, then slowly folded it before setting it squarely back on the table.

"Tell me."

"I want to build something." He held up his hands.

"Like a house?" She lurched with surprise.

He smiled broadly and shook his head. "No. Nothing concrete."

"I don't understand."

"Let's talk about you."

"Stop deflecting, will you, Luis?" Talia picked up her folded napkin from the table. Flapping it open, she waved it about before dropping it onto her lap. "Having taught at the university is prestigious. It makes my portfolio more appealing and has even opened some doors." Oops, why had she let that slip out?

"Portfolio? Opened doors?" Luis's smile quit and he sat straighter.

"Oh, I might as well tell you. I hope to return to school for my Ph.D. in art." She stopped short of telling him just where it would be. For now, she'd withhold that bit of information.

"What an excellent idea! Doctor Bonilla." He silently clapped his hands.

"Do you really think so, Luis?" The look on his face made Talia's heart pound with such love it turned her voice to velvet pudding.

"Well, your students will miss you along with the women who love your classes at The Creative Art Studio."

"I will miss all of them, too. I love the art studio, along with the owner and all her classes." She pulled her eyes from his and pointed to one of her paintings right behind him. It was of a Spanish Mediterranean courtyard filled with palm trees and flora. The canvas was painted with rich colors of umber, sage, mustard, and crimson. "Luis, as I have told you hundreds of times, my ultimate dream is to have my pieces hung in galleries instead of restaurants. I need additional training to reach the next level."

"That's my dream for you, too. I'll find you a top-notch school. Just leave all the expenses to me. I don't want you to worry about a thing. Just paint."

Oh no. Now he is being sweet. This just makes things harder. Then she noticed the dark circles under his eyes. Not wanting to add to any stress, Talia hesitated, making her voice tender. "Luis, I need to do this on my own, but thank you for your offer just the same. By the way, you look tired. Long work hours again?"

"Long hours *still*. I'm in the middle of a difficult work situation."

"Ah, there's always pressure being an elected official. What's it about this time?" Talia cocked her head to listen.

"I'm caught in a hard spot with the governor."

"Wow, the governor, now that is something new." She leaned forward, her hands trembling as she twisted the napkin on her lap. What words of encouragement could she use to lift his spirits? "I know you are doing your best."

"The citizens of Denton County are using this election year as leverage to bring down crime statistics.

They demand more wins from the prosecution. Now that fracking has been banned in the city limits of Denton, there are more problems."

"A hot button topic for sure. Which do you think is more hazardous, fracking or vertical drilling?"

"Most likely fracking. When the company is drilling, they go vertically and then horizontally. Here in Denton, they are directly under a hospital and a school as well as homes. There are wells within feet of homes. It can destroy houses, send poisonous gases into the air, cause earthquakes."

"But now that it's banned, what does your office have to do with fracking? You are a prosecutor."

"Yes, and my office goes after criminals—those who break the law in this county. For instance, I have evidence on my desk that an oil rig was recently damaged by someone who is a plant in the anti-fracking movement in order to make the protestors seem irrational thus discredit them."

"Impossible."

"Oh my dear, in politics, nothing is impossible. Big companies, big money. Big money wins elections. The oil companies are trying every which way to shoot down the ban since we are sitting on some of the richest shale in Texas. They are even camping on the doorstep of the new Texas governor for legislation that would make it illegal for individual cities to decide fracking laws, making it a state decision. Oil wells could be pumping again in Denton. Aside from how I feel about it, people forget I don't make laws. I enforce them. It's the trickledown effect down from Austin. But I can handle the pressure. After ten years as the D.A., I've learned to take it in stride."

"You don't seem like you are taking this in stride, Luis. My advice to you is to keep your antacids handy."

"I've started carrying them with me." He patted his pocket. "Outside of that, though, there is plenty of crime which doesn't always reach your ears because you are absorbed in your paints and canvas and students," he smiled adoringly, "and also in your lovely garden."

"Be good to yourself. Delegate some cases to your staff." She tucked the last bit of warm bread into her mouth.

Luis paused, then exhaled slowly. "That's a simplistic answer. Not every case worries me. Right now, it's just one in particular."

"Want to talk about it?"

Luis lowered his voice to answer, "In the last few months, six women have gone missing. It's all over the news. Surely, you have heard about it."

Talia cleared her throat remembering the recent newspaper headlines. "As a matter of fact, I have. Ransom, or are they just gone?" Wanting to hear more, Talia also leaned forward; a cold tingle went down her spine.

"There haven't been ransom notes for any of the women." Luis shook his head.

"Then the women are dead?" Talia held her breath.

"No bodies have been found to substantiate that. However, the perp leaves a highly unusual calling card. In all my years in law enforcement, I've never seen anything like this."

"What's a perp?"

"Perp is short for perpetrator."

"And he leaves a calling card. What kind?" Luis

sure knew how to get her attention.

"It's one of those details I can't tell you since it hasn't been released to the public. But let's just say it's quite clever." He winked.

Chapter Two

By the drained look on his face, Talia knew Luis wasn't about to tell her anything more about the calling card, but Talia also knew, given time, she was good at whittling things out of him.

"Okay, then tell me this, do you have any suspects?"

"We have just one suspect and, right now, he's only linked to the third woman, none of the others. That's a big, big problem. To give us more time to get the case together, I wanted him charged with the lesser crime of carrying an unregistered handgun. That we can prove. Instead, another prosecutor in my office charged him with three counts of kidnapping, hoping to get evidence after the fact.

"That's not how I work, and he knows it. That leaves us with a forty-eight hour window before his arraignment to get our case together. Unfortunately, that was twenty-four hours ago. It's not enough time to make it happen. Sam Brimley will be set free and soon. My office will take the full heat from both the public and the press."

"If the women aren't dead, then there's a good chance they're being held against their will, right?"

"There are endless possibilities of why they're missing. They could've left voluntarily, which the families insist is impossible, and frankly, I agree with them. With so many of them gone and a common calling card left, it's highly improbable. Too coincidental. Then there's the worst-case scenario. They might be dead and we just haven't found their bodies yet. And, as you suggested, they might be held involuntarily. For the present, it's all guesswork. Meanwhile, it was my formerly trusted assistant, Alex Monahan, who went behind my back to file court papers to go before the grand jury." Luis rubbed his forehead as if tired of running this through his mind.

"But why would Alex go against you, his boss?" She looked at him. "That doesn't make a bit of sense—oh, he wants your job, doesn't he?"

"Yes. Sam Brimley will walk in a few days and I will get the blame. Tee, we live in a Red state. His timing is spot on with the fall-out on the oil ban, coupled with the elections. The oil companies are backing his run for my job in exchange for his pull to get legislation through making fracking a state decision, not a local decision. Our little town faced down Goliath and won. Do you realize how impossible that was? Yet it happened here, so it might just happen all over the state. The oil companies are running scared. Before Monahan can win, he first has to discredit me. I'm the first link in the cog. You know, I thought I had the governor's endorsement in my back pocket, but now, it appears to be up for grabs." He drew in a breath and held it. "Maybe it's time for me to do something else with my life. Plan B."

"I don't believe that. You have done a wonderful job as Denton County's D.A."

"The voters will decide." He released his breath. "Even though jury instructions tell them not to, jurors tend to convict on emotion. They put too much faith in eyewitnesses who are usually biased and often flat-out wrong. Give me evidence. At the end of the day, cold hard facts and DNA are a prosecutor's best friend. Brimley just might be innocent but no one seems concerned about that. If there's injustice done to him, then many will suffer."

"So, Alex Monahan is using Sam Brimley to discredit you in order to win your seat."

"Exactly."

"You're a noble man, Luis Arroyo. Everyone looks up to you. And no wonder, you're a pillar of the community and a respected prosecutor." Talia reached across the table to squeeze his hand. "A man with integrity."

"Don't be so sure about me. Just like Monahan, there are shadows hidden inside of me, too."

"Not you, Luis."

"Yes, me, Talia. There are temptations in my life I've had a hard time resisting." Luis withdrew his hand to cross his arms over his chest.

"Temptations? Like what?" Her heart sank. His questionable words piqued her interest, yet made her worry at the same time.

The pixie server hustled back with a tall tea glass along with a carafe. She set them down in front of Talia, adding to the center of the table another large basket of baguettes with another small bowl of honey butter.

"Finally. I'm starving," Talia muttered.

"I think we're ready to order. We'll both have the large House Salad with the special dressing," Luis said passing the menus to the waitress.

"Put my dressing on the side, please. Oh, and I would love some of your Italian cheese bread with Parmesan. And a half order of calzones. Thanks, Remi." Talia's dimpled mouth smiled.

"You've got it. I'll bring you more water, sir," the waitress trilled, leaving the table.

"I'm anxious to talk to you, too, Talia, but no more about my work. I get that all day long. Let's talk about the future. Our future."

Talia suddenly panicked. Was he about to tell her he had picked out all the furniture for the condo? She saw it all now—sparse to the point of being cold, modernistic with lots of pops of silver. He had to be stopped. She held up her right hand.

"Wait, Luis…let me go first." It was time for her to launch her mission. Luis had momentarily sidetracked her with talk about politics and missing women. Now she was refocused.

It was good news to have Luis tied up in a new case. That made this the perfect time to jet off to France; he'd be too wrapped up in his work to spend much time thinking about her departure. Decision made; Talia would tell him now.

She breathed in deeply. "Luis, I really…" If she looked into his lovely russet eyes, she'd cave.

"Yes?"

His stare was fixated on the diamond engagement ring. She couldn't stand it anymore; his expression forced her to look into his eyes. Talia thought about all the lovely things he did for her—planted two hundred tulip and daffodil bulbs in her garden, suffered through a cooking class with her, personally cleaned her home when she broke her leg water skiing, held her hand at the hospital for days while her mama passed, and paid her papa's way back to Mexico, where he wanted to live after Mama died. Not only that but he was a great champion of her art, took her to girlie movies, called each morning to say hello, texted during the day to say "hope your day is going well."

"It's nothing, Luis." She figuratively rolled over. "Go ahead and tell me what's on your mind first. I'll wait." A dessert cart rolled right past and she didn't even care. With her next breath, she realized that all she cared about was being with Luis. Living with Luis and having babies. Talia knew that now.

Luis reached across the table for her hands and held them firmly in his. A taut silence followed. He stared into her face, and Talia's heart thumped. *What is he going to say*? When no words were forthcoming, she filled the air with her thoughts, "I'll never forget the day you asked me to marry you. You dropped to your knee right in the middle of the park."

"And you got upset because you thought my knee went out again." Luis chuckled.

"We had been jogging." Talia began to relax. "It was an honest mistake."

"I had trouble getting the ring out of the box."

"And then you dropped it in the grass." Talia's eyes misted with joyful tears, remembering how the tiny hairs on her arms stood up, electrified.

"It didn't take long to find it. Then I asked you to marry me." A smile spread across his face.

"Right in front of a group of bystanders."

"I like to think of them as witnesses." He winked.

"It was a great proposal," Talia gushed, trying to slow her fluttering heart. "I wouldn't have changed a thing about that day."

"Me either. You blessed my life, but Talia, there is something else I have to say."

"Go on." She dragged the steampunk pendant back and forth on the chain. The pendant was mixed media with assorted charm accents of hearts, flowers, and a moon, along with a paintbrush and some delicate Czech beads. The main feature, though, was an old skeleton key. It seemed to catch Luis's eye.

"Hey, love that necklace."

"Thank you. I made it."

"Ah, of course, who else? Your talent amazes me, yet again."

"And this is the key to my heart." She held it up and laughed at herself for being so conventional. This wasn't going to be her D-day in Denton after all. Now that she relaxed a bit, she recalled this restaurant had the best hot fudge sundae.

"You're the most extraordinary woman. There's no way for you to know this because I never told you, but when I got home that night after you accepted my proposal, I called everyone I knew to tell them the loveliest woman in the world was going to be my wife. *Mine*. Everyone was happy for us."

"We have such sweet friends and I love your family. They took me in the moment they met me."

"They all love you. No wonder, you're sweet, kind, thoughtful, and talented. Not to mention gifted. Brilliant," Luis continued dispassionately as if he were making a report. "Tee, you have an inner strength that's rooted in confidence. Don't ever lose it.

"You're flawlessly appealing and stunning…the total package. There is a strength within you which can handle anything life may throw at you."

"Don't tell me… That compliment is about to be followed by a *but*," Talia chided, feeling a wave of love for the man wash over her like a tsunami. He certainly had gifts about him that could turn a potentially bad lunch into the best lunch of her life. They'd work out the relationship kinks. She wanted to wake up with this man every morning for the rest of her life.

"Forgive me, Tee, but I just can't marry you." His eyes watered. Luis showed both grief and firm decision.

"Huh? You can't be serious." She froze. Her heart felt as though it was about to drop from her chest. When she found her voice, she whispered, "You are kidding me, right?"

"I'm so sorry." Luis bowed his head and became interested in a minute crumb on the tablecloth. "I really think we hurried this engagement. I cannot go through with this."

"We've dated for three years." Emotions writhed inside as Talia's voice caught in her throat. She was suspicious of his motives and, without thinking, gave her purse a hard kick. "This isn't a joke?"

"No, Tee. No joke."

"You don't love me anymore?" She hated the sound of her voice, so pleading, so pathetic, so needy. On the inside, she screamed, *please love me!*

He glanced away.

"Wait…a moment ago, you mentioned you have temptations and something about a shadow. Perhaps it comes by way of that pretty law intern in your office? What is her name?"

"Tee…of course not." He shook his head.

"Now I remember her name. Jade."

"This has nothing to do with Jade or anyone else. It has to do with us. This relationship isn't working. Surely, you know it, too. I have sensed dissatisfaction from you for some time now. You and I are in different places with what we want from life. I'm deeply rooted here. And you," he smiled deeply as he spoke, "you are a free spirit and still need to find yourself."

What just happened? A rock plummeted into her gut. The silence between them thickened. A transformation ebbed across Luis's expression. One minute, he compliments her, and the next, he breaks the engagement. What next? It was like trying to read a strange forecast.

Luis glanced at his watch as though he had an appointment. "Please say something, Talia."

"We are not breaking our engagement. *No*." She shook her head adamantly

"You cannot hold me to it." He pressed back tears.

"Hold you to it?" Talia swallowed hard trying to take in his hard words. She paused for a moment to gather her thoughts. "After careful consideration, I have come to the conclusion you are correct, Luis, our relationship doesn't work. I didn't want to admit it even to myself…until now." *Why am I saying this when my instinct tells me to grab hold and never let him go*? Pride wasn't a good attribute when your heart was breaking. But Talia couldn't beg. She refused to make a fool out of herself.

Luis appeared increasingly upset. "Forgive me?"

"You said it aloud. It's official. We're really broken up, done. Finished. Caputo." Talia answered in a strained voice. No longer would she reveal her neediness to him. There was a discordant chord echoing inside. She expected their relationship to take a new direction during lunch and to leave the Mellow Mushroom Pizza Restaurant with a sense of relief. *Where is the relief? The joy of feeling free?* Shock, yes. Confusion, yes. Pain, yes. But, relief, no.

Remi placed their house salads down in front of them, along with cheesy bread and her calzone. After refilling the water glasses, she asked, "Is there anything else you need?"

They shook their heads. Luis and Talia picked at their food in silence, staring down, too hurt to look up at one another. She tried to put a fork speared with lettuce, cucumber, and tomato into her mouth. But when she opened her mouth, the fork didn't go in. Instead, she blurted out in an unintentionally loud voice, "Luis, I never told you this, but I was to wear my mama's wedding dress and mantilla."

The busy room turned quiet.

"You will look beautiful in it someday."

"Someday, I will wear my mama's dress, but not with you, *si*. I spent a lot of time planning our wedding."

"Tee, please keep your voice down. I'll repay you for all expenses. Tell me how much you've spent."

"Forget about the money." Her voice quivered with insecurity. The woman at the next table looked sorrowfully at them.

Luis furrowed his brow tightly. "Of course."

"What did I say to change your mind? What did I do? Did I get you upset about fracking, or, was I not supportive enough about Alex Monahan? You found me lacking in sympathy." Slumping in her chair, the words stuck in her throat. Suddenly, a life without this man seemed tragic. She despised being rejected by anyone—artists, teachers, men, her family, but especially Luis.

"Life is filled with paths. We get on one and think we will be on it the rest of our lives. Not so. Suddenly, without any warning, that path ends and a new one sends us in a fresh direction. That's what happened here. I will always love you, Talia, but it's over." His voice was soft as she sniffled. "Please don't cry."

"Who's crying? I'm not crying. It's allergy season. Do you know how much ragweed is out there this time of the year?" Talia dabbed her tearing eyes with a linen napkin and then blew her nose into it.

"I know this is a hard time for you, especially without your mother. It's only been a year and with your papa returning to Mexico—"

"Please, do not mention my mama, or my papa." Talia swallowed her tears. She couldn't break down and cry in such a public place. *No, not here*. Those emotions were saved for the privacy of her home.

"After reassessing your goals and creating new ones, you'll feel so much better. A fresh perspective always energizes me. It'll do the same for you." Luis was formal and in control again. She detested him for it. He felt so far away. A curtain dropped between them. It was the end of the last act.

Time to leave. She searched the floor for her purse and found it open near Luis's feet. Its contents were spilled all over beneath the table. Scooping everything back inside, she stood. "I'm fine. Oh, and since we are no longer engaged, here's your ring back." Talia pulled it off her finger and held it out in the palm of her hand.

"Don't do that, I want you to keep it." His voice

was nearly inaudible.

"I can't keep it, Luis. It's not proper for me to keep it, especially since you are the one who broke up with me. It says so in my etiquette book. Wait, maybe you take it back if I break up with you? I can't think right now. I need to go home."

"Do with it whatever you choose."

"You're stubborn, but I am more so." She placed it on the table between them.

Luis picked it up and slipped it into his pocket. "If you ever want it back…"

"I won't."

"I will keep this for you until you change your mind."

"I will only change my mind about the ring if you come with it."

The napkin slid off his lap. Reaching for the napkin and finding the envelope from France, he asked, "What's this?"

This can't be happening. Talia flushed. "That's mine. What are you doing? Please hand me the paper."

Straightening his back, he unfolded the paper that held the words spelling her goodbye.

"It's from the Sorbonne." Luis's eyebrows creased together as he read.

"I just…" Talia couldn't think of a way to finish.

An awful silence buzzed in her head. He wasn't a speed-reader, which proved to be agonizing. He read it thoroughly, both pages, pulling it away each time she tried to grab it. It appeared as though he was studying the news. It made him wince several times. His expression chilled.

Now he would think she had planned to leave him

all along. Finally, he exhaled sharply and looked at her. "Wow, Tee, this is wonderful. So, breaking off this engagement isn't such a bad thing. You are landing on a nice pillow. Congratulations on your acceptance."

She bit her quivering lip.

"Well, then I guess that just about says it all." After refolding it, he held it out to Talia.

The Sorbonne letter went back inside her bubble-gum pink purse. She snapped it closed. Face burning with humiliation, she squeezed between the tables on her way out. Once on the street, she hurried toward her car. Her strappy heels hit the pavement with loud *clippity-clop* sounds as she made her getaway. Tears of regret streamed down her face. Soon, Luis caught up to her. "Wait."

"Go Luis! What more can we say to each other that won't simply be unnecessary pain? It's obvious we both came here today with the same purpose in mind and that was to travel in opposite directions. Let's just leave it at that. And please don't ask me to be friends with you." Her throat got so tight she couldn't squeeze any more words through. Luis's face became a blur, wavering like a heat mirage.

"Drive home safely, okay? Call me when you get there. If you don't, I'll call you, Tee."

She stared at him as a cold sadness wormed its way down her back. Luis was gone. Her world had shrunk.

Chapter Three

Relieved to be home, Talia turned into her drive on Locust Street and pulled the keys from the ignition. She sat silently for several minutes trying to absorb what had just happened. It was one thing to plan a break-up and quite another for it to actually happen.

As she reached for the cute purse on the seat beside her, she suddenly wondered how she had gotten here, because she couldn't remember anything—not a person, a stop sign, or any traffic, even crossing over University Street—but here she was, staring at her house, bushes, flowers. *How scary. Talia, you'd better start paying closer attention when you're driving.*

Talia shut the car door then noticed the For Sale sign plunked in front of the two-story, vintage cottage across the street. Although the place had been vacant for well over a year, she assumed the owners would eventually return. *Guess not.*

Curious, Talia crossed over for a closer look. Pots of dead flowers still adorned the porch's crumbling steps. With care not to step on any rotten boards, she walked the L-shaped porch, gazing through the filmy windows into rooms filled with antique furniture. She coveted each piece.

Circling around to the back of the house, a rusted-out radiator leaned against the clapboard. Without hesitation, she hopped up on it in order to peer through the rear window. To her delight, she could clearly see the quaint kitchen. It was perfect with white painted cabinetry. Even the farmhouse sink looked to be in good condition as did the original 1920s linoleum. Feeling brave, Talia had to see more, and after jumping down, pushed on the lopsided gate tangled with wisteria. To her surprise, the yard was huge. She walked around the house admiring the fretwork that badly needed repair. All the unexpected beauty it held made her want to see more. Since it was for sale, she decided to try the door but found it solidly locked.

The weather grew even more hot and sticky. Talia walked back across the street slowly and took a moment to look at her bungalow, examine it as a stranger might. Adorned with shutters and straight lines, the bungalow didn't have any of the delightful trim detail like the cottage house. It was also quite small with overflowing closets and cupboards. Yet, she loved it. Her refuge. She'd surely miss it while in France, but at least, it would wait right here for her return, not like someone else she recently knew. Not quite ready to step inside, she needed fresh air and bird songs to flush away the negativity of the day.

Talia entered through the side gate and wandered through her garden filled with interesting plant life. Due to the cover of the large leafy trees and low-hanging limbs, it felt cooler than the hot street side. The tranquil backyard held a shimmering pond with lazy-drifting lily pads. An errant frog leaped from a flat rock and into the water, sending a shiver down her spine. Surprised, she tried to see where the frog was hiding but saw only her reflection.

She strolled around the yard, pulling up weeds as

she went. Walking made her feel better, although she'd need to walk from here to Mexico in order to notice an improvement. As the sun began to blanche away with night rising—it would soon be the moon's turn to watch itself on the pond's water.

Due to all the panic and falderal about missing women, she locked the gate and scooted up the steps into the dark house. How good it was to be home. Safe. Entering through the foyer, she flipped on the cove ceiling lights, which gave off a soft, reverent glow against the furnishings of the tidy living room/dining room combination. The white-slipcovered couches, piled with embroidered, plump pillows, flanked an old adobe fireplace. A coffee table, made from an old door and neatly stacked with magazines yet to be read, separated the couches. Pictures her mother had painted long ago were hung on every wall as focal points. Throughout the space were skinny pots of colorful orchids.

The landline caught her eye. The light was insistently flashing. Talia hurried across the cool Mexican tiles and pressed play to start the messages.

"Hey, Talia. Call me, okay? I just want to be sure you're all right."

"Tee, are you home?"

"Hi, it's me again. Just checking."

"You really should be home by now."

"Call me now."

Talia sat on the arm of the chair as she listened to Luis's messages. "That's it, Luis? That's all you have to say to me? Yes, I am okay tonight, home safe and sound, but what about tomorrow night, and the next night, and next week? Will you call me then to see how

I am, or is your concern only for tonight?" She felt jittery, her heart fluttering in her chest, like a bird wanting to get out of a cage. She played all the messages a second time, listening to the kindness and worry in his voice, and the tears came.

Dazed, Talia walked to her bedroom where the double-sized bed took center stage, covered with a fluffy white duvet under a myriad of frilly lace pillows. As if pushed from behind, she dropped face down onto it and lay in the darkness with only the light of the moon sifting through the curtains. She remained scrunched in that position until she turned her head to the side. Hanging on the armoire was the vintage Mexican wedding dress and hand-crocheted lace mantilla. For months, she had searched for the perfect gown to reflect the culture that meant so much to her. An off-the-rack dress was nearly chosen until she remembered her mama's, neatly folded and preserved in her trunk. Now there was no need for a gown. It was perplexing how a few hours could change one's entire life.

The phone rang. Talia scooted to the side of the bed and picked up the bedroom extension. Certain it was Luis again, she cleared her throat, took a deep breath, and nonchalantly answered. "Hello."

"Talia you're home, good. Did lunch with Luis go well?"

"Yulan! Oh thank goodness. It's so good to hear your voice."

"Nice to hear yours, too," she said with uncertainty. "Tell me, did the break up go smoothly as we hoped? Or did Luis tell you to go and have fun, that he'd wait for you? But first tell me what you ate? I hear the restaurant has gnocchi with Parmesan cream and black truffle essence to die for." Yulan Yu was on a roll and Talia smiled as she waited for her friend to come to a stop.

"I didn't eat anything, but a roll. Something unexpected happened," Talia explained.

"This doesn't sound good."

"Luis broke up with *me,"* Talia blurted. Punctuating her frustration, she tossed a small bed pillow across the room. It hit her vanity, rattling several vintage Mexican perfume atomizers.

"Oh, sorry, but you knew this might happen when he heard about your desire to go to the Sorbonne."

"No, he broke up with me before then. I never knew I could feel this miserable."

"You need me. Why don't I come over for a girl talk?"

Imagining Yulan's wide almond eyes filled with concern, Talia swung her right hand to her heart. "You are the best friend I could ever have."

"You've got that right. I've known you were a forever friend, ever since I first laid eyes on you in the kindergarten room."

"I think it was because we were the only non-white students in the class."

"Even so, we've been at each other's side through it all, especially the boyfriends who have come and gone. Some were real idiots, do you know that?"

"Luis was different."

"Well, yes, he has a job and doesn't live with his parents. Two points in his favor. And he always treated you like a princess. Three points."

"You know, Luis is my first love."

"And we can discuss what happened when I get there. On the way, I will stop for ice cream. It always has a way of making us feel better."

"Don't you have work tomorrow?" Talia reached for the tissue box.

"Yes, but maybe we can have a sleep over? I can bring my blankets and sleep on the couch."

"I would love that, but for now, I want to be alone. Do you mind?" Talia hugged her knees like a little girl.

"Not at all."

"We will get together soon, okay?"

After the women closed the call, Talia stared at her parents' wedding picture on the bed stand. It was like rewinding time, working her way backward through life. If only she could feel their arms around her, one more time, to quell the ache. Talia scooped up the picture and held it to her breast as though her parents might return in that very moment and hug her right back.

Talia cried that her mama was in heaven and her papa in Mexico but she saved her hardest cry over losing Luis. She loved him even though he had planned their future without really consulting her. She saw her dreams wilt like spring flowers in one hundred degree heat. Her stomach and throat burned and ached with tears of anguish. She felt each tear washing the very life out of her body.

When the tears began to fade, she realized people we love never leave for good. We carry them with us wherever we go. Until today, Talia never thought about not seeing Luis again, even when she dreamed of Paris. Somehow, she always saw Luis in her life. But now, it was like something out of the movies, having to choose between Luis and painting. What was left behind would forever be mourned like holding her mama's hand as she passed, watching her papa as he waved walking away from her and onto the plane, and listening to Luis yell at her to slow down on the sidewalk as she walked away from him. All three left empty space. Memories were encapsulated in moments. There's no running back allowed in order to say different words, no use in wishing life was something it wasn't.

She felt thankful for the time she and Luis had spent together. Thankful her papa was back in his country he so loved. Thankful her mother watched over her. Thankful knowing she would pull through no matter what tomorrow brought to her doorstep. Thankful she had the Sorbonne—her escape hatch. There was tranquility in those thoughts of gratitude. Suddenly, she felt all right because she loved them and they helped shape her life and would shape it going forward. Her tears dried up. After silently pontificating, Talia felt a little better.

More clear-headed now, she knew something was amiss with Luis. Something he wasn't telling her. The conversation seemed to leap gaps between what he said, what he may have thought, and what he might have possibly meant. It kept her awake. She hated insomnia which always came during the worst possible moments. Her brain kept going around and around. It made her get up and walk the floor. Finally, she was able to return to bed and just as she was dropping off to sleep, drifting, the noise of a car pulling into the driveway drew her fully awake.

It was pitch-black. The clock read four a.m. A car engine cut out. A car door slammed. Someone moved outside her window. She bolted upright in bed; blankets fell from around her shoulders. It was several seconds before she realized it wasn't a dream. Someone was in her yard, was up by the house. Words concerning the missing women raced through her mind as fear leapt up as fire, thinking she was about to become the next victim.

She grabbed for her cell but immediately dropped it into her rumpled bed covers and couldn't locate it in the darkness. She reached for the landline and then, changing her mind, set it back on the cradle. Not wanting to turn on a light, her stomach lurched, the room spun. Talia gripped the edge of the mattress, trying to steady herself as she crept out of bed, one foot on the worn floor, then the other. Silently, she tiptoed on the edges of the boards, making sure they didn't squeak. With each step, her heart thumped hard in her chest. She leaned toward the window and lifted the edge of her curtain. She couldn't see anything but the bushes that needed cutting back. Then a car door opened and shut. An engine started. The car pulled out of her drive as headlights moved across the inside stucco walls of her home.

Fear snaked into the rest of her night.

Chapter Four

Sluggish from a sleepless night, Talia yawned and ran her fingers wearily through her hair.

"What is a five letter word for the name of a flower in shape of a star?" Talia asked herself aloud as she scratched her head with a pencil. "An aster!" Sitting on the steps to her porch, she heard a car pass and glanced up in time to see a sea-mist colored Jaguar cruise slowly past. Dropping her pencil, it rolled down a step and settled against her foot. Suspicious over the never before seen vehicle, Talia cupped her hand above her eyes for shade. At first, she thought the driver was checking out the house for sale, across the street.

The car stopped and the window rolled halfway down. His stare was upon her. It wasn't the house that interested him—it seemed to be her. Their eyes met for a split second before he smiled. It gave her the creeps and sent her back into the house to peek out from behind the curtains. The vehicle continued down the street. Just as she began to drop the curtain back in place, the Jag turned around and drove the wrong way, on the one-way street. Certainly, now would be a good time for a squad car to stop this man from endangering lives.

Undoubtedly, that showy, expensive car wasn't owned by anyone in this part of town. Besides, everyone who lived in Denton knew Locust was a one-way street. As part of the neighborhood watch, Talia tore an edge from the newspaper, stepped back onto the porch to see the car more clearly at the other end of the street, and wrote down the license plate number. She slipped it into her jean pocket as the car turned toward Bell Street.

"Oh, you-whoo! Talia!" June Clover, a midsized woman in her late fifties, pushed a wheelbarrow filled with gardening tools through the yard up to her front steps.

"Hi there, neighbor!" Talia set the paper aside and left the shade of the porch.

"Thank goodness I caught you. Now that school is about to start, you've been so busy that we hardly get a chance to visit anymore," June said in a Southern drawl, stopping long enough to pull a tissue from her green Bermuda shorts and mop the little beads of perspiration along her bleached hairline. An apricot-colored, standard poodle high-stepped along next to her.

"Hey there, Lulu." Talia patted the dog's fluffed pom-pom head.

"Wish there was a nice breeze this morning. Winds aren't stirring which means it's probably going to be over a hundred by mid-afternoon."

"Air conditioners are already humming up and down our street. Is your bursitis any better?"

"I woke up with the normal aches and pains, but I woke up," June prattled cheerfully. "I did have a headache, but a baby aspirin took care of that. My big toe was aching a bit, but then I figured I really should forget my pride and buy a larger size of shoes. Can't be a size five forever. I've surely expanded my borders in the last few years." June snorted as she patted her side and quickly continued, "Little Lulu and I are digging up some dead hydrangeas. The drought did them in."

"Look how clean you are! There's not a speck of dirt on you." Talia noticed.

"That's because I haven't started yet." She laughed at herself and then elbowed Talia. "My knees give me such problems. If I'm on them too long, I'm up all night in horrid pain. Oh, by the way, I need a favor. Is Luis coming over today? The UPS man delivered my new backyard grill this morning. I thought maybe he wouldn't mind taking it out of the box and putting it together for me. I'd do it myself but I hit my elbow the other day on the door as I was going outside and it's still a bit tingly."

"Luis won't be coming by to see me, ever again." She blinked back tears.

"Oh? Trouble in paradise, eh?" June reached for the younger woman's hand.

"Well, yes. We've broken off our engagement." Talia drummed the crossword puzzle gently against her thigh, trying hard to ignore Lulu's personal watering of her purple azaleas.

"I'm so sorry to hear that. And here I thought he was such a fine man."

"June, he is a fine man." Talia blinked.

"Well, after breaking your heart, he certainly can't count on my vote in this coming election. We girls must stick together." June gasped, cutting off Talia's sentence before leaning closer. "Was it another woman, my dear? If it was, you can talk to me all about it. I can write a greeting card to cheer you up and send it into Hallmark to see if they would like to publish it."

"I don't feel like talking, but thank you anyway."

"You can tell me. You see, I know all about these matters. I was engaged once myself, years ago, when I first began submitting greeting cards."

"Oh? What happened?" Having shared many backyard chats over the years, this was the first hint of romance, or passion, gone wrong.

June sighed and stared down at her double-knotted tennis shoes. Her face was drawn and unhappy. "It was because of an untimely *indiscretion...*on *his* part, of course." She bit her lip. "When I found out, I broke it off immediately, put on a brave face, made myself a cup of tea with two sugars in it, and then ran myself a nice bubble bath where I spent the night."

"I'm so sorry."

"I took a friend's advice and moved on. That's when I left the city to buy my home right here. I took up gardening and handing out store samples on weekends. Don't feel bad for me." June brightened straightening the buttons on her blouse. "I'm blessed with you for a good neighbor. Look, my knees are shaking already just from taking my garden equipment from the shed. Let's sit, shall we?"

The women sat on lawn chairs and June jiggled her leg as Lulu found a shady spot up on Talia's porch. Talia couldn't help but compare her broken engagement with her friend's, although as far as she knew, Luis had been true. "What happened to your ex-fiancé?"

"I wish I knew for certain, but surely, he's married with a passel of children by now. It's been thirty-five years since I last laid eyes on him. Eventually, I forgave him, but it was too late for us...for me." She shook away her melancholy while shooing a pesky fly. She poked at Talia's newspaper with her hand spade, leaving a trail of dried dirt. "Oh, you do crossword puzzles. Me, too."

"Yes, in fact, I was working one when I noticed a car in the neighborhood that doesn't belong. I wrote down the license plate." She patted her pocket.

"Good for you! We have such a good neighborhood watch going, even if it's just the two of us. No fear, you're perfectly safe with me next door. When my soap operas aren't on and I'm not working in my garden, I spend quite a bit of time looking out the windows. I log in license plate numbers and note anyone who doesn't seem like they belong before calling the police. I have sharp eyes and they're about to become even sharper. I just ordered a brand new pair of binoculars. The UPS man should be bringing them any day now."

Talia raised her eyebrows and spoke from the side of her mouth. "I feel safer all ready."

"Good. May I ask a favor?"

"Ask away."

"My tomatoes are still green but I noticed yours are ready for picking. I need some for the new salsa recipe I tore out of the magazine when I was in the doctor's waiting room."

"Sure. You need them right now?"

"Yes, my cilantro is fresh."

"Not a problem." Talia dropped the newspaper on the lawn chair and went to the shed for a small bucket. When she returned, she held it out to her neighbor. "Here you are. Take as many as you want."

"Oh dear, my knees are really hurting today. Would you mind picking them for me? While on my walk yesterday, I noticed the ripest ones are toward the back, near the bean poles and carrots." June nudged Talia in that direction.

Talia took the bucket and walked past her flowerbeds of heather and lavender, and on past the Mexican Petunia bush and the Butterfly bush that were in full bloom. They seemed to be the only plants doing well in the late summer drought. The air smelled of pond, sun, pine, and an unidentifiable putrid odor. *Dead animal*? Talia shivered as she batted a couple of fat, buzzing flies away from her face.

"Over there! To the right more—my right!" June flailed her arms pointing.

"All right, I see them," Talia called back, shooting a quick smile as she held the bucket in one hand and with the other covered her nose. When she reached the spot, she pulled tomatoes from the vine and carefully placed them into the bottom of the bucket. One, two, three, four.

"You might want to pull up some of your carrots for me, too." June waved. "It'll save me from going to the grocery store in this awful heat."

A bit annoyed over the woman's presumption, Talia weakly returned June's vigorous wave just as she turned, stepped, tripped, and stumbled over an unexpected rock. It was then she noticed flowers were drooping with brown edges. The vegetables looked poorly as well. On her way for the hose, Talia frowned at June who was busily cutting the tips of her herbs.

"You should try my recipe," June happily sang out.

Talia turned on the spigot and grabbed the end of the garden hose, pulling and dragging it along the ground toward the vegetable garden. The hose kept creasing and getting hung up on something making her stop and straighten it out. A buzz of annoying flies hummed around her.

Not watching her footing, Talia tripped again, but this time, she tumbled face down into the pole beans pulling the posts down on top of her. Tangled up, her wind was knocked clear out of her. Talia tried catching her breath, mad at herself for crushing so many of her plants. The water gushed out of the hose, soaking her as a swarm of flies burst into the air.

"Are you all right, dear?" June called, turning off the spigot, and coming closer. Now Lulu had wandered off the porch and sniffed the air in Talia's direction.

"Fine." Talia lay on her stomach and looked closely at what had tripped her. How unusual. It didn't have the normal markings of a branch. Instead, it was smooth and dark brown with bits of hair rising out of it. Puzzled, Talia's gaze followed it to where it jutted out and then disappeared into the undergrowth. It looked familiar but yet out of place. It wasn't a fallen branch. It was a fallen person.

"Hello? Are you all right…?" she asked still lying on her belly, looking closer. The naked leg had an arm draped over it. Fortunately, they were connected. In fact, they were an ensemble, attached to a complete body. But the body didn't move or answer her question. Long dark hair like tentacles swirled about the sickly, puffy face. Talia got to her feet, took a few steps, but dizziness overtook her and she sank down to the roots of an oak.

Okay, okay. Don't freak. It's just a matter of remaining calm while deciding what to do. If she closed her eyes and waited a minute to reopen them, perhaps the woman's body would be gone. Maybe she was seeing a mirage. Talia closed her eyes. But she knew she couldn't sit here forever with her eyes tightly closed. Little by little, she opened them, hoping for the best. The dead woman hadn't budged.

"Are you hurt? Should I call for help? I'd help but my knees are still hurting."

"Call 911!" Talia screamed.

"Oh my! Did you break your leg?"

"There's a body here between my carrots and beanpoles!"

"Is it a coyote? They have been a nuisance in our neighborhood since the new highway went in." June came closer. Her tennis shoes were heavy with mud, creating squeaky sounds with every step.

"Not a coyote, it's a person." Talia shouted, "A female!"

"A female?" June looked perplexed. "What is she doing there? Can she get up? Ask her if she needs something."

"Call 911!"

"You might be seeing things. Poke it with a stick."

"No way."

Talia abruptly stood, taking one last look at the figure. By the sound of the amount of flies and the pungent odor, she knew this woman wasn't okay. The woman was quite dead.

The emergency call was made with June using her cell. Uniform police officers not only quartered off all the flowerbeds, but the entire yard as they waited for the county detectives and crime scene investigators to arrive. Living in a small town, people would know where the body was found, but Talia reckoned the overhead news chopper would soon have it aired so the entire Dallas/Fort Worth area would be very aware as well. That meant Luis would know, too.

Talia sat on the porch steps as June energetically patted her back. County officials arrived, invading her space. The heat had been building all day, closing in, and now she felt she was breathing through a mask. Her throat was dry. Trying to speak, words caught involuntarily mid-sentence and disappeared. There was a bottle of water in the refrigerator, but for now, her legs would not cooperate so she could get it. They felt as though they were lifeless. The smell of the corpse lingered in her hair and on her hands. Even the shower with a fresh change of clothes didn't dislodge the odor. It was genuinely repulsive.

June seemed the opposite. It was as though she had forgotten all about the pain in her knees. The dead woman had somehow given her new life making her animated; her eyes sparkled as she cleared her throat numerous times just to be ready for any on-the-spot questions from a neighbor, the police, or a reporter.

"Do you think we'll make tonight's news?" June bubbled removing her muddy shoes.

"I hope not." Talia rubbed her temples with the tips of her fingers.

"Stop that!" June swatted her shoulder. "You're a heroine and I'm your neighbor. If it weren't for me needing tomatoes for my salsa, there's no telling how long that body would have been out there decaying. Your veggies would get a horrible reputation down at Saturday's Farmers Market.

This was Talia's first experience with a dead body out in the open. Prior corpses had been properly sanitized in funeral homes—well dressed, combed, and made up like they were just taking a lazy afternoon nap. This woman was decomposing. The smell was beyond compare and something she'd never forget. Perhaps this was one of the missing debutantes. Since the woman was left in her yard, would she be next? Luis's security condo with a doorman suddenly appealed to her.

A dark sedan with a flashing light arrived behind the white van with the words CRIME SCENE INVESTIGATIONS printed in black on the sides. The van maneuvered across the front part of the lawn, leaving long brown ruts on her beautiful green lawn. Passing traffic slowed to navigate around all the emergency vehicles while the drivers craned their necks to see what the excitement was about. News helicopters buzzed low overhead as search and rescue crews arrived. Reporters hurried down the road while talking into their microphones. Police held them back. They had work to do before questions could be answered and before the media would be allowed to get closer.

The D.A.'s sedan arrived. Once it pulled to a stop at the curb, the driver's door opened. Out stepped Luis in his dark suit, white starched shirt. Feet on the ground, he straightened his blue tie. There wasn't even a suspicion of a smile on his face, and yet, Talia's heart jumped at the sight of him.

Luis perused the scene, but his eyes stopped when he saw Talia. To her delight, his professional demeanor seemed to instantly melt. His face softened. Swiftly, he walked to her. It was the type of walk that said he still cared. "At first, I didn't believe it when I heard a body turned up in a vegetable garden. Then I really became concerned when I heard it was your vegetable garden."

"Believe it." She slapped her thigh from nerves.

"Are you all right, Tee?" He looked at her tenderly.

"I'm fine." She looked at Luis.

As though Luis might blame her for the pandemonium, June added, "We were only gardening."

Luis gave a quick smile and softened his voice even more. "Did you see or hear anything? Do you have any idea how this happened? What can you tell me?"

Talia shook her head over and over. Her teeth chattered. It was hard talking, putting thoughts together. "I just fell over a body." There was nothing more to add.

She couldn't help but ask, "You told me about missing women. Do you think she could be one of them?"

"DNA and the crime lab will have to determine that."

"Come on, I'll walk you inside, out of the sun, and away from all the attention. You need to rest. As soon as I know you are okay, I'll speak to the crime scene officers."

"Be sure to fill me in." Talia got to her feet but her legs felt like they were going through an earthquake when she tried to take a step.

"Lean on me, sweetie." Luis put his arms around her back to steady her. She felt a rush of gratitude as he walked her up the steps.

"Oh my goodness, Talia! There's news anchor Roy Campbell from the six o'clock news. What a doll. Maybe I should talk to him?" June patted her hands over her hair and then straightened her blouse, undoing the top button.

Luis guided Talia through the bungalow's front door. "Miss Clover, do not speak to any news person, only the police. Do you understand?"

June looked crushed, but agreed as she followed them into the house.

Luis helped Talia into her favorite chair and then went to the kitchen to grab a bottle of water from the fridge. "Here. Drink this and stay inside."

"Thanks Luis." She looked at him gratefully.

"Look, I have to get out there. I need to get a feel for the crime scene in order to do my job. If it's any consolation, the preliminary report phoned into me was that the body has been decomposing for a few days, and with the reports I've gotten on the way here, it doesn't appear she was murdered on your property."

"Just dumped here then," June supposed.

"Luis, wait. Why was she dumped here?" Talia paused, not liking the word dumped. "Let me start again, why was she left here? Why my yard?"

"I, too, find it interesting that she was left in the yard of my fiancée."

"Ex-fiancée." June nodded her head, seemingly unpleased.

"Tee, now that you are okay, I have to get out there," Luis reiterated.

"Yes, go ahead Luis. I'll be fine here with June."

"Good. Take good care of my girl, Miss Clover." Luis took the cell from his shirt pocket and started to scroll through his phone messages as he walked out the screen door.

"Oh my, did you hear what he called you? *My girl.*"

"I'm sure it was just an overreaction in the heat of

the moment."

"How was seeing Luis again?" June asked Talia in a whisper of female conspiracy. "Was it all you hoped it would be? It sounds as though you two are still together. Oh my goodness…do you think our property values will drop because of the body in your garden?"

Chapter Five

Talia leaned back in the chair, rolling a cool plastic bottle across her forehead. She looked across the room at June, who couldn't be removed from the crime scene with a jack hammer.

Luis was close. For a brief moment, he displayed real concern for her. Talia was determined to seize the moment and have a personal moment with him. Sleep would be forever elusive if she didn't. The porch was a good place to wait and catch him before he slipped away. She got to her feet and was reaching for the screen door handle when a woman, with skin the shade of dark chocolate, blocked her path. "Hello? I'm Homicide Detective LaRue Jackson. The Denton D.A. said for me to speak with a Talia Bonilla and a June Clover." She peered through the screen.

"Here, here," June answered, hurrying to the door. She gently elbowed Talia to the side. "Please come right in."

The detective's six-foot frame stepped into the room. The I.D. badge dangled from a silver chain hitting at her waistline. It didn't take Talia long to explain her role in discovering the body; she walked, she fell, she saw.

"Anything out of the ordinary you've noticed lately?" Jackson asked.

"I'm Miss Clover. Call me June. May I go first?"

June raised her hand.

"Certainly." The detective poised her finger on her iPad ready to take notes.

"No, nothing unusual." June shook her head.

"There is something. Last night a car pulled into my drive while I was in bed. I heard someone get out, and it sounded as though they came close to the house, before returning to the car."

"Talia, you never said a word to me about this." Then addressing the detective, June added, "She never said a word to me about it."

Jackson ignored her. "Did you look out your window, Ms. Bonilla?"

"No, I felt too scared to look. The car was in the drive only a few moments before it left."

"The body could have been dumped then," June figured.

"No. There was too much overgrowth. Blow flies, too," Jackson explained.

"I just remembered something, Detective. I don't know if it means anything or not, but, this morning, a car cruised the neighborhood—one I've never seen."

"We're on the neighborhood watch committee," June pointed out.

"Not even an hour later I found the body."

"Maybe it was the car from last night?" June exclaimed.

"Tell me about the car, Ms. Bonilla." The detective turned her back on June.

"It was a sea-mist colored Jaguar convertible. There was a bumper sticker on the back fender, *The Eyes of Texas are Upon You.*"

"Did you get a good look at the driver?"

"I couldn't see his face. Even though the driver's window was halfway down, the sun was in my eyes. Up to this moment, I thought he was looking at me, but do you suppose he was looking to see if the body was still in the garden?"

"Anything else?" Jackson asked, leaving the question unanswered.

"He wore a cap, rim down, hiding his eyes. Then he turned around in a driveway a few houses down to drive back down our street."

"He drove down this street—going the wrong way?"

"Oh, I wrote down the license plate!"

"May I have it?" Jackson asked.

"I must compliment you on your voice, Detective. You should know it's quite calming," June pointedly interjected. "It must come in handy for calming rampaging criminals."

Returning to Talia, Jackson continued, "License number."

"Of course, I put it right in…" Talia slid her hands down inside her pants pockets finding nothing. Then she remembered: After calling the police, she pulled off her clothes and shoved them in the washer, on hot, before jumping into the shower. After a thorough scrubbing, she changed into fresh jeans and T-shirt, the clothes she had on now.

"Oh no…the wash machine!" She leaped over Lulu, curled up in the middle of the room, and dashed into the laundry room, as the female detective followed. Slamming the agitator knob, she pulled open the lid and yanked out the pants. Turning the pockets inside out, Talia held soggy paper pulp.

"Sorry. It was written on newspaper which apparently doesn't hold up too well in hot water." Talia weakly joked as she looked into Detective Jackson's face, noting she was not amused.

"Can you remember any part of it? Think about numbers, letters."

Talia's eyes flickered and then centered on a corner of the ceiling. "Ah, let me think, let me think…do I remember?" She massaged her right temple. "Nope, don't remember—no. Sorry, but how hard can it be to find a sea-mist green Jag with a bumper sticker which says *The Eyes of Texas Are Upon You*?"

Jackson shoved the iPad into her large purse. "Try lemon juice."

"Excuse me?" Talia stepped toward the woman.

"Wash with lemon. It's the only thing that'll get the smell out of your hair and skin, it works on clothes, too. And I'll take those little shreds of paper; you never know what the lab might decipher. Put them in a baggie for me?"

"Sure, I'd be happy to." Talia raked through her kitchen drawers. "Um. This snack size bag should work." She dropped the paper flakes inside and zipped it closed, then handed it to Jackson.

"I'll be going to have a look in your yard now."

Talia and June stood quietly for a moment staring after her. Then the two women dashed to the dining room, kneeling below the line of windows. Their line of vision of the crime scene was positively perfect.

"I bet we can hear everything they say if we just open this window!" June told Talia pushing on it. "Help me get this old window unstuck."

"It's not stuck, it's locked." Suddenly feeling

animated, Talia twisted the lock at the top of the window and shoved it upwards hard, rattling both panes of glass. The women knelt down and peered over the windowsill, heads together to eavesdrop.

"Glad to see your knees are no longer a problem," Talia whispered.

"Marvels of over-the-counter healing are wonderful. And you seem better now, too. Luis was your pick-me-up. Aspirin was mine."

They rose up just above the windowsill. Detective Jackson judiciously walked around the perimeter of the vegetable garden. Her eyes darted back and forth from the body to the street and back again. Luis wore sunglasses, arms crossed over his chest. Today, his hair was parted on the side.

Squatting down next to the body, Jackson asked one of the officers, "Has the Identification Team gathered the evidence yet?"

"No, Ma'am, they have been waiting for you," a young officer answered.

"Good." She looked at him hard for the first time. "When did you get to the scene?"

"I was on duty when the call came in. It took me five minutes to get here."

"And you are Officer?"

"Officer Davila," answered the slender man with a sharp crew cut.

"You know, that officer looks familiar to me. I just can't place him," Talia murmured.

"Shush, if you keep talking, we'll be discovered."

"Is this where Ms. Bonilla fell?" She pointed to an area filled with smashed tomatoes and snapped beans.

He nodded it was.

"Fell right on top of the corpse. Looks like our dead girl here reached out and stopped the living so she'd be found. Who did this to you, Baby? Talk to me." Looking into her face, Jackson remained quiet for a few moments then glanced toward the house. Talia and June ducked, accidentally pulling the curtain rod down, bonking them both on their heads.

"Listening to police business, ladies? I have eyes on the back of my head."

The window slammed shut.

"You don't happen to have any wash for the line, do you?" June asked.

"My jeans and blouse should be done by now."

"I am sure they need a good airing, on the clothes line."

"Too late. The police pulled it down."

"Then it's time to be creative." June slowly moved the window back up a few notches. "Maybe they won't notice us this time. I'm sure they won't think we'd do something like this twice in a row, especially since we were already scolded."

A man wearing a badge with a suit moved closer. He seemed to be taking notes.

"She's been dead a while, Detective Chavez," Jackson said.

"Talia! That means you haven't watered your plants in days? In this heat?" June clucked her tongue.

"Forensics will tell us if she's one of the missing debutantes," Chavez continued.

"I want the results ASAP!" Luis commanded. "Tell the lab this is top priority."

Their voices trailed off, an indication they walked away.

"Be sure to have the CIS team vacuum the body before moving her," Jackson ordered.

Talia got to her feet and helped June to hers. They ran through the dining room, down the hall, and into the living room, following the movement of the officers.

June panted, "I never thought anything like this would ever happen to me."

"It happened to the victim," Talia corrected, looking out the front, having lost her nerve to pull Luis aside. It wasn't the right moment to discuss their broken relationship.

"You know, I may just have to split my evening tranquilizer with Lulu. I think she's probably as exhilarated as we are."

By now, Lulu was laying on her back on the sofa, feet up in the air.

"I don't believe excitement and exhilarated are the words I'd choose."

"What words would you choose?"

Talia thought for a moment before answering. "Murder and mayhem."

"Oh, look, Luis is leaving." June pointed out the window.

Talia's heart ached as he briskly walked toward his sedan, right past her bungalow. She ran through the house and was out the door and down the steps in time to see him drive away. A dull chill crept over her. Didn't he want to check at least one more time on her? She narrowed her eyes feeling crestfallen Luis hadn't bothered to step back inside to say additional words of comfort, or at least advise her to lock her doors and windows.

Before Talia knew whether to be angry or hurt,

before she really understood what he had meant when he referred to her as "my girl," he was gone. And a moment later, June and Lulu were too.

Talia looked around for evidence of Luis ever being in her life—a robe on the back of the bathroom door, his hairbrush on top of the chest of drawers, loose change dropped in a small, decorative dish, his cologne in the bathroom cabinet—but there was nothing. Luis was gone, and yet, he was still everywhere.

At last alone, Talia put on music, drank iced tea with three teaspoons of sugar, and took a long lemon bath.

Chapter Six

"Yesterday, there was a body face down in your flowerbed?"

"It was awful, Yulan. I cannot begin to tell you."

"Try."

Talia touched her forehead as though she had a headache. "I don't even want to think about it."

"A dead body was feet away from you, and you didn't call me?" the American Asian woman wanted to know. "I watch Nancy Place criminality show all the time on TV. This is just the kind of murder she loves to analyze. We both ask tough hitting questions, pay attention to small details, so you can understand we have much in common, but she'll never know about me—her greatest fan. I feel a sense of disappointment."

"Sorry, but you weren't my first thought." Dressed in white cropped pants and a simple navy cotton T-shirt, Talia fastened her vintage state fair bracelet around her wrist.

"Who was the dead person?"

"No introductions were made." For her sanity, Talia tried to make light of a horrific situation.

"Not what I meant." Yulan crossed her arms.

"The media hasn't released the name yet. A body in my yard is hard to think about."

"The corpse should be enough to take your mind off Luis."

"It's Sunday. I bet he's at his office working overtime on this case."

"I know that look."

"What look?" Talia asked innocently.

"You are planning to drive by his office to see if the light is on and if his car is in the parking lot."

"Mmmmaybe."

"Pitiful. Just pitiful." Yulan shook her head.

"You win. I will resist the urge."

"How are you feeling about the breakup? I know it's just been a few days."

"I've missed him every day. He's a big hole in my life, in the middle of my soul. One minute I am ticking along fine, and life is sweet, because I am going to study art in Paris, France. And the next minute, I am totally devastated to be without Luis. My emotions are all over the place. I am slipping and sliding. I love him so much, it makes me ache."

"The disengagement is new."

Talia stopped primping and turned to Yulan. "Disengagement? Interesting new use of the word."

"Between the body and the breakup, you do look worn out. Give yourself time to heal. I know—let's take some girl time together. Maybe take a trip over your Thanksgiving break." Yulan blinked hard. "A trip to see your papa in Monterrey."

"That's just what I need. Yulan, you've only been here a little while and already I feel better." Talia hugged her. "Thank you."

"I think it's my voice that soothes. Soft and low, like all my family, except for my cousin whose voice is like a squawking duck."

Talia pulled her hair up on the top of her head and

clamped it down with a large clip. Immediately tendrils began to fall.

"I'll look up times and prices for travel once you give me the dates. I have lots of saved vacation days. I can take off anytime."

"Are you really sure you want to spend it in Mexico at my papa's?"

"We are there for one another, remember?" Yulan moved from the chair to the edge of the bed. "Change of subject. Talia, you've got to tell me everything about Luis's case. It'll help to make up for the slight of leaving me out of the loop."

"Okay, let me think for a sec." Talia tapped her index finger on her temple. "At lunch the other day, Luis said the evidence is falling apart on their only suspect."

"Are you kidding me? Sam Brimley may walk?" Yulan's chin dropped.

"What? It worries me that you actually know this deviate's name." Talia put her hand on Yulan's forearm.

"All of north Texas knows his name. It worries me that you don't. This is a huge case and it's been in the media for months. I've seen his picture and listened to his sound bites when he screamed out, 'I'm innocent.' He's articulate. Gets right to the point. He's not the kind of handsome you'd notice if he passed you on the street. You're a smart girl, Talia, why haven't you heard about the disappearances of socialites before now?"

"It's summertime and my flowers have never been prettier—that is until it climbed well up into the nineties. A well-kept, weed-free garden doesn't happen by chance. And I also had been busy planning a wedding, remember?"

"Which reminds me, don't forget to change your online social status back to *single*. You mean, Luis actually told you the evidence doesn't fit? What's the evidence?" Yulan begged putting her hands together.

"You change subjects so fast, it makes me emotionally stumble. The *perp*, as Luis refers to him, leaves a unique calling card when he abducts the women."

"Oh my goodness, Talia, tell me about the calling card. I'm dying to know! Ooops, bad word choice. Sorry."

"Luis would never tell me information like that. I even asked. To get the particulars, I'd have to find them on my own, and I'm not sure how to do that, yet." The women faced each other like matadors in a ring.

"*Yet*? I like the sound of that word. Promise him anything, just find out."

"Since I'm no longer seeing him, I'm not sure how that will happen."

Yulan's eyes lit up in contemplation. "Maybe you left something at his place and need it back. And while you're there, you can snoop."

"I don't want to snoop. I need to get him out of my head. Thinking about Luis all day wearies me. So, today I am going to have some fun. The Arts and Jazz Festival is in town this weekend. Please come with me."

"I can't. This afternoon, I'll be at Lewisville Lake with Adie. Of course, there's no real point of going since I can't swim, but at least it'll be cooler than sitting in town where all that concrete heats up the place."

"I thought you didn't like spending time with your cousin."

"I don't. Life according to Adie is all about her. She discusses her latest diet plan, but she's a morsel too thin. She whines about not having enough funds to acquire the latest fashions, but she gets them anyway—thanks to her rich daddy. And of course, she parades her beauty, along with her perfect life, under my nose. Adie is the poster child for superficiality, but sometimes you have to see people you don't particularly care for when you're related."

"In other words, your mom has been needling you about spending more time with her, huh?"

"Yes." Yulan heaved a sigh while perusing the closet. "I wish I could fit into your clothes. Adie thinks I'm a fashion misfit. But, I wear a white lab jacket all day, so what do I care what's on beneath them? Oh, and—look at you. If I didn't know better, I'd think you were going on a date."

"No. No date." Talia waved her away, looking inside her closet. "Have you seen my purse? You know that pink one you gave me for my birthday?"

Yulan raised her voice to be heard through the closet wall. "When you move on, you move on fast."

"What? Of course not." Talia emerged empty handed.

"You look too hygienic to be going somewhere alone, without a purpose." Yulan spotted the purse next to the bed and held it up in the air. "Here."

"Thanks. Have you seen my car keys?"

"Windowsill."

"If Brimley didn't do the crime, then the person behind the kidnappings is still out there."

"Which means, there will be more kidnappings. The festival is in town. It makes the perfect opportunity for the perp to stalk his next victim. Snap pictures of anyone you talk to with your cell phone and then email to me, so I can turn it over to the police if you go missing." Her dark, almond eyes grew into wide circles.

"You know, that's right. In that case, you had better cancel your beach plans and come with me. That'll really impress Nancy Place." Talia held her pink purse in one hand and keys in the other. "Let's go."

"Stop teasing. You know I can't. Look, I've been carrying a whistle and a canister of mace to get the bad guy. Take it with you today just to be on the safe side." Yulan pulled the whistle on a chain from around her collar.

"I think you'll need the whistle more than me in case Adie needs the attention of a life guard and decides to drown in order to meet him," Talia refused as Yulan followed her out of the house.

"The FBI did a profile on this person just before Brimley was caught. They said it is most likely a Caucasian male who wants to be in the position of power. Has had bad relationships with women."

"How can he expect to have a healthy relationship with women if he keeps kidnapping them? He only has himself to blame," Talia teased as she locked her front door.

"Why do you joke in the face of serious matters?"

"In terrible moments of panic, a bit of laughter is a welcome guest. I just made that up. Pretty good proverb, don't you think?" She winked.

"Just be careful. My conscience is now clear." Yulan waved her hand above her head in the air. "If you end up missing, I'll feel unburdened for I did my part in warning you, and I'll attest to that fact when everyone searches for you."

Talia felt a sense of relief her friend wasn't going along. Yulan had a tendency to set her nerves on edge, always focusing on dreadful details, but figured that was due to working with microscopes, blood samples, bodily fluids, and test tubes in Parkland Hospital's lab, six days a week.

What she wanted was a day filled with music and good truck food to get her mind off the negative. No more talk about death and breakups. The women got into their separate cars and drove away.

Traffic was predictably heavy as she headed to the square. While hunting for a parking space, Talia clicked on the radio. '*Another Denton County woman is reported missing. The name is being withheld pending further investigation.*' Talia quickly snapped off the news. Perhaps Yulan was right. Today she meets a stranger and tomorrow she ends up missing. She could hear her friend saying, "I tried to warn her. The last I saw of Talia Bonilla she was holding her bubble gum pink purse—a birthday present from me. Due to my urging she emailed pictures of every man she spoke to that day. I have them right here on my cell."

With the Honda parked on Elm, Talia walked toward the town square. As she crossed the street, a familiar Jaguar wheeled about the corner roaring directly toward her. Ridiculously, she froze in place and held up her purse. The deafening squeal of brakes echoed between the buildings, as smoke blew up from the tires.

Talia stood alone on the hot blacktop as the sports

car screeched to a stop, inches short of her trim figure. Chills ran up her body and across her arms from fright. She remained frozen to the spot as the driver jerked the car into reverse, gears grinding, made a wide turn, driving slowly around Talia. Then it burst around the next corner.

She'd seen it twice now. First, it cruised down her street, now it blew down the street. Was there a body close by to boot? Talia had visions of feet sticking up from a city garbage bin.

Badly shaken, she turned right, where the streets were blocked off for pedestrians today. Talia found a seat at an outside café to peruse the brochure of the day's events. A hot breeze blustered past as she gazed around contentedly.

All of Denton appeared lovely, but particularly, this section of town with charming shops that were outlined by brick sidewalks. In between specialty shops, there were quaint restaurants and small eateries, all hung with colorful awnings and window boxes overflowing with profusions of geraniums, impatiens, petunias and other summer blooms. Talia admired the preservation of the old, reborn factories living and flourishing amid the background of the four-story stone courthouse. Street singers and fiddlers striking up tunes were a common sight. Although the town sported two universities, this particular area was like a village where people warmly greeted one another.

"May I get you something to drink?" the waitress asked beneath the rippling green and white canopy at Cartwright's.

"Yes, do you have raspberry tea?"

"No, just plain tea."

"That'll be fine."

Slowly, the café spot began to fill with people. Couples arrived. Friends sat together. Half the glass of iced tea was gone and she had nearly finished with the chips and guacamole when she noticed an attractive man seated at the next table. What caught her eye was the bouquet of orchids placed in front of him. Talia smiled. He smiled.

"Lovely flowers."

"Thanks. You obviously have an appreciation for them. Take them."

Perhaps in his early forties, his nose was slender making his forehead seem higher. Thin, misshapen eyebrows accentuated his long, sad face. She estimated him to be only a few inches taller than her.

"I was only admiring your flowers. They appear to be a mixture of Foxtail Orchids and Flutterby Orchids. The lace ribbon is a nice touch."

"It's Spanish."

"Of course."

"My girlfriend just broke up with me." He crossed and uncrossed his legs.

"Ouch. Sorry to hear that."

He got to his feet and slowly walked toward her, bouquet in hand. Holding his breath, he asked, "May I join you?"

Talia hesitated. She could almost hear Yulan admonishing her for speaking to a stranger. Only Yulan wasn't here, and it was the middle of a sunny day in downtown Denton, surrounded by hundreds of festival goers. "Certainly. Please."

He offered the bouquet again.

"It still doesn't seem right." Talia pulled back a

loose hair falling in her face.

"Juana, my ex, isn't in my life any longer. I'll only toss them in the nearest trash bin."

"No, don't do that. I'll accept them, gladly. Thank you."

"How about splitting a sandwich with me?"

"I can stay a little while, but I must warn you, my favorite group will be taking the stage soon in Pioneer Park."

The waitress took the order.

"By the way, I didn't catch your name."

"Marco Correa."

"Nice to meet you. I'm Talia Bonilla." She reached across the table and shook hands with him firmly. "Marco Correa? You must be the man who designed the Correa building downtown Dallas."

"I did have a bit of help." A smile swept his face.

She supposed she had seen him on the news during a soundbite, or his picture in the newspaper, but couldn't clearly recall. He was much younger than she previously imagined.

"Impressive. How many floors? Eighty?"

"Close, seventy-five. My office is the entire top floor."

"Of course, the eagle's nest. The view must be dazzling."

"Yeah, you can see for miles, nearly to downtown Fort Worth. Drop by sometime, and I'll show you the panoramic view."

"Thank you, but heights and I don't mix. If it were my building, I'd take up the entire ground level."

"Are you serious?" Marco raised his thick brows and quickly made his sandwich half disappear in two bites, while Talia nibbled self-consciously on hers.

"If I'm higher than ground floor, I get disoriented. It's as if a magnet is drawing me over the edge. I don't like roller coasters, or airplanes either. Sometimes not even step ladders. I get dizzy."

"But you're missing so much by allowing fear to rule you. If you ever feel daring, you have a standing invitation to visit me."

"Okay, but only an act of God would get me up there."

"How do you manage the Texas State Fair?"

"I go to the exhibits and stay off the fairway."

"Oh come on, the rides are great. You can't miss those. It's un-Texan."

"I've always been like this. The only ride I ever went on, other than a merry-go-round, was at the Kiddie Fair near Lake Texoma. Instead of a huge Ferris wheel, it had a much smaller one meant for children, and instead sitting on an open bench, I sat inside a birdcage—safe. I loved that ride. Years ago, when my mother's paintings were on exhibit at the fair, she ran across a vendor who created custom designed bracelets and had this one made for me." Talia held up her sterling silver chain bracelet with an attached birdcage. "I love how the door opens and closes. See? I am rarely without it."

"And I see a bird trapped on the inside."

"There is also a charm of Texas, a Ferris wheel, a hot dog stand, a boat, a teddy bear, and a camera."

"Cute. All the things you'd expect to see at a fair. There's a Mexican proverb, 'Though a cage be made of gold, it is still a cage.'"

"Yes, I know it well."

"There aren't many vendors anymore since so many artisans use online as a means to market their product. Are you an artist like your mother?"

"As a matter of fact, I am. I teach at a university."

"Right here in town? That sounds exciting. We're in complimentary fields."

"We are, but you are the philanthropist." Talia recalled reading about the millions he put into the arts over the years.

"As I have been blessed, so I bless others."

"Beautifully said."

Marco grew quiet.

"Thinking of Juana?"

"You caught me. We dated only a few months but I fell really hard. We planned on being married this summer." His attention went to a woman walking down the street in six inch heels, which seemed out of place in the laid back college town. A gringo, her hair reminded Talia of a dandelion gone to seed.

"Finally! Here you are, clear up in Denton." She rolled her eyes. "I've been looking all over for you. Don't you ever answer your cell, or check messages?"

"Misty, what are you doing here?" He ran his finger down the face of his smartphone.

"Hello," Talia said, but the woman didn't respond.

"I thought you might be at the Dallas Art Gallery, but the receptionist told me where to find you."

"Why would you think I was there?"

"I know about your fondness for that picture by Christina Alvarez. Anyway, there are documents back at the office that need signing. They should have been in last night's mail." Her tone was sharp, reprimanding.

Talia wasn't sure if she should feel prickles of

intrigue, or excuse herself from this awkward situation.

Marco's face flushed. "This will only take a moment. I'll be right back, please wait?" Taking the firecracker by the elbow, he shuffled her down the street, away from earshot. Talia carefully watched their features, trying to read body language. The young woman appeared vaguely agitated and nodded her head in agreement with whatever Marco was saying. In a few moments, Miss Firecracker walked away in a huff. Cheerfully, Marco returned to the table as though nothing out of the ordinary happened.

"It seems I have unexpected, last minute business. The corporate secretary caught some papers I need to add my signature to before tonight. It's important, or I wouldn't leave. Forgive me." Marco remained standing behind his chair.

"Nothing to forgive. Marco, thank you for the lunch."

"Please don't forget the orchids." He walked quickly away.

Talia headed on foot toward Pioneer Park, carrying the large orchid bouquet, and catching the eye of everyone she passed. But, what caught her eye were the courthouse steps that were overfilled with protesters, flooding out across the vast grassy lawn from there.

"In a shocking and unexpected move, Denton's D.A. Luis Arroyo dropped all charges against Sam Brimley this morning. We are speculating his release this Sunday afternoon was to sneak him out of jail, so the media would be caught unawares," shouted a man with a blow horn. Others waved placards, demanding Brimley's re-arrest. The angry faces gave Talia shivers. *Where is Luis during all of this?* She glanced about, but didn't see him.

Even though she had looked forward to this weekend for months, she found herself suddenly wanting to go home. Her mind was everywhere else—the Sorbonne, her classes at the university, her class at the Creative Art Studio, but most of all, on Luis. Feeling raw and exposed, she returned to her car.

When she arrived home, she couldn't help but notice that a realtor was showing the vintage house to a young couple. As she climbed out of the car, they waved.

"Seems like a friendly neighborhood," the potential buyer called.

Coveting the place for her, it was tempting to fib and say something negative about the area. Buying it was a pipe dream for so many reasons; she'd never be able to properly restore it was at the top of the list. Truth prevailed. Talia smiled. "Yes, very friendly, and this is the best part of town to live. She only needs a loving hand to make her beautiful again."

As Talia entered her bungalow, she found it to be naturally quiet, as always. Immediately, she arranged the orchids in a sizeable vase and placed them on the coffee table. It was then she saw the dog-eared pile of *Modern Bride* magazines stacked neatly on the chair. With a sudden surge of determination, she scooped up every last one, carried them outside, and dumped them into the trash. How she wanted to wipe those smiles from the cover brides' faces. But the trash compactor on the dump trunk would do that nicely for her. After closing the metal lid on the situation, she rubbed her hands together and walked back into the house for a long shower.

Slipping into her cotton nightgown, she powered up the AC and sat cross-legged on her bed reading—actually, trying to read. Thoughts of the day kept flooding her mind, pulling her attention from her book. First of all, meeting Marco Correa was more than an honor. What a shock to meet him with a bouquet of her favorite rare orchids. Was this a fate thing, or something she needed to be wary of? Certainly, he was a puzzlement and the secretary was clearly off the charts of sanity.

The worst part of the day was the protest. It wounded her. In the years living here, she couldn't remember ever having seen anything like it. The old courthouse, which now housed a museum, was a place of serenity where artists gathered to sing, or read poetry—the nice order of things that made Denton so unique, not this uncalled for madness.

Hours later, when darkness filled the sky, hunger hit. Talia ordered pizza, a large pizza with sausage and pepperoni. Then a smile spread across her face. "Wait, I need to amend my order. Make that a medium, with double cheese and anchovies. No meat."

Placing the phone back on the cradle, she smiled, realizing she had just pleased herself for once in the pizza ordering process. Talia simply loved anchovies and since Luis wasn't here to complain about the smell, she could revel in them without guilt.

Their relationship had been about pleasing him. Since that spiraled out of control, she could now do as she pleased from fishy anchovies to stressed furniture choices to messing with paints in France. Without warning, pain seared her chest from losing Luis. It caused her to melt into a chair. All that freedom of choice seemed such a small reward for losing someone she loved. How many tins of anchovies would she give up to win back his heart?

Thirty minutes later, the delivered cardboard box was in the center of her coffee table. She ate the warm, soft, gooey pizza directly off a napkin. Cheese hung from her chin and marinara sauce swiped her cheek. It was as though she had never read an etiquette book in her entire life. Finished with dinner, she tossed the carton into the outside trash but not before giving a left over anchovy mustache to August's sweet bride on the cover of the magazine.

Laughing manically, she shut the backdoor behind her. Just as she returned to the couch, she heard a clanking noise outside the kitchen window. Heart thumping, she rose to her feet and moved across the floor toward the direction of the sound. Talia lifted the corner of the curtain and the noise immediately stopped. A slice of a shadow shot past. Her fingertips snapped on the outside light switch, the single porch bulb cast a yellow glow into the yard. Talia yanked the curtains farther apart, looking as far as she could in both directions. Seeing nothing, she moved to the backdoor, and opened it. "Anyone out there?" Her voice shook right along with her hands.

A large, round object lay on the grass. Talia walked to the trash can's lid and picked it up. Neighborhood dogs barked, and in the mix, was Lulu's unmistakable high pitch. Talia turned to see June's window open and Lulu's head peering at her.

At her feet, the cardboard box lay with a few dangling gooey shreds of cheese hanging from the inside lid. Rapidly, she folded the pizza box several times to make it more compact, and then stuck it far down into the trashcan.

There, she thought, *you won't pop the lid up this time*. But, as she looked again into the trash. she noticed the August issue of Bride's Magazine was missing. In fact, digging deeper all the magazines were gone, every last one of them. Someone took them. *Why*? And the bigger question, *who*? The phone began to ring. Talia put a lid on the garbage and sprinted up the steps, back into the house, locking the door behind her.

Her heart stopped for a breath. The caller ID read Luis Arroyo. She picked up on the fourth ring. "Hi Luis."

One by one, she turned off all the house lights and walked room-to-room peering out windows, checking to make sure everything was locked tight.

"You had me worried, Talia. I called you earlier today to check on you, and when you didn't answer, I had visions of you lying outside by sweet potatoes."

"Sweet potatoes are a fall vegetable. I'd be lying among the summer vegetables."

"Okay, then lying out there by summer vegetables."

"Was I lying out there because I fainted from the heat?" Talia wanted to lighten up the conversation a bit while keeping it going.

"I almost drove over there to check." Obviously, Luis had chosen to ignore her pun. "Where have you been?"

"Luis, I didn't lose my life. I just lost you." Still irked about him taking off the other day without a word, she added, "It's none of your business where I was, but I shall tell you just the same. I was at the Arts and Jazz Festival." Talia sat back on the couch drawing her legs up beneath her chin. "I heard about Sam Brimley. Are you doing okay?"

"I'm doing just fine now that an innocent man isn't sitting in jail."

"Where do you suppose Sam Brimley is tonight since he is no longer sitting in jail?" Talia asked, thinking about her backyard incident with the trash.

"Free to go anywhere."

Chapter Seven

From watching the news, Talia feared Luis was on a downward roll.

The release of Sam Brimley, a week earlier, became the hot topic all over the Lone Star State. Enraged citizens called into radio stations and ragged about their disgust to the listening audience.

"Who does the D.A. think he is anyway?" asked one angry southern voice. "Sam Brimley is guilty and that Arroyo D.A. just gave his buddy the key to every debutante's front door."

Another caller suggested, "Let's set up a date between Brimley and Arroyo's girlfriend, if he even has one."

The voices continued, "Since he let a killer go, we can let Arroyo go this re-election. And our fine governor right along with him!"

As expected, the evening news wasn't any better, but Talia couldn't get enough of it. She sat on the couch in her bathrobe and messy hair, drinking a soda, eating chips, and holding the remote—while flipping between all the local stations. A thick coat of bitterness covered her tongue. On the local channel, the case was recounted in graphic terms. She put her soda can down and pressed the volume button up, up, up.

Even the grieving families were paraded in front of the cameras. Sobbing, they begged for the captor to release their beloved daughters, calling names over and over again, as pictures of her interacting with their family flashed on the screen. Each of the wealthy families had already hired the best private investigators their money could buy. Some bought themselves two. And there it was, the mugshot of the infamous Sam Brimley. Yulan was right about Sam being nondescript—brown hair, brown eyes, white male in his mid-thirties of average height and weight. You could pass him on the street and never know you had.

Finally, there was Luis on channel eleven's news, appearing drained but unflappable, on the court steps. He simply explained, "The evidence is inconclusive with no direct link to Mr. Brimley. Under the laws of the State of Texas, there was no reason to hold him any longer at this time. Meanwhile, let the residents rest assured that until the real culprit is behind bars, my office and the police department will not rest. This case is our top priority. Mr. Brimley has been advised not to leave Denton and to keep in touch with authorities."

"Lock up your Denton daughters," one man hollered looking around at all the faces.

A reporter screamed up the steps at him, "Hasn't he been charged with anything?"

"He was brought up on charges we were not ready to prove, whereas he should have been charged with one count of possessing an unregistered firearm."

"But doesn't that violate his parole?" another reporter asked.

"It does. We cannot go back and redo the charge at this point. I take full responsibility of this error."

"Oh, Luis, it's not your fault." Talia clasped and unclasped her hands. "Stop being noble."

“The district attorney’s office sounds as though it’s in a mess.”

Standing tall, holding a briefcase at his side, Luis looked as though he’d gone without rest for days. Reporters leaped forward firing more questions at him to which he only repeated much of his initial statement. Photographers reacted by snapping pictures. Undaunted by it all, Luis remained stoic. He went on to say he had not given up hope the missing women would be found, as well as the perp.

“Good for you, Luis,” Talia whispered. Tonight, she was seeing him through new eyes. He carried the weight of the county on his shoulders. Whatever he did, someone would always find fault. It was too much for him. Too much for any man. What would happen if suddenly he lost all control? Talia wanted to wrap her arms around him and tell him she was there for him. It hurt to see a fine, honest man like him going through this vicious ordeal. Her face was wet with tears. Her head filled with encouraging words she longed to say.

The police not only needed to find the one who did this, but they needed to find those sweet women. Every day, every hour, that passed, the hope of finding them alive became more and more remote.

“This cannot become one of those mysteries gone cold that we watch on TV years and years from now. Families will have no closure. There would be no body to grieve over. Always waiting for their loved one to walk through the front door—the not knowing that will never end.” She realized she had just had part of a conversation with only the walls to listen. Snapping off the TV, she rose to try and release some nervous energy.

Talia paced the floor of her bungalow, thinking there had to be a way to help. If so, she was determined to find it. Passing the worm-wood buffet, she caught sight of herself in the wide mirror above it. Critically, she took inventory of what she saw. Her hands were calm. Her dark hair pulled back into a tight bun, accentuating her high cheek bones. Her eyes reflected determination, and she felt resilient. On the buffet was a framed picture of her with Yulan, standing in front of the Dallas Arboretum from last spring. Talia picked up the phone and dialed her best friend.

"Hello." A sleepy woman answered.

"Yulan!"

"Talia? Is something wrong? Are you okay?"

"I'm fine. Why?"

"It's so late."

"I called to tell you that you were right."

"I knew I was. What am I right about?"

"Yulan, I need to find out about the calling card. There is so much more to this than what is being said on TV—but I have to figure out how to get into Luis's place to snoop."

"Great. I have been heard. What more can I ask of you? Tell me the plan." Yulan yawned loudly into the phone.

"I have no idea. We can talk more tomorrow so I can let you get back to sleep."

"It's okay. Glad you chose me to call."

"We share everything. Always have, always will."

"Yes."

"I will try to come up with a plan. When I do, I will call you back."

"Great, but make it during daylight."

"One more thing. We are going to replace the phrase *snoop* with the phrase *investigate*. It's more antiseptic."

Talia closed the call and went to bed. Would she ever be able to have a good night's rest again in this house?

Sleep came but so did the nightmare. It was bad. She felt trapped by lurking evil. Someone was coming for her. There was no way out. She tried screaming but no sound came out—just rasping, like a dying person.

I need to find a way out of this nightmare and find the path that leads back to Luis's heart.

****

The morning papers read, *An unnamed source at the Denton County Prosecutors' office is citing this as one of a number of cases in which the D.A.'s office has made another hasty decision and has released a suspect prematurely for having been arrested on the basis of flimsy, or flawed evidence.*

Talia finished her morning class preparation at the University, leaving her free to use her lunch break for research.

"May I help you?" the gal at the newspaper front desk asked.

"Hello, I would like to look at all the information on the disappearing women in Denton County." For some odd reason, she suddenly felt flustered.

"Disappearing women, you say?"

"Yes, they disappeared."

"Saying it like that makes it sound like an illusionist's act." She chuckled.

"Okay, the kidnapped women—debutantes." Talia fidgeted with her purse, glancing at the wall clock.

"What you need is in our Information Newsroom. If you go through those glass doors," the receptionist pointed to her right down the hall, "you'll find all our daily back issues on our web. It's a media library of sorts. Just go to a computer terminal and select the dates for the issues you wish to see and the monitor will bring it all up."

Once inside the room, Talia sat down on a padded chair and placed her purse on the floor between her legs. She typed "Denton County Missing Women" into the browser. Way too much information spewed up on the screen so she narrowed it by typing in Denton and dates of the last six months. Nearly fifty articles appeared. Talia wanted to read them all but there wasn't enough time before her next class. Drawing in a breath, she hit print, knowing it was going to be a big load and hoped a supervisor wouldn't hassle her about it.

The picture of the gal whose body she had stumbled over came up on the screen. Just today, the coroner, through DNA, identified the woman as Maria Salas. Attaching a name made it more personal, more real. A family mourned for her. A future snatched away.

Talia read the cause of death was inconclusive. Impossible to have seen her beauty in death, but in life, she had been lovely with her long hair and perfect smile. Talia read on and was relieved to see neither her name, nor June Clover's, were mentioned—only referred to as "bystanders." *Thanks, Luis, for keeping our names out of it, although I am not sure what June will have to say about it.*

The headlines read: *Kidnapper Takes Number Seven—One Dead.* Pictures of each of the missing socialites followed. They all had plenty in common—family connections, private schools, wealth, and such splendor of countenance. Talia studied their faces carefully. They could easily have been beauty queens or movie stars. The world once lay at their feet and hopefully, their feet now didn't lie underground. Talia printed off copies of everything she could find about the case. With two filled boxes, she asked for help to load them into the back of her car.

Once her class was over, Talia hardly noticed the traffic on either side of her as she drove home along I-35. She looked for the Jag in the rearview mirror. It was a relief when it wasn't there. At last, she reached her quiet street without a sighting, and within seconds, she was pulling into her driveway. Talia popped the trunk and was taking out the first of the boxes when she heard. "Oh-you-whoo!"

June sauntered over, swinging her metal bucket.

"Oh-you-whoo yourself, June. Coming for more tomatoes?"

"No thanks. We know how the last foray into your garden turned out."

"That we do. Say, if you're not doing anything, I could use your help." Talia walked up to her house, juggling her purse, keys, and one of the heavy boxes. The doorknob hadn't even turned in her hand by the time her neighbor arrived with Lulu.

"What do you have there?" June asked. "Oh no, don't tell me you're painting the kitchen again. I just remembered…there's a bad catch in my elbow."

"No fear, I am not painting the kitchen, or anything else, right now. I spent my lunch at the Denton News reading all the information on the socialite case. There are copies of articles in the boxes, including the girl who was out there." Talia nodded in the direction of her newly planted lemon grass, compliments of a privately-owned, organic garden center. "After I get the other box from my trunk, I thought maybe you might help me read through these so we can list the women by age, address, where they worked, by whom they were last seen. Anything that might give us a clue as to where they might be and who is responsible for their disappearance." Talia led the way into the kitchen, thumped down her information on the table.

"Personally, I'm thrilled to help," June chirped. "But shouldn't the police do this?"

"I'm sure the police are."

"Then we can help the police by doing the research ourselves."

"We're both personally invested because the girl was found in my garden."

June sat right down at the kitchen table and took out her reading glasses. Talia went to the car and returned with the last of the information along with Yulan, who stopped by to gossip. The three women settled around the table as Talia explained the research.

"This is so exciting!" Yulan sang out.

"I can't wait to dig in," chimed June.

"Thank you, ladies. Now let's get to work. There are three of us and seven women, one is dead. Two of us need to take two girls. June, you take three socialites to read about and then report."

June handed out pencils as Talia set the kitchen timer.

"I want three socialites," demurred Yulan. "I work quickly, and with detailed precision. No one can match me."

"Do you mind June?"

"No." She pressed her lips.

"This is going to take lengthy research which requires focusing on each detail. I'm hoping to find a common link. Let's be careful. Take our time. These girls deserve it. Okay, let's work an hour and see what we've got."

An hour of silent reading and note taking passed as the women divided the information into category piles—background, education, friends, and family. As they worked, Talia first looked at June and then at Yulan. They both were wholly committed to finding the link between the women, which would help catch the perpetrator. They read, scribbled, drank water, and rubbed their eyes. Yulan was the first one to break the silence.

"I'm ready."

"Tell us what you found," June invited.

"Two of mine came from Corinth and one from Shady Shores. Each attended private schools, but not the same private school. The one found just outside your backdoor, Talia, had started public school but then got kicked out for drugs. That's when she was sent to a private school. That record should have been expunged since she was a juvenile. Odd. June?"

"My two are from Denton," June observed. "One lived in the Historic District on Bell. That's just a street over. Oh, my. The other lived in a new subdivision. One went away to boarding school in the east and the other went to a private girl's day school in Dallas."

"What about yours, Talia?"

"One of mine is from Denton and one from Sanger.

Again, wealthy households and private schools, but none were the same school. What surprises me, after going to good schools, why didn't they go onto college? None of them had a formal college education."

"I'd say, the assailant came into their life recently which helps pinpoint the time element," June supposed.

"Their ages range from twenty-one to thirty-five so they all wouldn't have been in the same grade. But they are all Latinos whose parents are loaded, have connections to society, and none of them held what we would consider regular jobs," Talia said.

"I wonder why not?" June asked.

"They weren't the type to become doctors…they were the type who *married* them," Yulan said, nodding her head as though the idea was offensive.

"It says here, one was a part time etiquette instructress for a popular girl's school, while another was a judge for the Miss Texas Beauty Pageant." Talia read her notes.

"Oh, I just love watching that on TV. I wonder which judge she was. Is there a picture?" June shuffled through a pile.

Talia flipped through the articles. Finding it, she held it up. "The judge was herself a winner about five years ago. This is her headshot from the pageant." The Hispanic woman's hair flowed around her shoulders. On her head sat a large, diamond-studded tiara. Her smile was broad showing off lots of white teeth.

"Shit! That's my favorite judge. There's not a moment to waste. We have got to find her as soon as possible," June gasped. "I can't find anything about the occupation of the others. That's strange. Why would that information be left out?"

"Same here," Yulan said.

"Were you able to find out who the last people were who saw them?" Talia tapped her pencil.

"Yes. Right here it says, 'Ms. Rodriquez called her daughter the day of her vanishing, just minutes before she left for Neiman Marcus.' Here's another, 'Ms. Secundino said her daughter had just broken off with her boyfriend, but refused to publicly disclose his name due to society connections. The last time her daughter was seen was at the health food store in the vitamin section.' I wonder which store. I need one in the area that's more fully stocked," Yulan said. "And the last one on my list was last seen by her masseuse."

"And the women were last seen by a party planner, dog groomer, plastic surgeon, pedicurist, and yoga instructor. I don't see a common link between any of them other than the general area where they resided and their social standing," Talia said

"That's it! It's all about social standing."

"I agree, Yulan. That only takes us back to what we already knew." June took off her reading glasses and pushed them around on the table.

"Yes, so we've come no further." Talia sighed. "So much work and nothing gleaned."

"Except the time frame. It's current. Nothing from the past." Yulan spun the pencil around on the table. "I may be able to do more."

"How so?" Talia asked.

"I have contacts in Luis's office."

"You do?" Talia was thrown by that comment. "This is the first I've heard of it."

"I went to college with someone who works for him now. I may be able to get their families' interview information. They might have said something privately to the investigator that would help us in solving this." Yulan smiled. "Besides, working in a lab, we do a lot of work not just for Dallas County, but all the surrounding areas."

"Will your friend release it to you?"

"It's privileged information, so let's hope so."

"If that is all for today, ladies, I better get going." June put her reading glasses inside her shirt pocket.

"Me too." Yulan stood.

"I need to ask you a silly question, June. Do you mind?" Talia touched her sleeve.

"No, I don't mind. You can ask me anything." June seemed pleased.

"The other night—and I hate even asking—did you happen to take my bride magazines? I had some in my outside trash."

"Oh? Does this mean you and Luis have made up?"

"No, it doesn't mean that at all. I don't want them back. I threw them out, and not even an hour later, they were gone. It's perfectly fine if *you* wanted them, but a bit disconcerting if you didn't because that means someone was picking through my trash."

"It wasn't me. People go through trash in search of discarded treasures all the time."

"But it wasn't the night before trash day, so the barrels weren't out on the street. It happened in my backyard with the gate closed and latched…" Talia's voice trailed off not wanting to cause June more worry.

"Maybe, someone got a head start on trash day and you only think your gate was locked. There is known to be competition in Denton." June looked for her dog. "Are you ready, Lulu? Oh, Talia, do you want to come over and see my new bathrobe? With this murder activity in the neighborhood, we might be getting a peeping Tom, too. Bad luck seems to run in threes and so does criminal activity. I must be more careful with my appearance."

"Thank you, but not tonight. I'll look another time."

"All right, but if you change your mind, please don't hesitate. Oh, and I got my nephew to put together that grill for me, so see, we didn't need Luis after all," June said cheerfully, moving toward the door. "If you feel these trying circumstances call for a new robe, I noticed they have the same robe as mine in your size." June patted Talia's cheek. "You just never know what a day—or night—will bring."

"I appreciate all your help."

Watching June and Yulan walk out through the screen door, Talia knew it was time to get her mind on something other than death and lesson plans. She turned to her laptop and found a Latino event in Dallas.

Chapter Eight

Talia and Yulan strolled through the room of the museum that displayed the Latino artwork.

Long pieces of luminous fabric draped from the ceiling in flowing billows. Paintings of oil, watercolor, pen and ink sketches, and charcoals varied in sizes and textures against the stark white walls. Slabs of crude concrete and polished marble supported coiled sculptures.

"Isn't it wonderful? I love how the light appears oblique in this one." Talia pointed to a watercolor with the sun streaming through a window, upon the face of a child. "See how the artist drew the light emanating from the face instead of the window? Interesting. I want to teach this concept in class."

"There's no mistaking a real work of art. It just jumps out at you. Look at this painting at the end. The individual dots come together as one uniform piece of artwork, the colors are wonderful, but personally, I like the Korean method of painting with more subtlety."

"See, I knew you'd enjoy yourself once I got you here." Talia wandered through the room. "Each culture brings such richness to our lives. I have a dream I want to share with you."

"If it's about Luis, I don't want to hear so you can stop right there." Yulan covered her ears.

Ignoring her, Talia continued, "Picasso once said,

Give me a museum and I shall fill it. What if, instead of just one room displaying visiting Latino pieces, there was an entire permanent Latino Museum in some place central for all to see, right here in Dallas? It could also have an educational department filled with books and poems, videos and CDs. Imagine Latino music piped throughout the rooms. There should definitely be a section where people of all ages and nationalities experiment with various medias. It'd be a real cultural exchange, this hands-on museum."

"I thought you were tired of working with little children."

"Just because I don't want to be an elementary school art teacher, doesn't mean I don't want children to be exposed to art forms. Children need to be trained, as well as inspired, to reach their potential. Don't we want more del Corazon's in the world?" Talia smiled remembering Luis's words to her. It had been weeks since she heard from him. A dozen times she had picked up the phone to call him and then set it down just as quickly. What words could she say that would make a difference?

"Huh? Who? Talia, you still want to go to Paris, don't you?" Yulan asked suspiciously.

"Yes, I do. One dream doesn't cancel out another."

"Well, if you really have a vision for this to happen then put it in the suggestion box in the gift shop."

"I'll make my suggestion in way of a formal proposal. The place I have in mind would be a separate entity altogether," Talia joyfully said, studying another painting.

"Hold it right there. Are your thoughts only for Latino children? What about an Asian museum?" Yulan suggested.

"Luis has a cache of business names who can help sponsor to raise money."

"Ah, and all the roads before you circle back to your past. Let's make sure your museum has plenty of drinking fountains, in case someone gets a headache and needs to take aspirin, like me. Be right back."

Talia admired a sculpture by Carols Rael when she stepped back onto someone's toe.

"Ouch! Watch where you're going, will you? I think you broke my toe with those spiky heels."

"I am so sorry, excuse me." Talia whirled about to see Marco. A drop-dead gorgeous woman had her arm looped through his. *Juana?*

"Surprise, we meet again." Marco acted a bit giddy as he reached for Talia's hand. "I'd like for you to meet…I'm so sorry, this is embarrassing, but I've forgotten your name already."

"Talia." Making sure to clearly enunciate her name, she couldn't help but feel a bit miffed over his trouble with short-term memory.

"No, Talia, not yours. I remember *your* name." He turned to the girl hanging on his arm. "It's *her* name I forgot." The woman giggled uncontrollably.

"Crystal, silly boy." Even Crystal realized her dress was too short and tugged at the hem.

"That's right. Talia, this is Crystal Silly Boy," he said satisfied in the moment.

"No, I am Crystal *Favela*, you idiot." She tickled his side.

Talia held out her hand. "Hello, Crystal, nice to meet you." It was as though she had been pickled in perfume, making Talia sneeze multiple times.

"We just met today…by accident. He bumped right into me over in the Roman antiquities."

Perhaps his eyes were burning like mine are right now and he didn't see you, Talia resisted saying.

"Yea, and here we are. Talia, don't tell me you came alone? Join us." He offered Talia his other arm.

"No, thank you. I'm here with my friend, Yulan." Talia looked around.

"Did I hear someone say my name?" Yulan brushed up from behind.

"Yulan, I want you to meet Marco Correa and his friend, Crystal Silly Boy." Talia became part of the joke.

"Nice to meet you." Yulan narrowed her eyes at the laughter, looking from Marco to Crystal to Talia.

"Well, I've got to run along," Crystal announced. "Thanks for the tour, Marco."

"Aw. Say it ain't so. Do you have to run off right now?" Marco asked. "We just met."

"I told you I had to meet someone by one o'clock. Another time, Marco," she promised. Before walking away, she slipped her business card into his pocket.

"There goes a fun afternoon. Well, I'll just have to spend it with you two lovelies, instead." Marco looped his arms through theirs, giving himself the middle spot. "There's a painting I want you to see."

He escorted them down the hall and then shuffled them to the left. "Ah, here we are." They stopped in front of a macabre painting that took up the entire wall space. A golden cage filled with women of all sizes and ages instead of what should have been birds. Arms and legs stuck out between the bars, reaching for help, crying out into the eyes of the viewer to save them. So many eyes. Eyes were in hues of browns, blues, black, greens, and hazel. The cage dangled above a rushing waterfall, held to a thin tree limb by a thin crimson cord which was unraveling. Up from the water arose an out of proportion hand clutching a pair of scissors, wide open, complete with razor sharp teeth along either blade. One didn't need to be a prophet to know what was about to happen.

"Salvador Dali at his finest, don't you agree?" Marco asked.

"I'm certainly not a fan." Talia rubbed her arms.

"Gotcha. Although it looks like Dali's work, it's really not. This one is even a bit too bizarre for him. *This* one belongs to Christina Alvarez. I love to come here and spend hours looking at her artwork. I see something new each time. My secretary knows where to find me when I am not in the office. You remember meeting her, Talia."

"Yes. It was a memorable experience." She recalled Miss Firecracker. "And you actually spend that much time here?"

Marco nodded and then stood silently, deep in thought, admiring the oil.

Just how many times has he stood here, on this spot, looking at that? Talia wondered. The painting, although beautifully done, gave her the willies. She wanted to leave. Reading Yulan's body language, Talia knew her friend felt the same.

"This artist paints what she feels," Marco pointed out enthusiastically.

"Then she must not feel so well," Yulan murmured looking at her watch. "Glad we took the time to take in some culture. Now can we get something to eat, Talia?"

"Sure."

"Let's go to China Palace for all you can eat king snow crab."

Marco walked the women to their car. Yulan jumped into the passenger side as Talia said goodbye to Marco. "At first I thought Crystal was ex-girlfriend."

"Juana? Don't I wish? But I did as you suggested, I called her."

"What happened?"

"Juana reiterated her need for me to leave her alone in rather brusque tones." Marco shrugged, appearing vaguely amused.

"I'm sorry." She touched his arm.

"Well, that's life, huh? We should commiserate over margaritas sometime, Talia. How about making that sometime, tonight? After your fish dinner? After Yulan goes home?" He covered Talia's hand with his which she quickly withdrew.

"I'm sorry, but not tonight." Talia pulled the door handle.

"Please." Marco stepped in between her and the car.

"It's getting hot in this car." Yulan fanned herself with a hankie. Her head appeared as a ripe tomato. "When I get hot, my blood pressure goes up. If you don't turn on the A/C, I'm going to have a stroke. Strokes run in my family, except for my one cousin on my father's side."

Marco stepped aside allowing Talia to open the door.

"Come on," he pressed. "Have dinner with your friend, and then we will meet. Tell me where. We can drink water for all I care. I just need someone to talk to.

Someone who understands what I'm going through."

"Not tonight," she repeated. It was easy to refuse. Marco wanted company for his emotional state of loneliness, and psychologically, she wasn't going there with him.

"Another time?"

Her gut told her to tell him "no" once and for all, but what she said was, "Well, maybe." It left a door open she knew she should close tightly. He gave off strange vibes. Somehow, he didn't seem to be the debonair Marco Correa everyone spoke about.

Talia slid into the driver's seat. Turning on the ignition, she powered up the air conditioning. Yulan smiled as her dark hair blew back from her face. Someone banged on the driver's window. Talia jolted.

"Geez. Marco, again." Yulan gave him an angry stare.

Talia rolled the window down, thinking *what now?*

"Ah, hey…wait a minute, I need your number."

Digging through her purse, she found a crumpled grocery store receipt to scribble the number.

"Thanks." He whistled walking away.

"You're going to rue the day you did that," Yulan snapped while fastening her seatbelt. "There's something really weird about him…famous or not."

"He's got a bit of an ego, doesn't he?" Talia commented as she backed out of the parking spot.

"Talia, you're so trusting."

"That's not true."

"And you're impulsive, too. You hardly know Marco Correa, but I think he's disingenuous. You must be really lonely to put up with him."

"I'm not lonely," she protested. "Okay, I admit, I

made a mistake giving it to him, but I didn't know what to say when he asked for it."

"No, just say no. Practice with me. No, no, no, you may not have my number."

They began giggling.

"No, Marco. You may not have my number. No, Marco, I will not go out with you." Talia laughed hysterically with her best friend. It felt good.

****

After dinner, Talia dropped Yulan off at her place and drove home. As she reached the rim of the porch, her cell phone rang. She was about to answer when something drew her attention. There was a sheet of paper hanging from her front door. Moving closer, she read the large, block writing in sharpie print—I AM YOUR GUARDIAN ANGEL. FEAR NOT. NO HARM WILL COME TO YOU. *How odd.* Talia looked behind her and toward the street as if almost expecting to see someone. As she pulled the message down, the cell rang again. It was Luis. She unlocked the front door, then twirled herself into a chair. "Luis, it's so good to hear your voice."

"Nice to hear yours. When do you take off for France?"

"Not for a while. Next school term."

"That's great to hear. Then there's time."

Talia's heartbeat picked up. "Time for what?"

Does he want to see me? Has he reconsidered our relationship? Talia could only hope.

"I am cleaning out some stuff and found a bunch of art supplies you left here. Want them, or should I toss?"

Toss? Her heart squeezed in despair. "No, no tossing. I'll come for them."

"Soon, I hope."

"Is tomorrow soon enough?"

When they hung up, Talia reread the note. She didn't recognize the handwriting, but hoped it was from Luis and his way of making her feel safe. Talia began to cry. She regarded herself pathetic. But then she thought sometimes these breaks-ups just happen. The one left behind can't disentangle themselves from their feelings. She couldn't set herself free from thinking of Luis either. Maybe after a while, she would just stop trying.

Chapter Nine

The first thing she noticed was his bare feet.

He stood in the doorway wearing a pair of washed-out jeans and a blue pull-over shirt. *How casual,* Talia thought as she stepped with trepidation into the apartment, unsure if she was to grab her box filled with art supplies and run, or if he'd give her a moment to catch her breath. A moment to talk. A moment to say how much they missed each other. A moment for them to touch.

"I see you got yourself a haircut. Nice. You've reinvented yourself since the last time I saw you. Is this the improved lifestyle of the newly single district attorney?" Talia wasn't sure she liked the makeover. Silently, she questioned his motive.

"Don't get like that, okay?"

"Like what?" Talia reared back defensively.

"All negative."

"I'm not being—never mind, where are my supplies? I'll get them so you can get on with your day. And on with your life."

"You are in a mood." He shut the door and crossed his arms. They stood face to face for several moments.

She fought to withhold the stinging tears. "You have lost weight, Luis."

"A few pounds. Thanks for noticing." He moved the waistline of his pants up and down a little.

"!Un poquito! Looks like more than a few to me. Are you on some crazy diet for something like a marathon?"

"I considered running in the White Rock Marathon, but I'm under too much stress at work to take the time to condition for it."

"The race is not until December, months from now. Surely, this case will be behind you and you can begin training."

"I *said* I don't have the time!'" By the look on his face, even Luis seemed shocked over the tone of his voice. He spoke again, but quieter, "I'll run next year."

Not sure how to respond, Talia bit her lip. What a relief to see Murphy, Luis's St. Bernard, wagging his tail joyously at her as great waterfalls of thick drool cascaded from his jowls. Her attention gladly went to him.

"Murph! How are you? Oh, how much I have missed you, big guy." Talia knelt to greet the dog, snuggling into him. His wagging tail beat the air causing fur to fly as he licked her face. *At least Murphy still loves me.*

"That's your box on the table." Luis pointed to the cardboard container. He watched her play with the dog. Finally, he asked, "Want something to drink before you go?"

Talia shot a look at him. Already he was inviting her to leave. Well, she'd drink it slowly.

"Something cold…it's very warm out." Talia went to the table and thumbed through her art materials. From where she stood, she could see Luis getting her drink. "I appreciate you getting my supplies together for me. I'm starting a new project and searched all through my shed for these brushes. I'd forgotten I'd left them here. They're quite expensive to replace and I don't want to spend the extra money right now if I don't need to."

"Raspberry tea all right?" Luis turned toward her and then smiled his irresistible smile. What power it had, making her spirits lift.

"Raspberry tea?"

"I've made a pitcher just for you."

"For me? Oh, Luis, how nice of you. Of course, I'd love some." It was hard resisting the urge to throw her arms about him. Maybe she didn't want to marry him, but being in the same room with him still gave her a thrill. Talia went into the galley kitchen, then leaned back on the cement slab counter to watch him as he opened the cabinet door for a glass. Luis filled it with ice from the freezer door panel. Pouring the freshly-brewed tea from the glass pitcher into her glass, he handed it to her.

"Mmmm. Deliciosa," Talia critiqued after a long sip.

"Tell me about your new project," Luis said grinning.

"How do you know I have a new project?"

"Don't you always?"

"You know how I usually do trees, flowers, and animals? Rarely buildings. This time, I thought, I might attempt a painting of my house on canvas." Talia displayed her enthusiasm well.

"That's a breeze for you."

"Not really. I'm given to free form, and this will definitely be geometrical. You know I'm not so good at that. My proportions go askew." She laughed at herself.

"You're good at everything." He rolled his shoulders as if tension invaded his body. Talia observed that this case was bringing out new emotions in Luis, shutting down old ones.

"I seem to remember that the last time you complimented me, it was followed by a zinger. It's made me wary of your accolades."

"I'm sorry, Talia. It was never my intention to hurt you." The touch of his fingers on her face felt wonderful causing her to step toward him. He reacted by stepping away. His body language stung her.

"The past is what it is, today is a new day. I'm fine." Stopping the dance of emotions, she tossed off maudlin feelings. She searched her mind for something generic to say. "Have you seen the new Latino exhibit at the Dallas Museum?"

"No, but I've read the rave reviews in the Metro section. Have you seen it?"

"Yes, and it's beyond all my expectations. No rush to attend. It'll remain in Dallas for a while. Give it time and the crowds will be gone. I know how you hate them." *Now would be a good time to investigate for clues about his case.* Talia walked around the room, nonchalantly looking at everything, scanning out areas that needed to be searched. "By the way, I've taken an interest in your legal case."

Luis followed and held out the pitcher offering her more tea. "Which case?"

"The missing debutantes." She held up her glass. "Here is to finding them alive and well."

"Here, here." Luis held his glass high. "By the way, we know the name of the woman from your garden, it's Maria Salas."

"Yes, I read it in the paper. But the paper didn't explain how she died."

"My office isn't releasing that information to the public just yet," Luis explained without expression.

"Oh? Surely, you can release it to me?" She smiled coyly.

"Sorry." He laughed.

"Until the others are found, I'm nervous about going back out in my garden." Talia's empty hand went to the steam punk pendant featuring an old skeleton key on its small chain, which was around her neck, and began sliding it back and forth—until it broke. Sighing deeply, Talia wound the chain about key and placed it in the zippered part of her purse.

He laughed again. "How many chains have you broken by always tugging on your pendant?"

"One a month, I think." She paid his laughter back with a smile.

"Let's sit down and visit. That is, if you have a minute."

"Yup, just happen to have an extra minute with me." This was more like it. He didn't seem in such a hurry to scoot her out the door. She'd gladly stay as long as he'd permit. How she missed their tender moments. It was good being with him today, even if it was only for utilitarian purposes of picking up art supplies. Luis's well-defined friendship was irreplaceable. She wanted him and her freedom. It seemed he only wanted his freedom.

Luis led the way and they sat in chairs opposite one another. Minutes of painful silence followed. Glancing about the room, it looked the same as the last time she had been here as an engaged woman. Talia finally went to the bookcase where framed pictures of them together as a couple still remained. Thoughtfully, she picked up each frame, one by one, and gazed into happy faces that now seemed so foreign, so long ago in an alternative universe. With this still on display, it was nice to know he hadn't amputated her from his thoughts. If another woman came over, she wouldn't help but notice Talia remained a presence in this place.

A briefcase was open. It contained a pile of folders. She'd give nearly anything to get a look inside of them. Maybe she could see something everyone else had missed. "The media has been brutal on you. I think positive thoughts for you night and day, but I don't think I'm getting anywhere with them. I've read a few less than flattering headlines. How are you managing?" Talia nervously ran her fingertips down the ends of the folders.

"Talia, don't let it get to you because I'm fine. The media's hobby is unfairness." He crossed the floor to her. "And there are so many new cases for me to go over that I even bring my work home with me at night. It's spread across my desk."

Luis reached behind her. He was close enough for her to feel his breath on her cheek. Talia didn't budge; hopeful a kiss would follow. But to her surprise, he shut the top of his briefcase and then pressed down on the locks, before taking a step back.

She furrowed her brows. How curious, he didn't mention the work in the packed briefcase. But what else had Luis been doing? The thought of him with another woman made her silently fume with jealousy. It made her ill that he could be giving the kisses, which still belonged to her, to someone else.

"So-o-o, you haven't had much time for socializing." Talia spoke deliberately trying to sound dispassionate so he wouldn't catch on that she was in pain. It was none of her business should he resume dating, but how could she explain it to her heart if he had? It was a needy, desperate act to pry into his personal life—but she had to know. The thought of Luis preoccupied with work, alone at night, was welcome. Maybe she could find some rest.

"No socializing of any kind, unless you count walking Murphy in the park. There's no time. And, I'm just not ready. How about you? Seeing anyone special yet?" A look of concern crowned Luis's brow. Could he be exhibiting signs of jealously? If so, it'd please her to know she still lingered in his thoughts while absent from his side.

"No time for anyone right now. As your work, my art comes first." Talia breathed an internal sigh of relief.

"Ah, your art."

Talia caught a glimpse of a single folder sticking out from under the locked briefcase. "How many cases are you looking at?"

"A lot."

It was a silly move to make, but Talia began to tug at the folder wanting to see inside.

He slapped the top of her hand and put the folder into his desk. He locked that too and slid the key into his jean pocket. Now she knew where the golden information was kept. It may be hard to get to but she now knew where to direct her energy. *Thanks, Luis.*

"I'd love to hear more about that calling card."

"Oh?"

"Ah-huh."

"Nice try."

"It seems so top secret. So mission impossible. Okay, what can you tell me?" She leaned on her hand wishing like crazy she could have a look-see at all his files. She'd settle for the one locked up in his desk.

"A few years back, similar crimes were going on in southern Florida, near Miami."

"Then there's a connection between the two states? And where was Sam a few years ago?"

"He was in Huntsville Prison, right here in Texas, for dealing drugs. He's a low life drug dealer and addict. Not smart enough to pull off these crimes. The person who does this is highly intelligent and very well organized. Has a well thought out plan. Brimley doesn't fit that profile. Excuse me for a minute. I'll be right back." Luis disappeared into the bathroom. This was what she had been waiting for. Ignoring the locked desk since the key was in his pocket, Talia practically pounced on the briefcase doing her best to get it open, but the lock wouldn't budge. She kept glancing at the hands on the clock as she went through drawers and shuffled through papers neatly stacked in piles across his desk.

Talia tip toed to the bathroom door and listened. Running water. Her eyes flickered across the room. Where should she look next? Bookshelves. The books were placed neatly in rows. Every one was exactly the same measured distance between the book and the edge. There were no oddly misplaced papers sticking out of the tops of any of them. Such a neatnik, it was adorably appalling.

More minutes ticked by. She tapped on the door

with the back of her index finger. "Are you all right?"

"*!Bien! Un momento.*"

"Okay."

Talia sauntered back into the kitchen to rinse out her glass; it provided her with a reason to investigate in another room. She opened and shut each cabinet door, not really sure what she was looking for. His mail lay on the foyer's table. All junk. Glancing at the shut bathroom door, her forehead drew together in a mixture of tears and a frown.

Is he avoiding me? *Maybe I should just leave*. She could go to Paris right this minute.

Forgetting the box, she picked up her purse and headed for the front door, leaving with a heart filled with pain. Murphy walked around her and then plopped down on Talia's feet as a roadblock. "Ah, I miss you so much. Luis, too, but that'll be our secret, okay, Murph?" Patting his side, he looked up at her affectionately, then belched loudly.

"Oh my! You're excused." She tugged at an ear. The bathroom door squeaked open, at last, and she heard the sound of Luis's bare feet across the wood floor coming into the room behind her. *Please circle your arms around me from behind like you used to do. I will lay my head on your shoulder.*

Luis walked past her and sat in the large leather chair in front of the windows, facing her. "You aren't leaving yet, are you?"

It was then she noticed he looked feverish; his short hair was plastered to his head. His breathing labored.

"Luis, are you ill?" Talia hurried toward him.

"No, no, I'm fine. Just give me a minute. It'll pass,

you'll see." He wiped his face with his shirtsleeve. "How's school?" He was so good at changing subjects it made her falter. Besides hadn't they already discussed it? She'd play along.

"Good. Still thankful I'm not teaching elementary school. Nothing has changed there, but it's only the start of the first week of the second semester. Amanda Pudding, remember her?"

"Yes." He nodded without making eye contact.

"She recently signed a contract with Disney to draw animations. You can see I'm teaching my future replacements." She eased down into the couch.

"You're irreplaceable." Luis's voice was tender, soft.

"Thanks." Why was she suddenly feeling warm and so shy?

For a moment, a timid silence hung in the air. Talia finally looked away. Luis's look pricked her heart. Unexpectedly, she longed for him to kiss her, but he just sat there on his side of the living room so she cleared her throat. *You are the love of my lifetime. How do I find my way back to you?*

"Luis, sometime when you're feeling better, I'd like to discuss with you an idea I have for a Latino museum in Dallas." Talia sat up straight, hoping to break the romantic feelings that debilitated her.

"Tell me your dreams." A sparkle emerged from his dim eyes. "I want to hear all of them."

"My dreams? Luis?" Her heart thumped hard against her chest. He had never uttered these kinds of words before. *Suddenly, he wants to know my dreams.* "Well, okay. Here's one. Our Latino minority is now the majority, and we need to celebrate that. I think a permanent Latino art museum is the perfect way in which to do so."

"How can I help you?" he asked eagerly rubbing his hands together, already recovering from whatever had vexed him moments before.

"You attend fundraisers all the time. Would you teach me the fundamentals?"

"Sure, I can provide some direction, as well as contacts. And I may even know of a property in the city."

"Oh Luis, that would be wonderful. Where is it? Who does it belong to? Let's go drive by it right now. Murphy can come, too, and ride in the backseat. We can stop at Mister Frost's and get him some fries again." This is what she loved, working alongside of him. Luis was so full of ideas and creativity. What a team the two of them once made. *He inspires me and gives me energy. We are a team.*

"Hang on…before you start lining up contractors, let me check with the owner to see if he's interested in selling, or donating the land. There are some old warehouses on the lot that would convert nicely, or they can be torn down, depending on their condition. I know what a preservationist you are. It's a great location with plenty of parking. The property isn't in the best part of town, but perhaps the museum will help grow that area."

Tears glistened in her eyes. "This makes me so happy, Luis." She wanted to go to him. Sit in his lap. Run her hands over his head. Kiss his lips. Whisper intimate things into his ear. Maybe he'd run his hand up her spine and kiss her neck.

"By the way, how are things up by your place? Are

you ready for a house alarm?"

"No." Talia recoiled. "I don't like the idea at all."

"Whether you like the idea or not, there's an active predator out there and I want you safe."

"Okay, Luis, tell me the truth, what's the real reason you called me?" she taunted hoping he'd admit to his feelings for her.

"What other reason would there be? I not only call you, but I call many women living on their own just to check on them."

Ha, Talia didn't believe him for a minute. "Even June Clover?" She hoped to catch him in a lie, because she didn't want him calling to check on anyone but her.

"Yes, even June Clover, and if you don't believe me, ask her. I call Yulan, as well. Didn't she tell you?"

"No, she didn't. Neither did June," she answered with an equal mixture of surprise and disappointment. *Why didn't Yulan tell her? And June?* She had to speak again just to prove to Luis she didn't care. "According to what I've read, since I am not a debutante, I don't fit the profile. I'm also extremely cautious and I feel very secure with June right next door."

"Hum, June Clover and Lulu come to your rescue. Not much of a system there." He rubbed his brow.

"Okay, I'll consider an alarm if you'll just stop asking me about it. Next, you'll want to install those bars over my windows."

"An alarm gives you freedom and peace of mind. Leave it all to me. I'll call the company I use, to give you an estimate. Now that you won't be moving in with me, you must take every precaution, and spend the money to make your home safe." Luis pulled the cell from his pocket.

"Please, don't. I'll call someone to make the arrangements myself." Talia removed the cell from his hand. "In all the years I have lived in my home, only one corpse has shown up."

Talia turned toward the window. The Jaguar sat at a red stoplight. The sight of it made her curious. Just how many sea-mist convertible Jaguars are there in town? She could even see the white rectangle sticker on its bumper. Now would be the perfect time to bring it to Luis's attention. With a bit of luck, he'd open up more about the case.

Just as she was about to point the Jag out to him, Luis walked up to her. "What else have you been doing?" His touch made her change direction and he definitely had her complete attention now because he was within kissing distance. The fan behind them blew her hair gently into his face. His eyes studied her lips. Then he swept the wild lock of hair behind her left ear. The unexpected smile took her breath away.

"What's happened to us?" Her arms dangled awkwardly at her sides.

"No mystery there. It just ended." As his lips moved closer to her face, she felt his breath again. She closed her eyes and breathed. *Peppermint*. She loved peppermint. Blessed joy, another inch and their lips would touch. Tiny whiskers surrounded his wide mouth and sprouted up the sides of his cheeks. She licked her lips. Her eyes remained closed. She was ready.

Luis turned suddenly. "Let me help you take the box down to your car." The kiss had been cancelled.

Just as he put his arms around the box, he caught sight of her sketchpad. Intrigued, he picked it up and began paging through it, stopping on the drawing of him while he worked late one evening. The familiar curve of his back was captured perfectly. On the table sat a large cup of coffee with steam rising from it. More steam rose from his brow, depicting his logical thoughts.

"Here, you keep this as a memento." Talia carefully tore the sketch from the binding and handed it to him. She paused, hoping to evoke those sweet memories that danced around her head into Luis's mind. He held the caricature in his hand and looked at his watch. Coldly, he added, "Thanks. I'll take these things down to your car. I've things to do."

"I've got the box." She felt hurt, dismissed. His mood had changed so radically she wanted to know what was happening with him. Hotly, Talia picked up the box. It was heavier than she expected making her stumble.

"Let me get that for you." He seemed a bit unbalanced on his feet.

"I think I can manage better than you." Talia resisted. They struggled over who was taking the box. Talia didn't want to give. The old Luis would have no trouble, but this Luis was more vulnerable, somehow frail, with a point to prove. Finally, he won. The box was his. She felt his arm hairs against her arm, but the touch was anything but personal.

Angry with him, Talia decided to skip mentioning the Jag and followed him out the door into the hallway. In silence, Talia went to the stairwell as Luis took the elevator. Strange, he never took it before. He loved the extra workout the steps provided. But that was the old Luis. The silence continued as they exited the building and went outside into the bright sunshine of just another hot day in a string of scorching Texas days. There was no skip in her step as she walked to where her Honda was parked. After popping the trunk, Luis put in the box.

"Talia, there's something I want to ask you."

"So ask." She put her hands on her hips, disguising her disappointment with nonchalance.

"My lease is up. Would you mind if I moved into the Frye Street condo? I know we were to live there together after we married, but it's close to my office and this apartment is so small."

"Of course, I don't mind." Talia interrupted. "I was going to suggest it myself. I think you should move to the condo. Actually, it's silly not to. There's a lot more room for you. Move."

"But I gave it to you as my wedding gift."

"And I give it back to you as my break-up gift."

"You never really liked it, did you?"

"It's a lovely place; I just found it rather sterile. I love living in old homes. They have a soul."

"New plumbing and tile will never be able to compete with the allure of creaking wood floors and disintegrating pipes in the ground." He patted her back. "I'll have the lawyer draw up papers for a transfer of title, if you don't mind."

"Go ahead."

Talia got into the car and rolled the window down to call back to him. "Go to bed, Luis, and get some rest. Maybe you should see a doctor, too."

Thumbs up, he waved goodbye. She turned the wheel and was on the other side of the block when she wished she hadn't allowed Luis to keep that cute sketch of him. If she'd left it packed inside the box, she could've taken it to the framers to return to him as a gift. Now it was destined to be in a pile of other miscellaneous loose papers. Maybe even end up in some case file Luis would be going over late one night. But if it were framed, hopefully he'd display it alongside the other articles of memorabilia from their time. A small reminder of a special evening spent together, while serving as an additional barrier for any new female who may try to cruise her way into his heart.

On a whim, she decided to circle the block, and go back for it. On the first pass, her parking spot had been taken, and there wasn't another open space. On her second trip around, she was surprised to see Luis on the street.

Where are you headed? Out of nosiness, she decided to follow him. At the end of the block, a taxi picked him up. She followed for several miles, worried she'd be discovered, thankful she wasn't. When he got out, she quickly parked behind a truck, with just enough space left to watch where he went. Luis knocked on a peeling green door of a rundown brick structure, which seemed to be abandoned. Talia leaned over her steering wheel.

Surely, this can't be where Luis thought the Latino museum would go? Of course not, the building Luis had in mind was in Dallas. *So what is he doing here*? Finally, a woman appeared in the doorway and handed him a bag. She took one bottle at a time from it and talked to him. Then he reached for his wallet and pulled out money.

A few minutes later, the taxi returned. Luis got in and headed back toward his apartment. Continuing to follow him at a safe distance, while dodging behind vehicles along Hickory—not to be seen, she felt like a sleuth. Just her luck. Trying to fit in with the flow of traffic on one-way streets, she outwitted herself and lost sight of Luis. Twenty minutes later, she still couldn't find him, and just as she was ready to give up, there he was. This time, he was within a block of his apartment. It made her take hard sharp turns in order to keep from being discovered. On her last loop around, he had gotten out of the taxi and was a block from home. By now he was limping and perspiring heavily. The last thing she saw was Luis in the rearview mirror ambling sluggishly back inside his building. Tucked under his arm was a small brown bag.

Chapter Ten

A week had passed without another call from Luis. On her days off from the university, she turned her attention to gardening.

Talia kicked off her muddy shoes when she walked into the bungalow for lunch. The cell buzzed and cha-chaed on the counter. Holding it between her ear and shoulder, she pulled back her hair and set it atop her head, weaving a long narrow pencil through to keep it in place.

"Talia, this is Marco," he announced.

"Oh, Marco. How are you?" She was way too busy for chitchat. Maybe she should ring her doorbell and pretend she had company.

"Oh, Marco?" he mimicked her words and tone. "What's wrong? Tell me, we are friends, remember?"

"Aphids!"

"Ouch, I didn't know you swore."

"I don't swear. Well, not usually. If there is swearing, it will be done in my garden." Grabbing the pitcher of tea, she poured herself a glass, dropping several iced cubes into it.

"What? You lost me."

"Aphids are little winged insects that zap plants of their life, my roses and crepe myrtles have an infestation of them." Talia tilted the glass toward her lips. The cold rush of lemon felt heavenly flowing down her throat.

"Oh."

"You asked. But the rest of my garden looks pretty good. My vegetable garden has been relocated from its previous spot, due to an organic tragedy, that I do not wish to speak about. It is once again doing well, until the neighborhood varmints figure out how to get through the wire. Slugs and snails are under control." Standing on her tiptoes, she peered out the sink window, keeping a sharp eye out for anything that dared to trespass.

"Sounds like you need a break."

"Actually, I'm on a break, a lunch break. In a few minutes, I'll be back out there to dig a bog in the back corner of the yard."

"I'm not even going to ask about that one. So, you're a gardener?"

"Yes, I am. Some of my best friends live in my garden."

"You've lost me again."

"Salamanders, frogs, toads, garden snakes, lizards of all kinds, and as soon as the bog is ready, turtles. I love those guys. Birds, too. But you didn't call to hear about my backyard." Retrieving an apple from the refrigerator, she took a big bite and then wiped her chin to remove the juice.

"After all that work, sounds like you need a break. How about meeting me in Dallas for some lunch? I'm thinking the Grand Lux at the Galleria?"

"Sorry, nothing on earth will entice me to travel through all that traffic mess today. Anyway, I'm fixing lunch right now as we speak." Retrieving a jar of peanut butter, she shut the refrigerator door with the swing of her hip.

"How's life without your beloved Luis?"

Do men really say things like this? "Nothing I wish to discuss."

"It sounds as though you're hoping to get back with the D.A."

"Did I say that? I don't think so. I lead a very busy life—"

"You're in denial." He cut off her words.

She felt skewered by his. "Well, I must admit I'm worried about Luis." At the count of ten, she'd hang up. *One. Two.*

"So you're worried about his drug use, too?"

Three. "What drug use? What are you talking about? If you are talking about Luis, you have the wrong man," she spit back at him, but something in his tone stopped her from hanging up. She needed to know what he was getting at. Either Marco had fresh information on Luis, or he was trying to play her. If she didn't find out which, she'd be up all night trying to figure it out. When he didn't follow with a remark, Talia followed with one. "That's the most ridiculous thing I've ever heard. How do you even know Luis?"

"Who doesn't know Denton County's D.A.? Who doesn't know me? Listen, Talia, there's something I need to discuss with you."

"Marco, this conversation has worn me out." *Four, five, six, seven, eight, nine, ten.* "Listen, I have to go."

"Wait. Don't hang up. This time it's not…about Luis. Honest. May I come over so we can talk?"

Standing mid-center in the house, she could see into nearly every room of her bungalow. Her muddy footprints were everywhere. Piles of sorted clothes were in the hallway. Clean dishes sat in the wire dish drain waiting to be put away, furniture needed dusting, and the vacuum cleaner had become a deliberate stranger.

"I'm too tired, Marco, and I have too much to do." She fantasized about climbing into a warm sudsy tub. Later, there'd be a quiet candlelight dinner alone while watching some movie. Even better, there might be another black and white romantic comedy to watch. She had a nice life that a cat would enjoy. Maybe she'd rescue one.

"I really need a fr-friend." His voice broke as if he were weeping. "I saw Juana today."

"Oh my, how did it go?" Hearing sadness in his tone overwhelmed her. She knew exactly how he was feeling.

"Badly. I need to talk?"

She caved. "Okay, but you are coming to Denton. I refuse to drive to Dallas."

Instead of a bath, Talia settled for a quick shower and rebuked herself for giving in to meet Marco. After slipping into jeans and a pull-over top, she brushed her hair, leaving it wet, and quickly applied only blush and lip stain. For the final touch, she added large, turquoise slab earrings with French hooks. As she got into her car, she waved at June who was seated in a chair, on her porch, with her feet propped up, and a pair of binoculars in her hand.

"I see the UPS man came." Talia waved.

"Yes, he did. I can see clear down the street as though I am right there with them. It's like I can reach out and touch them." June held out her arm and pawed the air.

****

Talia waited at Jupiter House, a popular coffee house. The exposed brick walls were filled with students' artwork. Most were framed, while others were displayed on stretched canvases.

"You look gorgeous Talia." Marco whistled a shrill wolf call a few feet away. "Thanks for meeting me on such short notice."

Talia pointed to a chair, sipping her strawberry drink. "Want a smoothie?"

"I'll pass on the sugar." He pulled on the large belt buckle threaded through his pressed jeans. Even his shirt looked freshly pressed.

"Nice boots."

"Thanks. Just bought them next door at Princess*La*De*Da. They have tan and turquoise women's boots. Top brand. They'd sure look nice on you. Allow me to buy them for you."

"Thank you, but I really don't know you well enough to accept gifts. We are here to talk about Juana." Talia found his carefree demeanor puzzling when earlier, he seemed close to tears.

"I was one street away from my office when I saw Juana walking directly toward me. She pretended not to see me, but I didn't let her get away with it."

"What did you do?"

"I blocked her path."

"You stepped right in front of her." Talia reiterated, trying to envision this as she sucked harder on her straw.

"I sure did. Then she tried to walk around me, but I blocked that path, too. I won't be ignored."

"Really? You did that?" She lifted an eyebrow.

"I did." He seemed arrogant.

"You're quite stubborn." Talia began to feel uneasy. *What am I doing here, listening to this?* She was caught for a moment, going in between her instinct to walk out, or to stay. His words were offensive and scary. But, he was a highly respected Dallas entrepreneur. Certainly, she didn't want to humiliate, or offend him. Maybe he was just exaggerating what really happened in a lame attempt to impress. She relaxed in her chair. "What happened next?"

"Then she held up her hand. Seems she got engaged. The ring is so small it takes a magnifying glass to see the diamond." His forehead deepened into a frown.

"Engaged? *Already?* That was fast."

"Yea, she's in love with some handyman. Can you believe it? She chose a toilet jockey over me…a world-renowned architect, someone who designs and builds buildings!" He twisted his napkin and then tossed it at a trashcan, missing it completely.

"Easy, Marco. Let it go." That was enough. Talia stood and deposited the trash into the container. "This is rather intense. You have very deep emotions. Maybe you should talk this over with a counselor."

"I'm glad it happened because it made me realize what I have with you."

"Huh? With me?" She spun around. "There is no you and me. I'm a matchmaker of sorts. I've lots of single friends. How about I fix you up?" *After you get on meds.*

"Talia, you're the only person I'm interested in."

"Marco, I don't know you that well, but I'd say you're the type of guy who enjoys the chase, and then becomes quickly bored. Once you get the girl, all interest is lost." She sat back down.

"Talia Bonilla, you are like no other woman I've ever known," he said, with a hint of desperation.

Catching her breath over his admission, she cleared her throat. "Marco, I get the feeling that's a line you've used on many women. There's no romantic connection for me."

"Don't say that. Talia, after speaking with Juana today, I began thinking about how we met. Your passion of orchids brought us together. I buy them, you care for them…kismet. Keep an open mind. Let's give it a whirl, what do you say?"

"I'd say you're on the rebound, but there seems to always be a girl somewhere about your elbow."

"They're only ornamentation for Italian silk suits. Is it my age that puts you off? I know I'm older than you, but it can still work."

"I really think we are best as friends."

"A woman for a friend," Marco repeated. "Certainly a novel idea for me. I'll take it. Well, friend, what grand plans do you have for your life?"

Talia shook her head.

"Aw, come on Talia."

"That's my business and I don't like anyone to be in it." She hated it when people dug around in her life. Having heart-to-heart talks with Yulan, or June, were different. She needed that; it was a girl thing. Everyone else didn't know her as well. She wouldn't allow it.

"You're cute when you're upset. Sorry it has to be Luis who upset you."

"Luis? Where did that come from? Luis didn't upset me," she answered coldly.

He gave an awkward shrug.

Talia crossed her arms bracing herself for what he might say next. "You agreed if I came you wouldn't mention Luis's name. You went back on your word. You don't know Luis."

"I know Luis all right. Both you and Luis seem to put a premium on friendship. But I doubt you'd let a criminal out of prison, even if he were your friend." The words tumbled from his mouth.

"What are you saying?" Talia looked around for her pink purse. Had she kicked it off somewhere again?

"Sam Brimley."

The sound of the criminal's name used in connection with Luis made her wrench. Her mouth fell open and she blinked hard at the implication. "I beg your pardon, but Mr. Brimley is *no* acquaintance of Luis's. He is a criminal." Talia vehemently shook her head. *Ah, there is my purse*. Still shut tightly, too. No spillage. She snatched it up and hugged it to her.

"Are you serious? Or didn't you know? That's it, isn't it? Luis never confided in you. Luis and Sam are old high school friends from a private school here in Dallas. They both attended on a football scholarship."

Her mouth dropped open. "Impossible. If it were true, it'd have come out in the news."

"Be sure to watch channel 5 tonight at eight," he told her with a pleased grin.

"It's going to be on the news?" Blood rushed from her face. Her hands felt numb; she touched her mama's turquoise, Mexican-sterling pearls she wore about her throat. "How do you know this?"

"I have contacts."

"Now I know why Juana broke up with you. You're nothing but a loathsome, busybody playboy. A pariah who likes to make trouble." Rattled, Talia looked for her purse again, momentarily forgetting she had it already.

"Are you afraid to handle the truth?" Marco loomed over the small table at her. Wanting to run and hide, Talia stood. "I'm leaving now."

Marco also stood. "The sooner you face up to this, the sooner you'll find love again."

His words stabbed her like a sword in her back, making her grimace. How foolish of her to agree to meet Marco. *What was I thinking anyway*? Talia kept walking away from Marco. Her life had become falling dominoes. Turning about, she responded, "I don't like people saying disparaging things about Luis. Remember that!"

"Just think about what I said." His hand shot out and he grabbed her forearm pulling her toward him. His mouth formed a grim line.

She opened her mouth to cry out, but nothing came. She yanked away from him and continued down the street where he didn't follow.

Reaching her car, she got in, closed the door, and turned on the ignition, revving the gas pedal with her foot. Something Marco said did trouble her. *Could this Brimley person actually have something on Luis? Certainly not the Luis she knew. But lately, he acted odd.*

Consumed with worry, she missed her exit causing her to circle back toward Denton. There was that Jaguar again. It came up fast behind her, then beside her. She tried seeing the driver inside. The car accelerated and then pulled directly in front of her, slowing its speed. Talia looked at her speedometer. It was dropping from sixty-five miles per hour, sixty, then fifty-five, then fifty, careening down to thirty, and still slowing.

"What are you doing?" she called to the invisible driver just yards away from where she sat.

Slowing her speed to the Jaguar's, she signaled to turn into the right lane to exit. The Jaguar pulled into that lane in front of her as if they were one fluid movement. Talia drove up within inches of his bumper and prepared to jot down his license plate number, but this time it was missing. There was no tag on the car either. Why weren't the police stopping him?

Her exit was a fourth of a mile away; she deliberately remained tightly behind him. At the last second, she turned on the Loop 288 exit. Too late for the Jag to make the same maneuver. It continued northbound, disappearing into traffic. Talia's heart thundered in her chest, watching for the car to return. The driver knew exactly where she lived; that is what frightened her the most.

Now on McKinney Street, she turned right onto Locust. Home was in sight. It looked safe, quiet. Entering her cozy bungalow, she noticed everything was the same as this morning, just as she left it. Locking the door for the first time in broad daylight, she made certain the windows were secure and then she pulled down the shades and closed the curtains. Feeling frightened was a new, bizarre, foreign feeling. Maybe she should alert the police to the possibility of being followed. Picking up the phone, she searched the front of the phone book and found the non-emergency number.

"Denton Police Department." The female answered.

"Hello, my name is Talia Bonilla, and I need to report a suspicious car that may be following me."

"Is he following you now?" she sounded alarmed.

"No, I'm at home now."

"Did he follow you home?"

"I don't think so." Talia lifted a corner of a drape to peek. "No."

"I'll connect you with an officer," the female voice replied.

"Thank you." She felt so much better already.

Someone answered on the third ring.

"Officer Davila. How may I help you?"

"A car has been following me off and on for several weeks." Talia was cool, to the point.

"What is the make and model of the car that's been following you?"

"A Jaguar convertible. Brand new model. It had a license plate one time but doesn't now."

"What about a temporary one in the window?"

Talia closed her eyes trying to remember. "No."

"A dealer tag?"

"I didn't see one."

"What color is the car?"

"A sea-mist green with a bumper sticker on the right rear bumper. It says *The Eyes of Texas are Upon You.*" This information she was sure about.

"I'm typing this all in the computer and will give you a number to refer to next time you call." His voice was official. No need for her to be afraid anymore; Officer Davila was in charge and would make sure she was safe. After all, it was his job, right?

"Good. I'm very concerned about this." Talia decided to play her drama queen card just to be sure he took her seriously. "One of the missing debutantes turned up dead in my yard."

"Yes, I remember. I was on duty that day. In fact, I was in your yard."

"That's right. I feel so much better knowing I am talking to you. I think this Jag might have something to do with it," Talia continued pressing.

"Do you feel you need to speak to a police officer in person? I can send someone to the house?" Davila offered.

"No, no need. You have all my information." Talia blinked.

"Yes, ma'am."

"Thank you." Talia gave him her address and phone number for the report.

"The reference number of this call is #5551248792. Keep that handy. Thank you for calling. Remember, no fear. We are here to protect and to serve you. Give us a call if you need anything more."

"I appreciate that very much. Bye." Talia hung up the phone and put the number in the zip pocket of her purse.

No sooner had she closed the call than her cell rang again.

"Talia, I've a favor to ask."

"Anything, Luis."

"Would you mind coming over to pick up Murphy and take him home with you? I can't manage taking him outside for walks anymore. You have a yard."

"Oh my, Luis, I'll be right there."

Chapter Eleven

Marco and Luis were opposite ends of a pendulum. Gladly, she loped from Marco's damaging words by running to Luis. She always turned to him for everything so it seemed natural. She sailed toward his place in her bubble of happiness.

It felt good, normal, safe to be knocking on his door. By now, he had moved into the condo. Curious, she wanted to see him there, in the new space. Try to imagine what it would have been like with the two of them.

Pressing the bell was like setting off a fire alarm, only it was Murphy barking wildly from the other side of the door. The dog's breath came as short, sudden spurts against the wood, reading her scent. His bark swiftly went from a high alert to a blissful greeting.

"Hi, Murph." Talia stood staring at the old factory door as if she could see right through the metal. Remembering how Luis looked the last time made her nervous. What would she see this time? Talia pressed the doorbell. "Luis?"

"*Si, una momento, Talia.*" A weak voice answered. Slowly, the steel-gray metal door opened.

Talia gasped, immediately feeling embarrassed for having done so. She took him in, her gaze sweeping rapidly over him from head to toe and back again. His trousers hung on him, and his wrinkled shirt was also coffee stained giving the impression he had worn it for days. Then there was his hair; it was balding at the top and back. Luis's entire appearance was like watching a terrible transformation in a black and white horror flick. "Stop your crazy diet, Luis, will you?"

"I think I agree with you this time." His eyes darted to the far corner of the room.

By now, Murph sniffed up and down her legs, licking them as lollipops. She dropped her purse and keys onto the flooring to bend down. She rubbed his ears and allowed him as many face kisses as he wanted to give.

Luis's smile was shallow and he seemed blissfully unaware of just how bad he looked. "I hate to burden you with my troubles, but with all this work, I can't keep up with Murphy."

"Luis, can you even walk to the park?" She bit her tongue feeling she had said too much.

"Of course. It's Murphy I worry about. He pesters me day and night to take him to the park to run. I don't have time for even short walks. Please help me out here." There was a dreadful edge to his voice that was painful to hear.

"You and Murphy belong together like Calvin and Hobbes, but yes, I'll take him…for now. Where are his food and bowl? I'll need his leash as well." Talia watched Luis gather together Murphy's stuff. The man moved clumsily. "Whatever you're battling, you're losing."

Luis stacked the dog's items at the door. "No battle. Just lots going on in my world right now."

"Apparently," Talia observed. "By the way, be sure to use an old picture for your campaign posters."

Luis wiped his nose with a handkerchief and then stuck it back into his pocket. "Hate these colds. Yea, old picture will do. Thanks for the suggestion. But as far as anything else, you're making too much out of nothing. You're good at that."

"And you're good at minimizing my feelings." Talia teetered between rage and compassion. "Isn't there anything I can do for you? I can make you dinner."

"Please don't. There is a lot of take-out left over in the fridge."

"Not so fast. I want to see what you've done with the place." Talia stood her ground, feet planted firmly in the foyer.

"Help yourself."

High ceilings with steel beams were a striking feature throughout the space. Recessed lighting had been installed over the work areas in the kitchen. The spot was divided in two sections and shared directly on the other side with the dining room. Three brick walls held the foyer, kitchen, and dining room, guiding the guest toward the massive ground to ceiling windows, which made the fourth wall. That section served double functionality as his office and living room. The condo gave a sweeping sense of spaciousness. And the windows. How she first hated them, but what amazing light they let in for her paintings. She looked over her shoulder at Luis and suddenly realized that perhaps he had been right in much of his advice to her. It may have served her well to consider his point of view. Yes, she had to admit, even to herself that it was a lovely space, but for her it was too confining—perfect for Luis.

The metal stairs led to the bedroom and master

bath with a large walk-in closet. However, on the first level, she spotted a twin bed stuck beneath the staircase. By the rumpled covers, she suspected that is where he slept, which meant he was too weak to climb the stairs. Suddenly, she felt dizzy and had to sit. The sight of Luis, the realization of his condition, made her head spin. Fear. He was fading away before her eyes, and there was nothing she could do to stop it.

She looked up. There it was—the symbol of their beginnings. The large canvas hung on the wall; it was hers. That year the fall colors in Evers Park were too enticing not to paint. While dressing in comfortable and worn clothes, she had no inkling she was about to fall in love. A paint brush was wound through her hair to keep it in place on top of her head.

Her paper clipped to her easel, she added a swipe of ochre watercolor. The wind was just picking up when the Bernard loped up to her, spilling her paint on the grass and all over her clothes. Luis Arroyo soon arrived in old running shoes to retrieve his dog and say his apologies, as the empty leash dangled in his hand. If one looked carefully, they'd see the man and his dog in the distance, which she later added.

A rising star in Denton County law, Luis Arroyo could've had any woman but for a little while wanted only Talia. That feeling had somehow soured. So that was what lunch had been about that day at the Mellow Mushroom Restaurant; he checkmated the decision to end their relationship. *And this is how love ends.*

"Again, Talia, thanks for taking my dog for me." Luis leaned against the doorjamb with the same leash in his hand. This time he was playfully twirling it. Talia stepped forward to grab it when she heard a news reporter on the TV starting the report about the D.A.'s office. His animated voice pulled her right on past Luis and into the living room. "Are you on this segment?" She walked around the couch for a better view.

"Not me. I asked my assistant Jade Clark to go on in my place."

"Ah Jade. So now she is your assistant. You have much more experience than that young girl. You're much more fluent as well, and besides this case is yours, right? You know it better than anyone. Who else can speak on your behalf but you?" It was hard to accept the fact that, when Luis had an opportunity to defend himself, he passed it along to someone else.

"She'll be fine."

Those were brave words but Talia knew Luis was worried. She sat down on the couch.

A flattering five-minute intro of Luis Arroyo's achievements in the Denton area followed and then the story switched to Sam Brimley. It was an interesting, well thought-out piece, paced nicely. Sam sure looked guilty to her. Luis shook his head all the while.

"Boy is this slanted," Luis complained disgustedly as he wrung his hands. "The devil's in the details, and they're not giving them. This flimsy reporting would never stand up in court. In fact, it wouldn't even stand up against grand jury scrutiny."

"Well, it just may stand up in the court of public opinion," Talia said dogmatically.

The segment continued. "Here with me tonight is Alex Monahan who, up to this point, has been considered as Arroyo's greatest ally. But due to a turn of events, he has taken the opposite side from his boss and now from his sense of right and wrong has decided to run against…his old friend."

"Spare me. He's being overly dramatic," Talia protested. "And where is Jade?" She looked over at Luis who seemed as surprised as she that his assistant wasn't being interviewed.

"It'll be okay," Luis said. "Maybe she'll be on after Alex."

Alex was dressed casually for once. He smiled sadly and then said, "Well, I still can't get over how a fine, honorable man like Luis Arroyo would release Sam Brimley."

"Maybe because you bungled it!" Talia shouted at the TV.

"Sssh!" Luis sputtered. "I can't hear the TV if you are blathering."

"Blathering?"

Now the camera panned in for just a headshot of the commentator, as he continued, "Why would a man with previous convictions for drugs and armed robbery, and now with mounting evidence in the disappearance of seven women, one now dead, have all charges dropped? We called the D.A.'s office but he wasn't in for comment. So we turned to the past for our answers. We found them here, at Saint Mark's private Catholic school in Dallas. Although you don't need to be Catholic to attend, you do have to have money, and lots of it, to pay for the tuition. Although the Arroyo family was not rich, he had something the school wanted and that was his football athleticism. Sometimes feeling as if he were on the outside looking in, the other young men didn't always accept this young Latino man from the streets."

"From the streets? Your parents lived in an upper

middle class neighborhood." Talia flailed her arms.

"Sssh." Luis seemed composed.

Now a picture of his parent's house came up on the screen. "This is Luis's old house. It's a modest home just on the outskirts of a small town. Where he wants to go is into the lights of Dallas and into the ritzy neighborhood—"

"That's Denton, you creep newsman. Luis, that's where you lived going through college. I can't listen to this. Turn it off," Talia ordered.

"Then leave. I'm listening to it," Luis shot back.

Talia remained.

Again the camera panned to the headshot of the commentator. He gave little gasps of air in between his sentences as if there was a horrid plot brewing and the listener needed to really pay attention to what he was about to say. "On his team was another member who felt like an outcast as well. His name?" He took a dramatic pause. "I'll tell you right after this break."

The TV sound bumped up several decibels.

"Talia, I need to tell you something," Luis said.

"You know Brimley." Talia's heart ached for him.

He did a double take.

"Yes, but that isn't what I was going to say." Luis hesitated before continuing, "But now that you've brought it up, you need to know we were never friends. Not then, not now. I only knew who he was. Even back then, there was something different. Do you really think I would let someone out on cronyism?"

"No, you wouldn't." She met his gaze. "I believe you."

"Then that is all that matters to me."

"How dare Monahan say all those things? Can't

you do anything about it? Sue him! Sue the station! Sue that reporter and the station!" Talia was on her feet, pointing and yelling at the TV.

"Stop. Anger isn't going to change things."

Talia plopped down on the couch.

Luis sat beside her and held her for a moment. "I've recently come to the conclusion I can't control what people do, say, or think. I can only control me and my reactions…my thoughts and attitudes."

"I applaud your platitudes," Talia said acidly.

"It doesn't matter. All that matters is you and I know the truth."

"You and me?" Talia was startled by this admission. "Thanks for being included in your group of two, but that's not enough. Luis, you must stand up for yourself. You cannot allow misinformation out on the airways."

"When the time is right, the truth will come out. Let's not discuss this anymore." He turned away from her and hooked the leash onto Murphy's collar.

The program was back on. The reporter continued, "Suspicion of drugs. But is it true, or just another ugly rumor?"

"It is just an ugly rumor," Talia murmured at the screen. "Right, Luis?"

"Don't ask any more questions, okay?"

"Wait, you said there was something else you wanted to tell me. What?"

"I said not to ask any more questions. Talia, just take good care of Murphy."

"I will. But remember this is only temporary." Talia pointed her finger at him.

"Don't *you* forget it is only temporary," Luis

chided.

Talia led the dog out of the apartment, but he refused to go easily. She pulled him along, feet out, nails scraping the floor.

"You have a new home with me now, boy."

****

Back home, Murphy headed to the bedroom where he made himself comfortable in the middle of Talia's feather bed. The white duvet now had a dog centered on it.

"You know better than that. Luis never allows you on his bed. And you are not allowed on mine. Get down!" She pointed to the floor. "I said *down.* Down…down boy."

Murphy looked at her and then sleepily rolled over, stretching out comfortably.

"I give up. Welcome to your new home." She flopped down on the bed with him and began to stroke his ears. Pretty soon, Murphy began to snore. "I think this is a pretty comfortable bed, too."

Chapter Twelve

Talia came home from her classes to a small pool of water on the tiled kitchen floor.

Frantically, she checked the pipes in the bathroom and underneath the kitchen sink. About then, she realized it came from Murphy's water bowl that he liked to jump into whenever he heard a car. After adoringly scolding him for his habit, she tossed paper towels over the water, clipped the leash to his collar, and out they went for a walk. The more she walked, the tighter her shoulders seemed to become, caused by concern for Luis. Not only had their relationship completely changed, but he had too. Talking it out with a trusted friend might help.

Along the way, she called Yulan, but no answer. Returning home, Talia knocked on June's door, but then noticed her car was gone from the drive.

At home, she sat on the floor across from Murphy while he ate his kibble, lamenting her woes to him when the doorbell rang. There stood Marco with a six-pack of soda and a large pizza.

"Marco?"

"I've come in peace. I had my first counseling session, today." He gave a wry smile.

"I am so happy to hear that."

The expression on his face said he had put their recent conversation behind him. "I've brought dinner.

Hope you haven't eaten. And I really hope you like anchovies."

"No, I haven't eaten, and I love anchovies." Surprising herself, she felt happy to see him. Loneliness could be a bitter pill. Needing to spill her guts and emotions to anyone who stumbled across her path, Marco would have to do.

Murphy stood feet away, head bent down low at what he considered to be an intruder. "Murphy, stop that."

"You never mentioned a dog." Marco stopped short, not sure if he should take another step.

"This is Murphy, Luis's dog. Murphy, this is Marco. Be nice, Murph." She touched his head. "I'm babysitting him. It's a beautiful evening so let's sit on the front porch."

Talia lit a citronella candle to keep away the late season mosquitoes, which refused to die until the first frost. Murphy plopped across Talia's feet and drooled in great puddles.

Marco offered him a corner of the pizza. Murphy had the food in one quick snap of the teeth.

"Leave the finger," Marco howled.

"Looks like you made a friend."

"Anything that big, I want to befriend."

Music oozed from the old radio, in the living room, through the open window.

"That old tube radio still gives a nice sound. I like it," Marco said. Tonight, he seemed at peace with the world and himself. It was a nice change.

In turn, she felt at ease with her feet up on the porch rails and a cold drink at her elbow. "I had it restored, has all original working parts. Great pizza."

"Here's to great anchovies on a great pizza," Marco added.

She half-heartedly responded to his high five with a weak hand slap. Marco was so corny and childish in ways, no wonder he never married.

"Not many people like these little guys!" Talia dangled one before popping it into her mouth.

"Their loss. That means more for me. Listen, I'm sorry for upsetting you the other day," he admitted. "I was very rude and careless with your feelings."

"No harm done," she responded in a small voice.

"Talia, thank you. Most women would have taken advantage of me and jumped at the chance to have a relationship with a famous architect who has power, influence, and money, but the counselor showed me how important it is to be over Juana before starting a new relationship."

"Good."

"Maybe you and I could get to know one another better, that is as friends? I'm sorry I upset you. I was way off base."

She looked down at her hands and the tomato sauce that had dripped on her white blouse. She took a paper napkin, tried wiping it off, but only smeared it more. "I appreciate your apology, I do. Unfortunately, you may be correct about Luis." How she despised her tears.

"Not sure what you mean?"

"He might be on drugs." *Oh gosh, why did I even say that?*

"Let me be your friend." He leaned forward.

"Thanks. I need one right now."

"Come on." Marco stood and pulled Talia to her feet. "Let's go listen to some jazz at Dan's Place."

Talia pulled back. “No, not in the mood.”

“Don’t tell me you don’t like jazz.”

“I love jazz.”

“Good. I’ll have you home in an hour.”

“Okay, okay. But I’ll drive my own car to make sure I’m home in an hour.”

****

It was nearly dark when she headed for home. True to herself, she stayed one hour and, to her surprise, found she fully enjoyed herself. Maybe Marco was right; she needed to get out and away from her thoughts. But she couldn’t shake the awful feeling of having betrayed Luis by verbalizing her fears to Marcos, of all people. She revved her car and took the long way home on the interstate. Getting off at the exit before the town of Sanger, she wound her way through the Denton backstreets. Luis had enough trouble without her opening her big mouth.

When she arrived home, a truck with large letters reading Home Securities, sat in her drive with Luis’s black sedan right behind. She scowled.

“Luis…” She spat his name out, hitting the steering wheel with her hands accidentally honking the horn. Nearly falling out of the car, she snapped at him, “Just what do you think you’re doing?”

“Making sure you’re safe.” He walked toward her. “We’ve been waiting on you. Where have you been?”

“It doesn’t matter where I’ve been. I didn’t know you were coming. Besides, my safety is no longer your concern. And yet, here you are invading my privacy, disregarding my wishes.”

Appearing embarrassed with the two security men waiting to gain entry into her bungalow, Luis took a hold of Talia's arm and walked her to the side yard. "Listen, indulge me. There are too many whack-o's out on the streets. You're a prime target…a single, attractive woman living alone. For goodness-sake, a dead woman was found outside your house. I can hardly sleep at night with the worry."

"You have sleepless nights about me?" She was just about to admit she had sleepless nights too when his watch fell off his wrist hitting the ground.

Talia picked it up and went to put it around his wrist, but even with the links tightened all the way, it still slid half way down his hand. She grasped his arm. Shoving his sleeve halfway up his arm, she was astounded to see how skinny it really was.

"You look anorexic." She withdrew feeling sick.

"Are we going in, or not?" hollered one of the security guys. "It's late."

"Please," he whispered. "My parting gift. Let me do this one last thing for you."

"Parting gift? You sound as though I will never see you again."

"Don't read too much into what I say."

"Oh all right, I give up. Go ahead inside." She tossed them the keys.

"Wait." Luis handed her a new flashlight. "Put this in your glove compartment. I also have a new car kit to keep in your trunk in case of a break down."

"Thanks." Her voice turned soft.

"I can't always protect you."

"Don't you see that's not your job?"

Once inside, Talia sat in a kitchen chair barely watching as Luis walked the installers around the inside and outside of the house. Murphy followed as they raised and lowered windows, went through the attic, hammered, and reached into vents. Silently, she admitted it would be nice to have this added measure of protection in the evenings while she slept. At least until this perp was caught. Still, it made her feel imprisoned.

Two hours later, the nasty deed was complete. Officially, she was wired to a local security company who now monitored her house. The installers explained the system to Talia, leaving the manual for her to review. From the corner of her eye, she watched Luis leave, walk to his car, get in, and drive off without so much of a goodbye. Again. What had she expected anyway, she treated him terribly. He was doing all he could to make sure she was safe and his reward was her ire.

Talia picked up her alarm clock and frowned at its time, past midnight. Obviously, Luis had a timeline for this, and clearly, he had to pay overtime. Here she was wide-awake with oceans of concern. She did all the normal things she tried when she couldn't sleep—drink warm tea, eat cold cereal, read her new book. Nothing. She was exhausted, but still awake.

She pulled out her photo albums and sat cross-legged on the bed paging through them. She looked carefully at the pictures of Luis. She stared hard at his face noting the smile, the happiness in his eyes. The Luis of long ago when long ago was only months. Her dearest love was disappearing before her eyes. She leaned back on her pillows and closed her eyes, comparing that Luis with the Luis she recently saw—the one with the sunken face, protruding cheekbones, emaciated body, and dark circles under his eyes. Marcos's words kept booming in her ears.

Giving up, Talia traded her bed for the couch where she went over the notes she, Yulan, and June made. Time to focus. She knew when a young woman disappeared, something important was left. What could she do to find out what that was? It would provide another valuable clue into the case of the missing debutantes. Nerves shot, Talia shuffled the papers back into order. Murphy began nuzzling her in the way he always did when he needed to be let outside. Talia slipped a jacket on over her bathrobe, feeling the need for a brisk walk.

After a successful walk around the block, she hopped behind the wheel of her car, with Murphy in the backseat, and headed toward a fast food place near the auxiliary road. At Mister Frosty's, she ordered super-size fries and a chocolate malt. For entertainment, she drove to Luis's condo, finding a parking spot directly across the street. A yellow glow came from behind his windows. His silhouette moved about.

"That's our guy, Murphy."

After they had finished eating, Talia drove slowly around the courthouse square and admired the thousands of tiny white tea lights in the large gnarled trees. Talia smiled at them as she turned onto Locust and headed north toward home.

Opening the back door of the bungalow, she heard a horrific blast accompanied by swirling lights. The alarm whelped like a ship on fire. Flipping open the five-inch thick manual, she looked for how to turn it off. PUNCH IN THE CODE. That's right! She did so and there was immediate silence. The phone rang.

"Hello?"

"This is Home Securities Systems. Your alarm has

gone off. Are you all right?"

"Now that it isn't going off anymore, I'm fine."

"I need your code word."

"Caged."

Chapter Thirteen

It had been a few days since the alarm was installed, and yet, even with Murphy, she had a hard time sleeping. Each small noise—the rumble of a car driving past, a pop of the house, the clank of Murphy's collar—quickened her startle reflex. Just when she started to drop off, she'd jolt awake fearing an apparition of Maria Salas might hover. Timidly, she'd slip from bed to peek out the window hoping another body wasn't being dropped in her yard. The sun rose above the horizon. Its soft light sieved through the delicate lace curtains in her bedroom.

Questions brewed about Luis's comment concerning his 'parting gift.' This time she'd get the answers. *Is it too early to call Luis*? Better yet, she'd go to his condo and face him. When she finished dressing, her resolve was dissolving. There was a strong possibility he might refuse to see her which would be really hurtful.

A phone call was best. She picked up the landline and dialed his number. There was endless ringing. Not even his voice mail picked up. Then she tried his office. Jade answered.

"Hello, this is Talia Bonilla. Has Luis Arroyo arrived at the office yet?"

There was a moment of silence before the answer. "No, Mr. Arroyo has resigned."

Talia's knees buckled. The world seemed to crumble beneath her feet. "Resigned. That isn't possible. I just saw him yesterday afternoon, and he never said a word. Are you sure?"

"Of course, I am. He resigned yesterday morning. The memo went out in inner office email last night. Someone is cleaning out his office as we speak."

"What about his re-election?" Talia panicked. A hundred questions loped through her head.

"He withdrew his name. It's all over the news." Her voice seemed too controlled.

"Can you tell me why?"

"I simply am not allowed to say. Only that he no longer works for this office."

"Was he fired?"

Silence.

Hanging up the phone without saying goodbye, Talia turned on the news. After sitting through international news, local news was next.

"Amid a flurry of accusations from the news report which aired on this station, D.A. Luis Arroyo tendered his resignation effective immediately. Alex Monahan is acting D.A. until elections. What was his first order of business? Issuing a new warrant for the arrest of Sam Brimley."

Talia bit her lip wondering if Luis had dropped the ball on this one. What was going on with him anyway? Her stomach churned. Talia tried both Luis's cell again, and then his landline, but they both kept ringing. No voicemail option. Now all Talia wanted to do was crawl back into bed and sleep all day, but with a long-standing lunch engagement, she couldn't.

Talia dreaded facing Yulan and her cousin, Adie,

knowing the talk would eventually turn to relationships, and relationships meant failed ones, and failed ones meant Luis.

By eleven, the women were seated at LSU Burger on West Hickory. Yulan ordered double bacon cheeseburger with fruit salsa and cinnamon chips, so Talia and Adie did, too. The conversation seemed easy. No one brought up the latest news on Luis. Talia couldn't decide if it was the result of politeness, or if they hadn't heard about his resignation yet. Time and lunch would tell.

"Isn't anyone going to ask me how things are going between Daniel and me?" Adie asked with a smile.

"I will." Talia volunteered putting off the inevitable. "How are things going between you and your new boyfriend?"

"I broke up with him," Adie announced, which took the conversation to the failed relationship talk. "Don't you want to know what happened?"

"No, we most definitely do not." Yulan shook her head. "Some things need to remain private."

"Of course, we want to know. What happened, Adie?" Talia said, hoping the conversation would focus on Adie and remain diverted from her.

"Daniel insulted my father." Adie nodded her head up and down, and even Yulan had to agree that was unacceptable.

"What did he say?" Talia asked.

"He said my father favored me too much."

"Oh." Yulan rolled her eyes and bit her lip. She settled her eyes on Talia. "Changing the subject from the preposterous to the serious, should I mention the latest developments in Luis's office?"

"I don't want to talk about it." Talia shook her head while holding her breath, bracing for unsolicited opinions.

"Why did Luis resign?" Yulan pressed.

"He has very good reasons. I'm sure of it." Talia wanted to appear as though she knew what they were, when in fact she didn't even know where Luis was.

"We may no longer be researching the kidnapping cases either, isn't that right?"

"Wrong. It still needs to be solved."

"What research is that?" Adie wanted to know.

"I've been gathering background on the missing women. Yulan and my neighbor, June were helping me."

"We need to finish what we started," Yulan insisted.

"I don't want to help so glad you didn't ask me to do anything. Talia, I hear you broke it off with Luis," Adie interrupted.

"Luis broke our engagement."

"Ah, I see. Some jerk. Yulan told me all about it." Adie clasped her hands together in a romantic gesture as Talia shot her best friend a questioning look. "So you're being comforted in the arms of another?"

"Regardless of what Yulan may have told you, he is not a jerk, and I am not being comforted in the arms of anyone. I merely met a new person."

"A male person." Yulan cleared her throat. "Marco."

"A male person who has become a friend. Nothing more."

Lunch arrived. Yulan shoved a cinnamon chip into her mouth, then grabbed another chip scooping up a topping of salsa. “Mmmm, I’m in heaven. This fruit salsa is the best ever. I think I taste a bit of avocado in here. Makes for a nice subtle taste.”

“Tell us about your new friend, Talia.” Adie pushed. “Since he is just a friend, it shouldn’t bother you talking about him.”

“There is nothing to say.”

“So the new guy in your life is named Marco? Are you sure friendship is all you want with Marco?”

“Yes, it is,” Talia said sharply, having had enough. “And, Yulan, I don’t appreciate you gossiping about me to your cousin.”

“Adie got it all wrong,” Yulan defended herself.

“And how does your heart feel about Luis?” Adie persisted sitting erectly while nibbling purposeful lady-sized pieces of salad.

Tears rushed to her eyes. She dabbed at them with her fingertips

“Here.” Yulan handed her a tissue. Talia repaired the damage the tears did to her face with a bit of powder from her compact.

“What does Marco do for a living?” Adie asked.

“He’s supposedly a famous architect,” Yulan said.

“There is no supposed about it. He is quite well renowned.”

“Tsk, tsk. What a foolish girl you are for letting Luis go. I, for one, would have married when he first asked. No long engagements for me. No telling how many pretty girls will be waiting in line once word’s out he’s available again,” Adie crooned.

“What about you, Adie?” Talia asked, turning the conversation away from her. “Has anyone taken the place of Daniel?”

“Are you kidding? There’s always someone ready to fill the spot of *current* boyfriend. I walk down the street and men hand me their phone numbers, just begging to get into my life. I have two, maybe three, new possibilities just from getting here this morning.” Adie looked over Talia’s shoulder and broadly smiled. “Make that four possibilities. Look. A server inside the restaurant is waving frantically at me to get my attention. I see you.” Adie waved back with one hand as she dug through her purse for her business card to give him.

The other women turned to see. “I don’t think he’s trying to get your attention, my cousin. See the spray bottle? He’s just washing the windows.”

“Oh.” Adie turned red-faced. “Okay, we’re back to three possibilities.” She set the card down on the table. “More than you have, cousin.”

A car backfired, making the women jump.

“Talia, did you hear? Another socialite went missing. That now makes seven counting the dead girl whose body was recovered in your garden.” Yulan continued in a low voice, “The picture of the latest one was in today’s paper, and she looked very familiar to me. I just can’t place her yet, but I will. According to that TV reporter…Nancy Place, there are no new leads in this case. The police are warning women in the area not to go out at night alone. I hope you’re not, are you, Talia?”

“Of course not.”

“Boo,” someone yelled from behind them.

The women jumped and all screamed.

Marco roared with laughter as he brushed up from behind the women. “Hi, ladies. I was in the neighborhood for lunch when I saw you here." He twirled a metal chair around backwards then sat down.

"Hi, Marco," Talia greeted.

"So you are Marco." Adie smiled approvingly. "The architect."

Whispering to Talia, Yulan said, "Speak of the perp and he appears."

"Ssshhh."

"Mind if I join you?" He signaled the server.

"Looks to me like you already have," Yulan replied evenly as she forced a smile revealing a piece of cilantro caught in her teeth.

"Marco, you know Yulan, but I'd like for you to meet her cousin, Adie Yu."

Flower-like Adie blushed. "It's so nice to meet you." She offered him her small, perfectly-manicured hand.

Marco nodded without taking their hands. "It's hot today and I'm thirsty. I see you ladies could use a refill on your drinks, too. But the server seems to have disappeared. Don't worry I'll find him." Marco went into the restaurant.

"Talia…why did you tell that creep we were having lunch here? It's supposed to be just us girls," Yulan angrily asked.

"I didn't tell him."

"I, for one, am glad Marco is here," Adie added.

"I much prefer Luis to this new one," Yulan said.

"Hey, I'm back so you can stop talking about me now." Holding a white towel over his arm, he poured ice water from the silver pitcher with the other, clicking his heels.

"Thanks for the warning," Yulan commented

dryly.

"What else may I get for you ladies to eat?" He held an order pad in his hand.

"What are you doing, Marco?" Adie laughed, totally delighted. "We don't need a thing. Talia, you never mentioned Marco was so charming."

Just then a restaurant employee walked up, not at all amused with Marco's antics. He abruptly snatched Marco's pad and towel; a server behind him took the pitcher from his hand.

"Please sit down, sir, and we will take your order," one of the servers suggested.

"Well, it's about time," Marco taunted.

Yulan kept an eye on Marco. She ate quickly, letting the others occupy the conversation. Marco tried too hard to be funny while Talia grew quiet. Adie hung on every word, Yulan looked as though she was holding back a scream.

"That's it. My meal is finished and I'm leaving," Yulan announced plopping her fork down. "Server?" She waved one hand in the air and wiped her mouth on a paper napkin with the other. "Check, please."

"Oh, I'll get the bill, it's my treat," Marco quickly offered.

"No argument from me. Thanks. Come on, Adie." Yulan pulled at her cousin.

"But I'm not ready to leave," Adie protested as she pretended to accidentally drop her card on Marco's lap.

"Wait, we all planned to spend the afternoon together," Talia protested while watching her friends walk away.

"I, for one, am glad they're gone." Marco studied Talia's face as if he were smitten. "Where'd you like to go? Name it. Paris, France, Rome, Italy. Did I ever tell you I have a private jet?"

"I do need fresh fruit. Want to go along with me to the Farmers' Market?"

"I've never been. I'd love to tag along," Marco offered enthusiastically. "Thanks."

They walked down the steps to street level.

"Follow me in your car. Where are you parked?"

"It's the green one right across the street." He pointed.

Talia froze as a ball of frost formed in her throat. There was the sea-mist Jaguar. So it was *Marco* who had been shadowing her, scaring her? It made total sense. There was no way she was going to take another step in any direction with him. Marco reached for her arm, but she stepped away.

"Is something wrong? You look upset…as if you have seen a ghost."

"So, that green car is yours?" Talia snapped. Quickly, she contemplated calling for help, but hated scenes. She wanted to get as far away from Marco as possible and then find that Officer Davila.

"Yup, one of 'em. I have five cars, various makes and models, dating back to the 1950s. Isn't this a beaut?" Marco proclaimed, as he cupped his hand over his eyes to shield the brightness of the sun reflecting off it.

Her heart rate skyrocketed. "I'm not going anywhere with you. You're the one who's been following me. Stay away from me, do you understand?" Talia fled down the street, hearing his footsteps close behind. It was hard to breathe. She felt as though she was suffocating.

"Following you? What are on earth are you talking about?" Marco chased her and grabbed her arm again, spinning her about. His jaw tightened. Talia wrenched her arm away from his hold. Frantically, she dug through her pink purse trying to find her cell phone so she could take a picture of it, but couldn't find it in the mess.

Just then a muscular man in a tight yellow shirt wearing jeans and a Rangers baseball cap, shading his eyes and part of his face, came rushing over to them. "Do you need help, ma'am?" He shoved himself between them, separating the two.

"Do I, Marco? Do I need help this man's help, or were you just leaving?"

"I'll leave right after you explain your irrational behavior."

"I don't think she needs to explain anything. Beat it, mister," baseball cap man said.

"Wait, just a minute," Talia told the man. "I do want an answer."

"I'll wait right here until you get an answer you like." Baseball cap man kept his eyes on Marco.

"Thank you." Talia turned back to Marco. "Tell me, why you've been following me in that Jag?"

"Jag? I don't have a Jag. I own that green Porsche two cars down from the Jag." He pointed. "See, right there."

"The hunter green Porsche." Talia blanched.

"Yes, I just told you that. I bought it last week. Oh forget it! You're not worth the trouble." He waved his arms in the air and crossed the street.

"Thanks for your help, I really appreciate it. I think I am good now."

"Any time." He clapped his hands together as if about to make a sports play and continued on down the street as Talia caught up with Marco.

"Marco, please listen to me. I'm sorry. I thought you were the driver of the Jag. That car has been following me."

Ignoring her, Marco opened the car door. Talia shut it on him. "It's just I've been so jumpy lately. My life is falling apart. Luis broke up with me, a dead woman shows up at my place, and now another woman has disappeared."

"Goodbye, Talia." Marco climbed into his car, revved the engine, and backed out of the space.

She wasn't sorry to see him leave. As for the Jag, Talia figured the smart thing to do would be to stake it out.

After Marco drove off, she noticed the Jag was gone, too.

All Talia wanted to do was return home. She found her car and got in, turning up the AC. *It's October, how can it still be ninety-three degrees?* Driving home, her cell rang.

"Are you still with that creep?" Yulan asked.

"No." Talia didn't want to say more. The afternoon had been too exhausting.

"Good. I wanted you to know that just this morning I heard from my friend in Luis's office. He feels more inclined to speak to me now with Luis gone from office, and his successor in charge."

"Oh, please tell me, Yulan."

"There is a common name between the missing women."

"And the name is?"

Chapter Fourteen

It was early morning.

Talia wrestled with the dough, pressing it down on the face of the cool marble slab. It served as a remedy for her raw emotions. Unbelievably, after all this time and hard work, Yulan's contact didn't know the name. It was a well-guarded secret, which only a few were privy too. The code name was "Big." It sounded like the romantic lead's nickname from some TV show, only this guy was lethal.

Where is Luis anyway? Since resigning, he left town—or so it seemed. For the past few weeks, since his resignation, he had been unreachable. His car wasn't where he always parked it and his place was always dark. The absent voice in her heart was deafening. Couldn't he at least have given her a two-minute phone call, if not for her, then for the sake of Murphy? What if there was an emergency with the dog? Luis hadn't even told her the vet's name.

With a tight fist, she pounded and pounded the dark dough, thinking there'd soon be nothing left for her fists to beat. Finally, tying it into a knot and sprinkling it with streusel, she popped the Pan Dulce bread into the oven. After cooling, she wrapped it up carefully in a clean linen towel.

Then she remembered it was Luis's all-time favorite. Perhaps she'd try reaching Luis again, right now. If he didn't answer this time, then that would be it. She promised herself she'd never call again.

"Yes, one more time will be all right won't it? Just one more time," she promised herself.

Her heart gave a hop when he answered. He sounded good; he sounded like Luis. Her Luis. Thank goodness.

"Finally, Luis, is it really you?" she gasped thrusting her hand over her heart.

"Hi, Talia," his voice was strong and rung with joy. "How's Murphy?"

"What? You only want to know about Murphy? What about me? Aren't you concerned about how this single gal is doing living all alone with a serial abductor still on the prowl? You haven't forgotten all about the predator since leaving office have you?" she teased.

"How are you?" he asked warmly.

"Wonderful. Second semester school starts today. My first class is at noon. By the way, where have you been?" Talia had to know while trying not to sound too nosey.

"Miami."

"You went on a vacation? Alone?" She held her breath, waiting for the answer.

"No time for a vacation. Remember I told you there was a similar case in Miami?"

"Yes, now I do."

"That's why I went…to speak to the lead detective on the case and read the files. I'm back as of last night."

"I just baked a Pan Dulce," she told him in her most sexy way.

"Chocolate?"

"Is there any other kind?"

"You know it's my favorite. Is it all right to ask about Murphy now?"

Wild with desire to see him, she quickly formulated a plan. "Yes. He's the reason I'm calling." She imagined Luis's smile.

"He's all right, isn't he?"

"Oh, Luis, he's so not himself." Talia looked at Murphy leaping wildly after falling leaves in her large backyard.

"Depressed?"

"Not sure I would go that far but he needs to see you." *I need to see you.* Murphy dug furiously in the bog uprooting many of her wetland plants; he turned about with a frog hanging out of his mouth. Talia knocked on the window for him to drop it. He looked up, dropped the frog, wagged his tail, and began to dig again, but in a new spot this time. He loved her garden and was quickly destroying it. "I'm bringing him by for a visit."

"When?"

"Now. As soon as it cools."

"Talia, that's not such a good idea. Not now. Not today," he protested.

"Well, the chocolate bread is ready today. Murphy is ready today. I am almost ready. It seems you're outnumbered. Just a visit and we'll not stay long, promise. Bye!" She closed the call before he could squeeze in another word. Hurrying outside, she checked on the frog that was now under the water in the pond. After checking he was no worse for wear, she grabbed Murphy by his collar and ran the hose over him. Great chunks of muddy clay still clung to his undercoat, but there was no time for a complete bath. "What a mess."

Quickly showering and changing into a turquoise skirt with an alluring side slit, she buttoned up a white linen blouse that accentuated her figure. Then she pulled her hair into a ponytail as she angled her feet into new patent leather shoes. After drizzling an icy sweet glaze over the dessert, she carefully covered it with wax paper and placed it onto a cookie sheet. Then with the other hand, she caught Murphy by the nape of his neck to clip the leash onto his collar.

Talia felt optimistic and sexy driving to Luis's. Murphy felt the excitement too, prancing all over the backseat, licking up the windows, and shedding profusely. His fur and mud spattered the seat.

She easily found a parking space and then led Murphy out by his leash. The cookie sheet in her left hand, the loop of her bubble gum purse swinging from her arm, Murphy pulled her along by her right hand. "Have you learned nothing from hours of dog training?" she complained.

As soon as the elevator doors opened, she released his leash, allowing Murphy to wildly sprint down the long hallway. He began to bark and scratch at the door, smelling Luis on the other side.

Blowing loose strands of hair from her eyes, she formulated her plan. Everyone seemed to either know what was going on with Luis, or had formulated their own notion. More than anyone else, she knew Luis's character. Any criticism didn't make sense. Caught in a maze of deadends, she had to once and for all find out the truth for herself.

She stood at the door. Knocked. Waited. Finally, the door flung wide, and there he was. Luis wore familiar dark trousers and a white silk shirt—it was just old enough that she remembered how the fabric felt against her cheek when he took her into his arms. His hair was still thin, but carefully combed back. He looked good. Rested. It seemed as if he had added a few pounds to his frame. It did her heart good to see him like this.

Murphy howled with delight then ran circles about his master. It was quite heartwarming, bringing tears to her eyes. Luis dropped to his knees and hugged the dog around his neck. But just as quickly, he drew back. "Yuck. What did you get into Murphy?" Luis exclaimed looking at his now muddy clothes.

"I did my best to clean him. It's nothing, really, just a little bog. I'm happy to see you, Luis."

"I'm happy to see you, too. Come on in." Luis stepped back.

"Enjoy." Talia kissed his cheek then set the cookie sheet on the granite countertop.

Luis smiled broadly as he scratched Murphy's ears. Talia noticed he looked at her adoringly. It was nearly like old times. "Gosh but I've missed the two of you. Bog, did you say?" He pulled some dried mud from the dog's underbelly.

"Bog is like a wetland."

"I'm familiar with the attributes of a bog." He tossed the crusted mud into the sink and then ran water after it. Grabbing a yellow kitchen towel, he dried his hands. "I bet it was fun digging. Wish I could've been there. Would love to have helped."

"Wish you could have been there, too. Would have loved your help."

"What do you need for your bog? I want to be part of it. A way to thank you for taking such great care of

Murph."

"That's not necessary."

"Tell me, before I get you something useless."

"Okay, I would love a turtle. I need one before the weather gets bad so it can acclimate."

"Done."

"The bog is my latest backyard project. Murphy helps. Whatever I do, he undoes. It's become a partnership. And we've both missed you." She meant her words, running her pointer finger over the bridge of his nose. "So very much."

"I'd like to see your bog sometime." He spoke softly, looking into her eyes.

"Murph and I would like that just fine. I imagine finding time won't be a problem anymore. I heard you are no longer the D.A."

"Quitting was the only right thing to do." Luis took a giant step back as his demeanor shifted. "There's too much gossip swirling around with Brimley and the re-election business. Fracking, too. Sounds like the new governor might be overturning our hard-won election of banning. Meanwhile, the town needs to get on with business. I need to get on with life."

"What's next for you, Luis?"

"Not sure." He moved his hand a little, as if he was going to take hers, but then he stopped.

"By the way, Miami seems to have done you worlds of good." Talia turned to saunter to the large windows and looked out. "The view is lovely from here. See, one doesn't need to be high above the street for it to be pleasant."

"I had that in mind when I bought it for us." Luis stopped short. "We sure seemed to tango a lot when we were engaged, didn't we?"

Talia asked him silently, *Would you dance with me one more time?*

As if momentarily paralyzed, Luis stared at her. Could he see the love she held tightly inside of her? What she saw in his dark eyes was only leftover pain from a love that might never be again.

After a long pause, he said, "Thank you for the dolce. Talia, I hate to do this to you, but I have an appointment." Appearing uncomfortable, he walked past her, toward his briefcase.

"Oh?" She turned about.

Luis wasn't saying more.

"Okay. I really can't stay myself. My first art class this semester starts in an hour. Murphy is coming along with me today." Talia glanced about, wondering how to stall.

"My Murph is starting class? Hey, boy, be good and give me a full report tonight. Don't give your teacher a hard time. Tomorrow, I'll polish an apple for you to give her." He hugged the dog's neck not worrying about getting dog hair on his clothing. Another thing she found so irresistible about Luis; *he is so unpretentious.*

"Really, I need to be walking out the door this moment." He leaned back on the bookcase, not seeming to be in any hurry at all.

"Well, then Murphy and I'll be leaving. But you really should change your shirt before you leave because I can see the mud on it."

"Good idea." He scooted around the wall of the hallway and she heard the squeaky movement of the tambour doors open. The phone rang and Luis was finishing buttoning the fresh shirt, when he picked up his cell. "Hello? Yes, Mr. Correa. I got in last night and I have those figures right here."

Her skin pricked with fear; Talia couldn't move. "Mr. Correa?" she whispered to Murphy who immediately pricked up his ears.

Luis nodded his head and covered the receiver. "I got a call from him while I was away. He wants me to do a couple of jobs for him. I need the work so why not? What? Yes, I'm still here." Luis turned his back to her as he went through a briefcase. It was a new briefcase, not the old one he used as D.A. Where was the one which held the secrets?

What was Marco up to by hiring Luis? There were answers to be had and she suspected this place might hold some of them. Taking full advantage of Luis's distraction, Talia tiptoed about. She didn't think she resembled a spy, but still acted like one. Pushing aside books, she didn't even find dust. Next, she slid open another drawer. Her hands reached about on the inside for anything unusual and came up with hardcopies of emails sent and received on the debutante case. Quickly, she scanned them, resisting the urge to shove them into her purse. The preliminary reading didn't give any new information other than what was already public knowledge. Quietly, she closed the drawer and then slid open the one beneath it. Her fingers searched frantically, finding nothing that didn't belong.

Then she hit pay dirt. There on top of his desk was the folder, finding it interesting he still had it right here. Not letting another second tick by, Talia opened the cover and there it was—a tiara. *How perfectly chilling*. It had to be the calling card.

The adrenaline rush from discovery made her head buzz, her skin tingle, her blood rush, and her heart pound. Never in a million years would she have thought of something more splendid. Now she skimmed for information. There, in Luis's handwriting, were the words—*In each case of the missing women, a diamond-studded tiara was left. They all matched perfectly. Individually, designer made. Center peaked with both clear and showy crimson diamonds. Set into a sterling silver setting. Measurements: 5.5 at the highest point, and 8 inches across.*

Tiara! That was the calling card. The kidnapper took the debutante and left behind a tiara, a symbol of her place in society. Perhaps a place he could never achieve; therefore, the caliber of the female he wanted would never be interested in someone like him. Excitement bubbled. She couldn't wait to share the discovery with June and Yulan. With three duplicate pictures, Talia figured Luis would never notice if one was missing. She folded one and slipped it into her pink purse. Next, she read the list of shops in the northern Texas area that carried tiaras but the shopkeepers all agreed this was custom made. Luis had visited each place and signed off on the investigation. Knowing he could be off the phone at any moment, she needed to work faster. If Luis caught her, how could she explain her behavior?

"Okay, will see you later. Bye… Talia?" Luis called down the corridor.

Footsteps came toward her. Talia shut the folder and centered it the same way she found it.

"Hi." She stepped breathlessly around the corner and directly in front of him. "I'll leave as soon as I use the restroom."

Behind the bathroom door, she twisted the lock. The medicine cabinet was ajar. Slowly, she opened it. Pushing the items about she saw the usual assortment of expected items—floss, eye drops, bandages, rub for sore muscles, razor, and cream, but now four pharmaceutical bottles sat at the top.

One by one, she turned them slowly about in her hand to read the labels. Captopril, Natrecor, Digitoxin, and Atenolol. Frantically, with seconds ticking away loudly in her ears, she searched for a pen in her purse, but all she came up with was a broken pencil and an exploded pen. That's when she thought about her camera phone. She took pictures of the bottles, making sure the pharmaceutical names were front and center. Carefully, she replaced the bottles, with front facing labels, as she had found them. Unhurried, she closed the cabinet and flushed the toilet at the same time to disguise any noise. Washing her hands, she then dried them. On the way down the hall, she took a quick peek inside the closet door that still stood open, revealing coats and jackets.

Luis stood at the far end of the living room looking out at the square. He appeared vulnerable. How she wanted to put her arms around him, lay her head against his back, and tell him she was here for him, to lean on her for a change. Instead, she gently placed her hands on his shoulders.

"What kind of work are you doing for Mr. Correa?" It sounded strange to her ears to listen to herself referring to Marco in this formal manner. What would Luis have to say if he learned she had become friendly with such a strong campaign contributor and now his new employer? Marco was behind something and, whatever it was, it meant no good.

"He's looking at out of state properties to widen his architectural business. I'm doing preliminary grunt work for him," Luis innocently explained.

Talia was suspicious. Maybe Luis was really checking Marco Correa out as a suspect as he worked for him. She certainly would do that. After all, he had just returned from Miami doing work on a case to which he was no longer connected.

"Okay, well, we'll be going now." Talia dropped her hands to her side and gathered up the dog leash. She led Murphy from the apartment. Her visit with Luis had gone better than she had hoped.

As soon as she got into the car, she dug for her cell phone and flipped it open to call Yulan, who picked up on the third ring. "Guess what? I was just at Luis's. I know the calling card. It is cool beyond words."

Yulan squealed, "Oh my goodness, I have to know. Tell me, Talia, I beg of you."

"A tiara."

"A tiara? Brilliant."

"I even have a picture of it."

Yulan practically swooned.

Talia removed the picture from her purse, took a picture of it, and then texted it to Yulan and June.

"How did you get this information without Luis seeing you?"

"While he was on the phone, I found the case folder and went through it."

"This is a proud, proud moment," Yulan congratulated her. "Next thing you know, you'll be joining the Nancy Place fan club right along with me.

We can go to conventions together. By golly, that tiara is gorgeous. Looks expensive."

"Now delete it. No one can know about this."

"Done."

Talia whistled her way up the steps of UNT's CVAD building, Studio of Visual Arts and Design, with Murphy in the lead. Quickly disappearing in between the doors, she still had just enough time to research before the students arrived.

Murphy curled up beneath her desk. She turned to the computer and opened the cell phone to read the names of the bottles. Talia typed in the prescription names and pressed enter. There before her eyes the words *congestive heart failure* blew across the screen. Flabbergasted, so many things fit now. Reading through the site, she learned about ACE inhibitors slow progression of heart failure. The medications he was on helped his blood vessels to expand, lower blood pressure but it also caused crazy side effects. With absolute clarity, she knew Luis had displayed them all—tiredness, hair loss, lack of energy, chills, nausea, vomiting, and stomach cramps. *Should he be taking all these drugs?* Someone tapped on her office door; the dog barely picked up his ears.

"Talia, sorry, but there's some rather bad news."

"Bad news?" Her heart dropped.

"I just got a call from Denton Presbyterian Hospital. It's Luis. I am so sorry." Dr. Hancock's wet eyes and sagging shoulders expressed how he felt.

Badly shaken, Talia rose to her feet. "I just came from Luis's. He was just fine. He's dead?"

Her heart pounded and breathing increased. Already perspiration crowned her forehead. "It can't be.

Someone got this wrong. Not Luis."

Dr. Hancock took her hand. "Luis collapsed outside his building, just a little while ago. Paramedics were called. He's still alive. They found your number in his cell. May I drive you, or call you a cab? You shouldn't drive."

Talia grabbed for her purse. "I'll be fine. What about my classes?"

"I'll cancel them for you today," he quickly offered.

"But it's the first day of the second semester?"

"All right. You have a point. I'll take your classes and tell them what a treat they have for you this semester."

"You are a dear man, Dr. Hancock. Oh, no! I nearly forgot about Murphy. I can't take him to the hospital with me, and I don't want to run home with him first.

Dr. Hancock grimaced looking the large dog over from head to toe, evaluating the situation. "I'll take Murphy, too. I assume he doesn't bite?"

****

Talia stiffly sat in the lounge of the hospital waiting for news, counting the tile patterns stretching across the floor. The staff hurried about in their usual professional routine while the air was scented with disinfectant, death, and medicine. Finally, a short, slender physician, Dr. Fuentes arrived holding her clipboard to the chest of her white coat and sat down. Fortyish, her hair was lightly dappled with gray, and a smile tried to put her at ease amid the chaotic atmosphere. She appeared intelligent and confident which immediately filled Talia with hope.

"Luis Arroyo collapsed this morning in the doorway of his building and a call was made for assistance. We have him stabilized in the emergency room. He's on the way to a private room now."

"Then he will be here for a while?"

"Yes. One of his heart valves won't close properly and it's leaky, seeping into his lungs. A new drug is on the market and we're putting him on it today. We're adjusting his meds now, but we'll keep him for a few days to make sure there are not any reoccurrences in the meantime. He'll be heavily sedated all day and won't even know if you're here. My advice is to let him rest, get some rest yourself, and come again when he's awake and alert."

"Is he dying?"

"We are hopeful this is only a setback."

Talia watched the doctor's mouth move as the words made sounds in the air from her lips. She knew the words, but it was difficult to put them together in order to make sense. Luis was critically ill and had been for a very long time; at least, that is what she understood. She hadn't known. "What's his prognosis?" Frightened, she cringed, feeling her body fold into itself.

"Since we caught Luis's heart disease early during a routine exam, there's an excellent chance for a normal life. We can treat him through drug therapy or surgery, but we're going the less invasive way for now," Fuentes explained.

"You said he was sleeping, but I really need to see for myself that he is fine. May I go in for a moment?" Talia begged.

"I don't see any harm in that. Just don't disturb

him. He needs to sleep," the doctor warned standing to her feet.

Talia picked up her bubble gum purse and walked down the hallway of diamond shaped red and white linoleum squares. The light coming through the window was diffused, a yellow glow filling the room. She pulled the curtains halfway across to stop the sun from waking him. Luis appeared so small and vulnerable in the white hospital sheets. The metal side rails were up as if he were an animal that may escape if it weren't for them. Talia touched his short hair.

"Luis, I'm here," her voice was intentionally low as she gazed into his sleeping face. Standing on tiptoes, she leaned over the bed rails, kissing him gently on his brow. Turning to the doctor, she pleaded, "Allow me to stay for a while. I want to sit with him, hold his hand. He doesn't know I'm here, but I do. He'd do the same for me."

"It sounds like this is where you need to be."

The room was void of flowers. She made a mental note to bring bouquets. Every so often, Luis moved his arm or twitched a foot beneath the sheet; her eyes shot in his direction each time he made a single sound, hoping he would awaken so they could talk. That never happened. The IV slowly dripped from the plastic bag down the long tube and into the back of Luis's hand. Leaving him was not an option. Not anymore. She loved him. That meant she'd never leave.

Talia peeked through the curtains at the emergency parking lot. At least there was no familiar Jaguar in sight. It all looked normal. She watched people across the street seemingly leading such ordinary lives, and it caused her to wonder if her life would ever be the same again.

Just as Dr. Fuentes said, Luis slept all day. By evening, Talia headed back to school to pick up Murphy and get her lesson plans ready for the following week. In case Luis needed her, a faculty member could sub. His family still lived in South America and couldn't make the trip to the States. The idea of Luis needing her to help him through this time made her glad.

Walking into her office that evening, Talia was anything but delighted to see Marco seated at her desk. Two greasy bags of takeout food sat on her class syllabus. *How could he be so careless?* Marco's mere presence irritated her. She just wanted to write lesson plans, speak to Dr. Hancock about a sub, get the dog, pick up some folders, and leave for the evening. With a hundred things on her mind, Marco was not one of them.

"It's about time."

"Did I forget something? I don't believe we had plans." Talia didn't try to hide her annoyance as she moved the bags onto the gray linoleum floor.

It was irritating Marco thought it was all right to be comfortable by sitting in her chair, meddling in her things; touching the special pens she wrote with, opening her books. Messy at home, she was meticulous at the office and knew even when a paper clip had been moved. She wanted to find out why he hired Luis for his special projects when he had nothing but obvious disdain for the man. However, she knew she had to approach that with subtlety, or she'd never get a straight answer.

"I thought I'd surprise you, but I was the one

surprised. No one seemed to know where you were, so I decided to wait for you."

"What made you think I'd come back today?" Talia sat down on the chair meant for visitors.

"Murphy." Shoving off from the floor with his feet, he spun her desk chair about once on its axis.

"How did you know Murphy was with me?" Looking about the room, there was no evidence the dog had come to work with her. Her calendar was flipped open to a week earlier. She slammed it shut. "You're stalking me."

"Chill out, Talia. Hancock told me you were out, didn't say where, but said you'd return for the dog."

"How long have you been here?"

He looked at his watch and indifferently answered, "About three hours."

His answer made her do a double take. "Just when do you get your work done?" she pointedly asked. At this time of the day, the cultural arts building was nearly empty. "Or, is that why you hired Luis, so he could do it for you?"

"So you know? It was just a matter of time until you did. Luis has talents. They're being put to good use, as a favor to you. Instead of yelling at me, you should be thanking me for keeping him gainfully employed. You are welcome."

Talia backed from his reach, as he tried to touch to her face.

"Actually, I cleared my calendar just for you. You're my top priority for tonight."

"You should have checked with me first." Needing to feel in control, Talia moved to the other side of the room. "All my free time will now be dedicated to helping Luis recover. There'll be no time for any lunches, or dinners, spur of the moment visits, or even phone calls. Not anymore."

"How can you put our friendship on hold so easily?" He shoved the chair out from underneath him and began pacing. "Whose shoulder are you going to cry on when he tosses you away again? Or, should I just fire him and get him out of both our lives?"

"No, don't." Fear spread across Talia's spirit. She didn't want to ruin things for Luis. Not when he was so excited about the projects and new opportunities.

A knock on the open door drew their attention. Amanda Pudding stood at the doorframe, seemingly puzzled.

Talia felt relief. It showed in her voice. "There's my star student…Amanda, hello."

"Ms. Bonilla, we all missed you in class today. I needed to see you, and Dr. Hancock told me you'd be back. I lost the rubric he gave to us for the project. Can I get a new one? I want to be sure I'm doing my project correctly since you weren't in class to explain it." Her blonde hair flowed down her back.

Talia searched through the folders on her desk. Finding the right one, she pulled the chart and handed it to her. "This is a particularly difficult one, but I know you can handle it. I am not sure when I will be back to class, but someone just as competent will be filling in for me."

"Hey, aren't you going to introduce us?" Marco smiled at Amanda who was quick to return it.

"No time for introductions. Amanda has work to do. Go home, Amanda, and get it done." Just like she wanted to protect Luis from Marco, she felt even more protective about Amanda.

"Come on…" Marco pressed.

"Amanda, this is Mr. Correa." Talia felt cornered.

"Are you related to the Correa of the Correa building?" How alert and intelligent her face appeared in contrast to the man she addressed.

"The one and only, but you can call me Marco." He beamed with delight, having name recognition. "I was just on my way out." The greasy bags were dumped into the metal trashcan and landed with an echoing thump. "Are you up for a cup of coffee?"

Amanda giggled girlishly which emphasized the age difference. Whipping her hair back as if she were in a shampoo commercial, her cobalt eyes sparkled.

"Again, I think she has a very difficult assignment to complete. You need to start this evening," Talia answered for the young woman. Then she nervously tapped her pencil eraser on the desk.

"Ms. Bonilla is right. I need to work on this project."

"That's right." Talia smiled. "I expect continuing excellence, and so does Disney. Don't let either of us down." She frantically waved good-bye to the girl who remained pressed against the door jam.

Undeterred, Marco quickly suggested, "May I drive you home then?"

"My car is out in the parking lot. Thanks any way."

"What a coincidence. Mine is there as well. We can walk out together. Safety in numbers."

"Great," Talia called after them. "Be sure to say hello to Jorge, the night watchman for me. Remember he sees *everything.*"

Chapter Fifteen

Bedrails down. Luis sat upright in his hospital bed, smiling at Talia, who sailed into his hospital room like a spring breeze, with a bouquet of freshly cut yellow lilies on her arm.

"Wow, Luis. I didn't expect to see you looking so well after yesterday." Her hope swelled. Relief flooded her worry and pushed it out to sea.

"It's amazing what the right cocktail of meds can do." Accepting the flowers, he leaned back into the thick, white pillows. "These are beautiful. Thank you."

"They are from my garden." Her heart rate quickened.

"I guessed as much." He breathed in their scent. "Perfect. Tee, they're perfect."

It'd been so long since he said her name like that she became lightheaded. It gave her hope. Maybe he remembered some of the good things about them. Maybe there was even a part of him who missed her.

"Look through your bouquet. I added one little surprise, just for you." She gave him a coquettish smile.

Luis searched through the bouquet. There it was…a single blue bud. Snapping it from the stem, he slowly placed the flower in her long dark hair. The stargazer lily appeared as a seashell, on dark waves.

"What are you doing here so early? Don't you have a class to teach, or a dog to let out?" He tried to act displeased, but the shine in his eyes gave him away.

"I'm where I need to be, by your side." Turning, she popped open the door of the metal side table looking for a container. "I guess I should've brought a vase for these."

"The nurse can find one."

Talia returned to his side and kissed him on his cheek.

"I miss you," he said.

She kissed him on the lips, closing her eyes, taking in his touch and the splendid way he made her feel.

"When I am well, we need to go somewhere, just the two of us. Get away for a bit to rekindle us." He pulled her next to him on the bed and kissed her deeply. "Where should we go?"

She used a laugh to cover her confusion.

"I'm serious. I've missed you so much." He held her to him. His hot breath against her neck stirred her feelings. "Life can be short."

"It can. But Luis you make me dizzy with all of this. I thought we were broken up. And you are here in a hospital bed, talking of vacationing and—" She held her tongue.

He laid back into his pillow and gazed out the window, releasing a puff of air.

"I want to ask you some questions and need answers." Talia took a deep breath, praying for strength.

"Ask me anything."

"Tell me, how long have you known about your illness, Luis? Did you know when you broke our engagement?"

His eyes seemed to turn from brown to mahogany

in the light.

"Talia, I sensed your hesitation to marry me. When I discussed the wedding or honeymoon, you drifted. If I had told you about my heart, you would've felt obligated to stay. I gave you an out…you took it."

"No. You opened a door and pushed me out." The words fell from her lips. Emotions between them always seemed to turn so quickly.

"Well, you should be very happy now…you're free." Luis crossed his arms.

"Ecstatically happy, too, it seems." Talia shook with fury. She grabbed her belongings and hurried out of the room. At the end of the hall, she stopped. Her fingers grasped around the handle of her purse. She bit down hard on her lip. Not one day had passed since she decided she would remain with Luis. But now, here she stood with wounded feelings, ready to fly away.

"Take a deep breath," Talia whispered to herself. "Put yourself in Luis's situation. He needs you." She twirled on her heels and walked right back into the room. Luis looked surprised.

"The doctor said your condition is treatable." Talia still held her purse against her chest. She stared at the floor reflectively. Her black hair fell forward shielding her face.

"With a price."

"What are you talking about?"

"Forget it." He looked away.

"Tell me, Luis. Please. Enough secrets." She crossed the floor and sat at the end of the bed. "Truth…please."

Luis picked at the bed sheets. Tears formed in the corners of his dark eyes. "Chances are that the medication I'm taking to save my life will prevent life."

Talia felt puzzled.

"It most likely will leave me…sterile." His voice was haunted and saturated with guilt.

Talia stared ahead as the meaning of the words sank in.

"No babies." The words made her feel as though she were falling off a cliff in the darkness, not knowing when she would hit the ground. She spoke in a low voice, as though someone else were in the room, someone she didn't want to overhear. "That was something I needed to know so we could have decided our future together, Luis. Stop making our decisions for me. It's time we make them together." She scooted toward him and held his hand to her face. "Let me be with you through your illness. It's what I want."

He gently tugged on a strand of her hair.

"Do you still love me?" Her eyes fluttered against the tears crowning her eyes.

"I will answer that when I'm well enough to do something about it."

"Loving me is the only thing that really matters." She began to weep.

"You say that now in your youth. But later, babies will matter."

For a moment, neither of them moved. She looked at him longingly and noticed he didn't recoil. Without a word, he put his arm around her shoulders and pulled her to him, her face against his chest. She breathed in his essence and felt lighter. She was safe here, completely safe with him. But something was still niggling her. "The day at your apartment when I came to pick up my art supplies?"

"What about it?"

"I followed you."

He crinkled his forehead. "Where?"

"To a broken down building where you knocked on the backdoor." She twisted the hem of her blue dress.

"Now I know what you are talking about. Dr. Fuentes sponsors a free clinic across town and it's open two-days a week. I needed a new prescription."

"So, your drugs are legal? Prescribed?" Worry eased.

"Of course, honey." He played with her hand, kissing her fingertips one by one. The other hand ran up her stocking leg under her ruched jersey dress. Her skin prickled by his firm touch.

"I see you are feeling better." She nuzzled closer, enjoying his touch. Something was missing from his arm. She glanced about the room for it. "Where is your watch?"

"I lost it." He shrugged.

"You lost your Rolex? That doesn't sound like you. The only thing you ever lost in your whole life was your baby teeth." She sweetly smiled.

"It'll turn up, but if not, I don't really care." Luis thoughtfully stared up at the ceiling. "I always heard that during times of illness, people re-evaluate their lives. I'm no different. In between doctor visits, I spent a lot of time looking over my life, asking myself what more I could have done to help others? Asking why I hurt the woman I care so much about?"

"Yes, why did you hurt me?"

"To save you from a greater hurt later."

"You were wrong. I want to share every aspect of your life, not be shut out."

"And Paris? What about The Sorbonne? Didn't you leave me out of that decision?"

"Forgive me."

"What is next for you, Luis?"

"Clean air. Clean water. Good land. I want to be part of the Frack Free Denton movement. I'm sure they can use a lawyer."

"But the oil companies were defeated in the vote."

"The new Texas governor is going for legislation that will turn over cities' individual rights in favor of state control. What ever happened to *government for the people, by the people*? I would like to bring legislation that makes the people decide without special interest groups overturning it. But, that takes time. I also want to lobby for more money for the mentally ill. I bet you don't know Brimley is mentally ill. The State of Texas is the bottom state in the U.S. in providing care and resources. There is so much good to be done that I cannot do as D.A. I've refocused my goals. Tee, I want to do something meaningful before my life is over. I want to matter."

"What about your job with Mr. Correa?"

"That's just eyeing some property for him to expand. A few months' worth of work till I'm on my feet," Luis said. "We've been friends for many years. He's a good man."

"A good man?" Talia nearly fell off the bed. Well, she certainly knew a side of the man that wasn't so good. She wanted to blurt out everything she knew about the man but thought it would do more harm than good to Luis's recovery. Another time, they would have that conversation, not today. For now, she would spent time with Luis, in bed together, fully clothed, arms around one another. When he fell asleep, she left for home.

Not the least bit tired, she sat on the couch, going over the case files with Murphy curled at her feet. Talia called June and Yulan for a three-way chat.

"There are so many matching tiaras. Where could they all have come from?" Talia reached for her tea.

"Maybe we should spend a few weeks traveling to all the stores in the Metroplex that carry them?" June suggested.

"The police already covered that." Talia stared at the photograph. "They came up with nothing."

"Everything seems to be online these days. Try finding it there," Yulan suggested.

Talia turned to her laptop. Reaching the homepage to one of the most popular sites, she typed in the word tiara and narrowed her search from there. "Ah, here's an interesting seller's name…princess*charming."

"Sounds like a true Prima Donna. It fits. Try her tiaras." Yulan giggled.

Scanning through the seller's individual tiara auctions, Talia said, "Looks very close to her designs. I'm going to email the seller." Almost instantly came her reply. Talia read it aloud to the women.

*Princess*charming, "Thanks for your interest in my custom made tiaras. I ship not only in the U.S., but also worldwide. If you'll send me a picture of the tiara you're referring to, I'll be able to tell in a glance if it's one of mine. I did get a rather large order."*

Talia, "How recently was it, and can you tell me the shipping address?"

*Princess*charming, "I don't give out information about my clients."*

Talia explained her need to know.

*Princess*charming, "Send me a picture and I will get back to you."*

Talia scanned the picture, emailed it, and then waited for the response, which didn't arrive.

Yulan said, "Adie is beeping in the other line. I better go and see what she wants."

"And I better get some coconut oil on my face before it gets any later."

The women closed their calls.

Twenty minutes later, there still wasn't an email response. While showering, Talia decided to give it another day, but at midnight, she still sat in front of the monitor, in her cotton nightgown, checking for email. Surely, multiple orders for the same style of tiara from the same client had to be something a seller would remember. If the tiaras matched, she hoped the seller would disclose the address where they were sent, putting them one step closer to solving this mystery.

That is, if princess*charming didn't also tell her client about the inquiry. *Then what?* Eventually, she knew she would have to tell Luis about the swiped picture. But, perhaps, he wouldn't get too upset knowing she used it to further solve the case. A bang at her front windows made her leap. Talia slowly crossed the room and turned off the lights. She looked through the peep hole in the door, where she saw Yulan standing on the porch.

Talia turned on the outside light and unlocked the door, forgetting all about the set alarm. As the door opened, the alarm shrilled loudly. Yulan's hands covered her ears, while Talia frantically punched in the code. Then she looked up and down the street, hoping she hadn't woken up the neighborhood.

"Wait till I tell you about Adie." Yulan stomped into the foyer.

"You scared me!" Talia showed her into the living room. "Sit down and tell me what Adie did? It must really be something to get you over here so late and I, for one, cannot wait to hear."

"Remember when I had to get off the phone because Adie was on the other line?"

Talia nodded.

"She had just gotten home from a date. Not just any date but the best one of her entire life. And it wasn't with Daniel."

"Okay, I know who the date wasn't with, but who *was* it with?"

"Marco! This is clearly your fault."

"Whoa…Adie and Marco went out on a date?" Talia gasped. Marco was circling people in her camp. This couldn't be good.

"Adie gave him her phone number on one of her little calling cards, and I hold you personally responsible for her actions since you are the one who brought him into our lives."

"I didn't fix them up. It's just a date. Besides they are both adults."

"No, it's more than a date. Adie thinks she's in love now."

"Must've been some date."

"Well, I don't like the guy. There's something strange about him. I know these things. You always said I had great discernment."

"No, that's wrong. I always said you were great at disconcertment." Talia tried calming her. "Marco is a lonely guy, emotionally needy…like Adie. Perhaps they'll fulfill a need in one another. And besides he's prominent, rich, well-educated. Adie could do much worse, you know?"

"Adie Yu has all the money she'll ever need."

"Exactly, and therefore, she makes a prime target for a man wanting to marry for money, but Marco has plenty of his own."

"Not only is he a creep, but now, I am fully convinced he's the kidnapper." Yulan pulled a newspaper from her tote and waved it up in the air. "Here, we have the latest victim."

Unfolding the newspaper, Yulan handed her the front page news with a picture of the latest victim. "I told you she looked familiar to me. Do you recognize her?"

Staring into the face of the pretty girl, Talia thought the woman in the photo did look vaguely familiar. She studied it more closely, but couldn't quite place her. "Who is she?"

"Does Crystal Silly Boy ring a bell? She went missing the day after Marco introduced us to her. Her parents no longer live in the area so they just reported her missing."

"No way! Let me see that," Talia gasped and snatched the newspaper. "You're right. It's the girl who was with Marco. Was a tiara found?"

"It doesn't say. Talia, I tell you he's behind all of this. You've got to believe me."

"Yulan, I have something to tell you, but don't go all crazy on me, promise?"

"Just say it."

"Marco hired Luis to work for him. He's having

him look at properties in different cities for his company to expand." Suddenly, it didn't seem so suspicious when she said it aloud.

"So what? This information doesn't relate to the case. It simply doesn't meet the standard." Yulan finished her words with a shake of the head.

"Think about it. Marco insinuates himself into my life, and then hires Luis to work for him, and gets Adie to date him."

"I don't see the connection with you, except for the body in your garden. I wouldn't be surprised if he put the body in your garden. Listen to me, ban him from coming here, talk sense to Adie, turn Marco into the police," Yulan demanded.

"We have no evidence. You and I are running on high-octane emotion. Let's formulate our plan." Talia paced back and forth. "I know…I'll call Marco to ask if he's seen the paper and gauge his reaction."

"Before you hang out your investigator's shingle, I still think we should call the police." Yulan reached into her pocket for her cell.

"I'm calling Marco right now," Talia sang out as she pushed in the numbers on her landline. "It's ringing."

"It's late," Yulan sang back.

"I don't care," Talia sang back.

"I'll pick up on the bedroom extension." Yulan thundered down the hall, flailing her arms above her head.

Talia knew when she picked up by the click sound. In a moment, Marco answered.

"Hey, Marco." Talia tried her best to act calm. "Sorry for calling so late."

"Talia, what a nice surprise. I didn't think I'd hear from you again."

"I called to say I'm so sorry to hear the news."

"What news…?"

"Ask him, ask him." Yulan peered out of the bedroom with her hand over the receiver.

Talia waved back while nodding her head.

"Then you haven't heard?"

"Haven't heard what?" Marco asked with a long noisy yawn.

"Remember that day we ran into you and Crystal?"

"Yes. What about it?"

"She's disappeared." It wasn't hard to act sorrowful.

Silence.

"Marco, are you still there?"

"Yeah. I can't believe it. When did that happen?" He sounded genuinely shaken.

"The day after the museum."

"Wow, that's awful. What else does the newspaper say?" Marco wanted to know.

Talia looked at Yulan for help, not having read the article.

Yulan made a cutting sign over her throat, mouthing words she couldn't quite get.

Talia turned her back to the frantic Yulan, who was jumping up and down again.

"Hello? What else does it say? Talia? Still there?" Marco asked again.

Talia shrugged her shoulders as she answered, "The paper is vague. You know, they are stingy when it comes to information."

"Let me grab today's paper and have a look. I'll get

back to you tomorrow sometime."

"Okay, but it's the Denton paper." She hung up.

"Now call the police," Yulan insisted.

"Not so fast. I was watching a show late last night. The man on the program never asked how his wife died, so he became an immediate suspect." Talia looked at the paper in her hand. "But Marco is looking in today's paper."

"I don't follow. And since when do you watch crime shows? That's my hobby. Call the police. That's what Nancy Place on Court TV would do."

"Yulan, we don't have a thing to go on except he knew her. Let's don't cause any trouble for Marco just yet. Anyway, I have evidence that he is innocent."

"What is it?"

"It's me. I've been with him on several occasions, and I'm still here. In fact, so are you and Adie."

"But we are certainly not debutantes. All the women taken were Hispanic. But I am Asian."

"You made my point. I am Hispanic and I have been with Marco numerous times."

"Don't confuse me. I do research lab work and need all my brain cells. Yeah, but you aren't a debutante."

They both stared at each other for a few minutes, breathing slowing, until Yulan broke the silence and asked, "By the way, how's Luis feeling?"

"When Luis comes home, I want to make dinner for us. You come, too. It'll cheer him up so much. It'd be a favor to me as well, to help us through those ill at ease silences we sometimes have."

"Maybe." Yulan arched her brows above her oval eyes. "That depends on the meal. What are you having?"

"How's this—a big pan of Mixiotes de Pollo. Green tamales, Luis's favorite. And a side dish of Tilapia."

"What's for dessert?"

Talia snorted, "Black bottom pie."

"I'll make an Asian salad for me to eat."

In the darkness, Talia and Murphy walked Yulan back to her car. "I feel better about Adie now. I just realized Marco won't last long with her."

"Oh…why not?"

"She has a short attention span. The only thing that lasts long is her shopping sprees."

Chapter Sixteen

Clattering up to Luis's door with their food dishes in hand, Talia instructed Yulan, "Don't you dare say one word to Luis about when we met Crystal Favela, or about her death. I don't want him to worry about anything."

Luis released the door. "I thought I heard talking out here. Welcome, ladies. Where is my Murphy?"

"Murphy was tired and decided to stay home to rest. It's been such a big day in my backyard for him." Talia also wanted him home to sound big and scary to anyone who might try getting into her house. Always grateful for Murphy, she hated the fact she now felt better with a house alarm. Luis had been right about that.

"Are you ready to take him back?"

Luis scrunched his nose. "Not yet. But soon I hope."

"You still have visiting rights so drive on up and see him anytime," Talia teased.

"Thanks." Luis sweetly played along. Filled with energy, Luis was animated. "Talia, I have an extra special surprise for you tonight. Stay right there." Luis turned off the lights and walked into the darkness of the living area where he flipped a switch. The room immediately became illuminated with thousands of tea lights. A white wooden bench swing was suspended in midair, hanging with chains from the steel beams above it. The windows provided a perfect view of downtown Denton.

"Wow, this is amazing, Luis."

"You did this?"

"Come sit with me, ladies."

It was as though they had stumbled into Wonderland. The three sat on the swing and pushed off against the window ledge of the old brick wall. Back and forth they swung.

"What do you think?" Luis felt proud of his surprise.

"I'm enchanted."

"It's better than the park. No muggers, or—" Yulan said right before Talia pinched her.

"Ouch! Why did you do that?"

"I saw a fly."

Over dinner, Luis had another surprise. "Remember that piece of land I mentioned might be good for your project?"

"Uh, huh," Talia answered with a mouth full of crunchy Asian salad.

"I don't have anything in writing yet, but I have the owner's word he'll donate a piece of his land to the city for the Latino museum. There's an old factory on site that you can use for the museum. You can start looking into contractors for estimates to renovate it. I've made out a list for you. We can use both the land and the building for collateral to obtain a loan and get started. I'll help with fundraising."

"This is incredible news! You must tell me who the philanthropist is. I want to meet him, to personally thank him."

"Well, he is a celebrated architect and lives nearby in Highland Park. You know his name, Tee. I do business with him." He stood to pour the women more ice water with slices of fresh floating lemons. His words proved to be more chilling than their drinks. "The man you want to thank is Marco Correa."

Yulan choked on her water making it spurt out of her mouth. Luis ducked. "Are you all right, Yulan?"

Talia patted her friend's back.

"Is there something going on here I am unaware of?"

"This most generous Marco Correa is dating Yulan's cousin, Adie."

A curious look crossed Luis's face. "Really? How'd they meet?"

"A long story. Let's have some of my black bottom pie," Talia suggested.

After dinner, the three resumed their places on the swing with icy lemonade. "Time to catch up on the news." Luis reached for the control.

Both girls grabbed for it, making it slip from his fingers, then drop to the floor. Yulan snatched it up, not wanting Luis to see the news about Crystal. "Let's see something else. Nothing happened in the world today."

"True and nothing happened locally either, did it, Yulan?"

"Absolutely not. Today was a very boring news day. Let's not waste our time. I bet tomorrow will be the same way too." Both women nodded their heads in agreement.

"The TV Guide says there's a good mystery on tonight, but there's also a game. Ball game or mystery?" Luis asked.

"Mystery," they both happily chimed.

Halfway through the movie, the heroine screamed and then proceeded to ascend the stairs as the villain chased. "I don't get it. Why would a person run upstairs when they're being chased? You only get trapped up there. If it were me, I'd run outside and get help that way," Talia mused.

"You would?" Luis asked.

"Yes, I'd never allow myself to be trapped."

"You've actually spent time contemplating this, Tee?"

"Of course. Never ever run up."

"What if your exit is cut off?" Luis questioned.

"There are phones, cell phones, bathrooms with locks, and buildings with windows, places to hide," Talia pertly explained.

"I'm glad to hear you are such a resourceful young woman." Luis squeezed her hand.

"Yes, I am. So, you no longer need to worry about me." She kissed his cheek. "You just got home from the hospital and look exhausted. Yulan and I had better get going so you can get rest."

Just as Yulan walked out, Luis pulled Talia to the side and whispered, "Tee, I didn't want to tell you in front of Yulan, but Marco Correa is a married man."

****

Talia stood on Dallas streets with her hands on her hips looking up at the tall building knowing she had no other choice but to go to the offices on the top floor. Just the thought of it made her stomach lurch, but calling Marco to meet her on the first floor would make her lose the element of surprise.

The mission was twofold. First, she wanted to

thank him for his generosity to the Latino community and secondly, confront him about being a dating married man and deceiving poor Adie Yu. Most likely his beloved Juana broke off with Marco when she found out this tantalizing tidbit about marriage. It was all beginning to make sense to her now. And how dare he tell her he was falling for her when he was married all along. *What a jerk.*

The front doorman was female. “Welcome to the Correa Building. I hope you have a pleasant visit.”

Talia read her nametag. “Thanks, Cecelia. I do, too.”

The air inside the complex was refreshing, echoing the feeling the pink Italian marble of the lobby’s floor, walls, and ceiling provided. Enclaves of rich wood furniture were huddled together on fine Eastern tapestry rugs, defining separate areas for islands of conversation. Pillars of this elegant marble shot up three stories in the foyer. It was a grandiose setting which took on more of an appearance of a palace than a downtown Dallas building housing hundreds of multifaceted businesses. With southern heat outside, it was northern cool inside making her wish she brought a sweater.

Since there wasn’t a directory on the wall, Talia went to the front desk to be sure his offices were still on the top floor. A young woman with dark hair, done up in a bun, greeted Talia. “Hello, I’m Yessica, how may I help you?”

“I’m looking for the offices of Marco Correa.”

“His offices encompass the entire top floor. Just go all the way to the top.” Yessica pointed toward the elevators. “Someone there will be able to assist you.”

"Thanks." Sucking in a deep breath of courage, Talia stood in the corridor looking at the line of elevators watching travelers come and go. Finally, she stepped through a pair of pewter doors and into the metal coffin. Regret was immediate. The fourth wall, entirely made of glass giving a panoramic view to the city, faced her. By the time she reached the top, if she survived the heart attack, she would be able to see not only all of Dallas, but pretty near all of Fort Worth to boot. She didn't want a bird's eye view of either.

Breath caught in her chest as her arms went numb. Talia felt certain the elevator would somehow dislodge itself from the side of the building, careening down, down, down to the pavement far below, shattering the elevator and spilling her guts all over downtown Dallas. Diving over a dozen people, she went for the large red buttons on the panel. Frantically jamming the OPEN button with the flat of her hand, the doors finally obeyed.

"Excuse me," she told the gentleman she accidentally elbowed in the stomach, and the other whose toes she squashed on her exit. She heard an elderly lady grunt in pain, but Talia was back in the lobby. A familiar looking gentleman stood a few feet away, waiting for an elevator. He wore a baseball cap, which seemed oddly out of place in this building. She had seen him before.

"Pardon me." Talia lightly touched his sleeve.

No look of recognition crossed his face but he seemed pleased to be of assistance. "Yes?"

"Is there any elevator that is enclosed on all four sides, without one wall being a window to the entire world?"

"Why, yes, there is," he chuckled. "There's only one with that type of view and it is…"

"That one. Just my luck. It's the one I picked. Thanks."

"Squeamish of heights?"

"Very."

"You must not be any fun to take to the State Fair."

"I never miss Big Tex. I avoid the rides, but enjoy the food, music, and exhibits. I even have an old bracelet from one of the state fairs. See?" Talia held up her arm. This conversation seemed familiar.

The man laughed when he saw the vintage piece. "Very nice."

A ping and another elevator opened spilling its contents of riders into the noisy corridor. He stood back, allowing Talia to enter first. She smiled. He smiled, then entered. Talia suddenly remembered and thought to herself. *Hey you're the same guy who protected me from Marco! What're you doing here?*

Even though the building housed dozens of offices, the coincidence put her on edge when she suddenly realized he might also have been the same man on the street holding the newspaper that day in front of the Mellow Mushroom Restaurant. Trying to gather the meaning of meeting him so many times and places, her brain shut down for every thought except fear as the silver doors slid shut. *I'm trapped in a coffin.*

Up, up, up into the sky, it shot as a bullet. The entire trip was made much worse each stop, allowing people on and off, prolonging the arrival to her final destination. It provided more time for things to go wrong on board her missile. She concentrated on the lit numbers on the panel above the door. Nearly to her destiny, one last stop for the exit of the man who began this journey with her. As he exited on the 56th floor, he turned and said to her, "In the future, there's an express elevator in the lobby that goes straight to the top floor, it's called The Rocket."

"Thanks." She was alone, no one left to break her fall. The last most terrifying floor of all was next. At last, the shiny pewter doors opened, and she weakly slithered out and into a modernistic style offices exclusively for Marco Correa, quite different from the grandiose European foyer, which lay floors beneath them. A bevy of gorgeous women seemed to be everywhere—answering phones, keyboarding, straightening magazines, and pouring coffee for the guests waiting in the lounge area. Yup, this was Marco's own little kingdom.

Ah, there was Marco's secretary at the receptionist desk. Miss Firecracker herself. The placard read, *Receptionist, Ms. Misty Trimmings.* Behind her was an entire wall of Birds Eye Maple wood with the words Marco Correa Designs & Engineering written in mahogany, outlined in silver. Extraordinary. Talia still had elevator knees when the woman spoke.

"Hello and welcome to Correa Designs. How may I help you?" Misty greeted in a sprightly voice, cocking her head to the side repeatedly.

"Hello, I've come to see Mr. Marco Correa," Talia sweetly answered.

"Do you have an appointment?"

"Mr. Correa told me to drop by anytime."

"Your name?" she asked as if she already knew the answer and was just checking her out, enjoying the front desk power.

"Ms. Talia Bonilla. I'm here about the Latino Museum."

Seeming persnickety, the receptionist snapped, "But *do* you have an appointment?"

"It never occurred to me to make an appointment. I'm sorry about that, but I'm sure if you tell him I'm here, he'll be glad to see me. We're friends." Nerves were settling as irritation climbed.

"Mr. Correa never sees anyone without an appointment. It's a rule. He's a most important man." Each word was emphasized.

"Would you please check with him?" Talia firmly asked. "I'm sure he'll want to see me." Was she like this with all clients? Or just with her? The woman just stood there staring blankly at Talia. "I said, *call* Mr. Correa."

"Would you like for me to make an appointment for you sometime tomorrow? Is morning, or afternoon the best for you?"

Never making eye contact, she paged through an appointment calendar on the desk.

"No, not tomorrow. I'm here today. I refuse to leave until I speak with him."

As though Talia was a dog needing to stay, Miss Trimmings held up her pointer finger and invisibly held her to the spot. With the other hand, she held a receiver to her ear. Talia heard her whispering words like "Unstable" and "Restraining order." The energy dropped from the animated woman's face and she became cherry colored. Quietly, she set the receiver back down. "He'll see you now."

Talia arched an eyebrow. "I thought so."

The receptionist stepped rudely in front of Talia

causing her to nearly stumble into the paneled wall. The blonde stopped in front of the large door before tapping.

"Come in," a deep voice answered.

Turning the knob, Miss Misty Trimmings pushed open the door revealing an oversized space. Talia walked through and the receptionist closed the doors behind her. In a moment, an elderly man pushing seventy with thick white hair and sleek eyebrows walked from his private bathroom. He held out his hand to her in greeting. Clean-shaven, Talia imagined his plump round cheeks to be soft to the pinch.

"Oh, excuse me," Talia demurred. "I'm in the wrong office. I was looking for Mr. Marco Correa." She turned to leave.

"Ms. Bonilla?"

"Yes?"

"How do you do? I am Marco Correa. How lovely to finally meet you. Our mutual friend, Luis Arroyo, is a great fan of your work. And I think your plan for the Latino Museum in Dallas is brilliant. I should have thought of it years ago. I also should have thought of meeting you a long time ago when he first told me about you. Please take a seat and make yourself comfortable. Forgive my manners, what can I offer you to drink? I have a fully stocked bar." He swung open a maple wood panel revealing an array of sparkling glasses and crystal decanters filled with various tones of dark liquor.

"Um, no thanks. I could use some ice water, though." Talia felt confused as if she had opened a door into the twilight zone. The office itself was quite intimidating and this man masquerading as Marco Correa definitely had her stumped.

"Not a drinker, eh? Ah, I've a better idea." Mr. Correa pressed a button.

"Yes, sir?" The animated voice came through the desk speakers making Talia squirm in the leather seat, as butterflies swarmed in her stomach.

"Ms. Trimmings, would you bring us some of your wonderful homemade lemonade?"

"Right away, sir."

"Ms. Bonilla, I've had your educational background, as well as your fine work since college, researched. Your talent is not only exceptionally bright, but it is also quite varied. With all your knowledge and wealth of background, I'm surprised to find you so young. Nonetheless, I'm pleased to help with your future dream. No, I'm more than pleased. I'm *thrilled.* I also am privy to the fact you were just accepted to The Sorbonne, which is a point of concern for me since I would want you to be in charge of acquisitions."

"My term begins fall of next year."

"What inspired you to pursue this worthwhile project, and what all do you envision for this museum? Mr. Arroyo has explained much, but I want to hear it directly from you." He made her feel she was the only one in the world and what she had to tell him was of utmost importance.

"Excuse me again, but I'm confused. I'm here to see Marco Correa, the *architect*."

The man's eyes went from friendly to puzzled. "I am Marco Correa, the architect." Shortly, a small, narrow smile wrinkled his face. "Ah, you must be thinking of my son. His name is the same as mine and he uses it to his advantage when meeting lovely young women. There's a picture of him on the other side of the room. See it on the shelf?" He nodded his head in the direction. "Is that who you expected?"

Talia stood to her feet and walked across the imported rug until she reached the bookcase filled with a collection of pictures, some spanning back more than forty years. Picking up the largest photo, she saw it was the Marco she knew, clearly with his father. How he resembled him.

"My son keeps my wife and me on our toes. He carries my first and last names, yet he isn't anything like me." Turning around, he added, "On the back wall, you'll see my framed buildings. Now, would you like to see what Marco has built?"

"Yes. Are they here, too, on the wall?" She gazed around the room.

"Come, I'll show you." Chuckling, Mr. Correa walked to the window where Talia joined him. Looking out across the grand expanse of Dallas high rises, she was ready to see which the younger Marco contributed to the landscape. There certainly was a grand smorgasbord from which to choose.

"Look up, my dear."

Talia blinked with confusion.

"See that narrow ledge above us, about six feet down from the top of the building?" He pointed upward on his own building.

Talia craned her neck to see. "Yes, very decorative."

"Well, that five inch railing goes all the way around the top. Now you've seen the mark Marco has left on this city. I build stunning monuments and he builds a useless decorative trim."

"Many people desire those simple touches, I for

one, are among them. Mr. Correa, please forgive me. I confused you with your son." Talia softened even more. "Surely, his wife doesn't appreciate the confusion, either."

"Ha! Wife? My son has no wife. If only he did, but he enjoys the single life far too much to marry. He's what I would call a *Parrandeo*. Ah, he'll never settle down."

Talia spun about at the sound of rattling ice cubes. Misty pushed an elegant silver teacart loaded with a pitcher of lemonade and two matching crystal goblets. Having slipped from her little jacket, she revealed bare arms, nicely muscled. Obviously, she lifted weights. Many weights. Picking up an eight-inch ice pick, it was frightening to watch as she whacked away at the ice cubes until they were reduced to shavings.

"You've met my receptionist, Misty Trimmings."

"Yes, we've met. Hello again," Talia said graciously smiling.

"Hello."

"Of all the receptionists in the entire world, I have the one who makes lemonade. She does it from scratch. Squeezes the lemons with her hands and sometimes adds a pinch of her secret recipe."

"Oh, and what would that be?" Talia cleared her throat, feeling uncomfortable.

"Not telling. That's how it stays a secret."

Marco presided over the lemonade, first pouring Talia a glass, and then another for him. After a long sip, he announced, "Almost perfect. I also have a secret recipe. But I am willing to share. It's bourbon." He winked and pulled from the crystal decanter on his desk. After adding a few shots, he tasted it. "Perfect."

"Miss Trimmings appears to be a woman of many talents," Talia agreed, feeling more and more uneasy as the woman grimly peered at her. "Thank you. Maybe it wouldn't hurt if I had just a dab of bourbon added to mine as well."

Mr. Correa uproariously laughed and poured two shots into her drink.

Misty curtsied before she left, as though Mr. Correa sat on a throne instead of at the edge of his desk. Closing the office double doors behind her, the air suddenly seemed lighter, but it could have been the bourbon that made it seem that way. In a moment, Talia heard a creaking noise. She turned in time to see the office door open a few inches and remain. *How odd. How rude*. Misty was just outside the door listening. She turned back to look at Mr. Correa who hadn't noticed.

Talia spent the next thirty minutes talking animatedly about her vision of the museum as Mr. Correa added his to it. He took notes while scribbling sketches on a pad of yellow ledger paper. Talia was fascinated how his mere pencil scratching quickly turned into pieces of art, themselves worthy of framing. *Would he think me strange if I asked for them to hang in the museum?*

"Before I forget, I have some papers here for you to sign." He opened a large top drawer and pushed papers about.

"So, this is really happening?" Talia hardly could believe it.

"Yes, it is. Now, if I can only find those documents." Exasperated, he closed the drawer with a slam and went to the next drawer until all the contents of each had been examined. Again, he pushed the button for his secretary.

"Ms. Trimmings, I'm trying to locate that contract and the deed for the museum land."

"They were sent out yesterday to Mr. Arroyo per your request." The voice came from the doorway and not the speakerphone, which added a comical air when Mr. Correa continued speaking into it.

"Ah, that's right. I forgot. Thank you, Misty, for being so efficient." He turned the speakerphone off and turned to Talia. "I'll have Luis get the papers to you. My accountant has set up a non-profit foundation. I nearly forgot, I'm forming a board and a fundraising committee soon. Please honor me with becoming a member."

"Yes, of course." Talia agreed draining her second glass of lemonade along with Mister Correa's unsecured, secret recipe. She felt tipsy.

"We're seeking public and private grants from foundations. The Latino community has been waiting too long for this. We can open it in stages. Let's start with packing the foyer with artifacts and paintings while the rest of the building is being worked on. That way we might be ready to go in months instead of a year or more. I'll need you here to oversee it and not in Paris painting. I'll have my CFO call you, Talia, and explain how to leverage the property to get construction financing. He also will be happy to introduce you to many of Dallas's society ladies who will jump at the chance to take up a new cultural cause."

"Oh, let me handle the society ladies, please, Mr. Correa?" the voice from the hallway pleaded. Feeling confused, Mr. Correa stared at the speakerphone realizing it was not turned on this time.

"Nonsense," he spewed. "I need someone with class."

The door banged shut.

Talia stood and offered her hand. "I really must be on my way. Thank you for a delightful afternoon and a generous donation. Here's to a wonderful and long friendship. What a miracle to have this large piece of land so centrally located along with ample parking. I can see you have thought of everything."

Walking out of his private office, Talia was again overwhelmed by the number of women working for Mr. Correa. The receptionist sprang from around the corner hurrying toward them, desperate to spoil their camaraderie. Obviously high-strung, Misty toddled over to talk to them as if she were struggling against the eye of a hurricane.

"Miss Trimmings, thank you for putting up with my unexpected visit to Mr. Correa. Next time, I'll be sure to make an appointment first."

"Talia, you come and see me anytime you want. No appointment necessary," Mr. Correa groaned while glaring at Misty.

"I made a mistake and thought Mr. Correa's son was the person I came to see," Talia tried to explain.

"Oh, that explains it," Misty sighed. "Marco always impersonates his father."

"Ms. Trimmings, isn't there anything you need to be doing at your desk?" Mr. Correa called out to her from his office door.

"What would it be? The phone isn't ringing."

"Miss Trimmings, would you please point me to the direction of the stairs? I've decided to walk down,"

Talia said.

"Don't you mean the elevator?"

"No, the stairs will be fine. I like walking." Talia knew she had to walk off the effects of alcohol before getting behind the wheel of her car. Not to mention she was scared out of her wits to tackle another elevator experience.

"I'll show you, follow me." Once out of earshot, she continued, "Marco is so over protected by his mother. To her, the sun rises and sets on him. No girls allowed if you know what I mean. No girl is good enough for him. Like me, you have to learn to take what Marco says with a grain of salt."

Chapter Seventeen

Talia pushed through the door allowing it to slam it behind her.

Feeling loopy from the drink, a migraine built behind her eyes. The stairwell she descended filled with echoes of doors opening and slamming shut. Mysterious ghostly steps and laughter could be heard bouncing along the walls—just no people appeared. As Talia started down the second set of steps, a door opened a floor below and two incredibly gorgeous women came up the steps, passed Talia, and went into the Correa offices. Looking around, there was no one else. She kept right on descending the stairs. Occasionally, there was a window on the landing between floors but it was small enough to ignore its view, large enough to allow natural light to filter in.

Choosing to rush down the next flight of steps, and then spinning about on the landing to quickly descend the next flight, made her even more light-headed. Finally, on the twenty-fifth floor, a door behind her opened and banged shut. Checking once more for a human form, she became startled when she saw a familiar man wearing the baseball cap. She stopped. But, was this the same man?

Seeing Talia, his feet began paddling down the steps after her. Not liking the speed he approached with, or the expression on his face, she clearly panicked; it had to be him. Reading body language, Talia loosened her grip on the long steel railing, allowing her to move down faster. Her feet beat against the steel metal steps, moving rapidly.

"Wait up!" he called to her. "I can't keep up."

"That's the idea!" She violently trembled from sudden fear. She needed answers only he could provide, but not in this empty tunnel alone, just the two of them. After speeding down several more stories, she was ready for the elevator, any elevator. She flung open the door to the nineteenth floor and darted out into the hallway where she bumped right into the younger Marco Correa. Totally out of breath as she threw her arms about him, her heart still raced with alarm.

"Wow, Talia." He squeezed back tightly. "You've had a sudden change of heart. I like it."

"Nice to see you, too," she said giving him a slight shove backward. It was nice to hear the heavy footsteps continue to pelt down the stairs past the floor.

"Have you been drinking?"

"Just wobbly from the stairwell." She hiccupped.

"What are you doing here?"

Suddenly, she remembered she was angry with him and shoved him again, but this time much harder. "I came to see you."

"Take it easy. But if you want to get rough, there is my private office."

"Well, you weren't in the offices of Marco Correa a few minutes ago. But your dad sure was."

"Oh." He ran his fingers through his hair. "You found me out? I'm glad, takes the pressure off."

"You lied. I went into his office expecting to see you and found him. Fortunately, your father overlooked my error and made me at ease."

"Dear ol' dad. He's quite a man, don't you think? Why'd you come here to see me anyway? You have my cell number. If you would have called, I could've just dropped by your place."

"I came in person to thank the real Mr. Marco Correa for the land and buildings he donated for the museum, it's something that can't be done over the phone. And in the process found out there are *two* Marco Correas. You're not the one I owe a note of gratitude after all. You're just a guy imitating his dad."

"Ouch," he chided, covering his head with his arms. "Don't hurt me."

"There's another matter I need to discuss with you." Glancing about, Talia realized the public arena was not the place.

"We need to speak privately."

"Didn't I already say that? Follow me to my office."

"You don't have an office."

"As a matter of fact, I do. I run a small side business of my dad's that is fairly lucrative. Right this way." Marco led Talia down the hall to a small end room with his name on the door.

"What does your company do?" Talia stood with her hands on her hips looking around at the small room.

"We're a vintage ornamental architectural company," he told her, offering Talia a leather chair. She sat down as he took his chair behind the desk where a clear view of the city could be seen. "Look at me…I'm a one man show. I acquire and sell vintage architectural accessories. If a client wants a piece to be replicated, I can do that as well. I personally design antique ornamental railings, gates, planters, and trim. When a building is about to be torn down, I salvage the pieces. My salvage warehouse is a few blocks from here…packed out with stained glass, doors, tubs, sinks, gates, pediments, and so much more."

"*Bueno*, Marco. It appears you've been quite successful on your own, so why do you feel you have to impersonate your father?"

"I don't. His name just carries a lot of weight in this town. And I didn't tell you I was *the* Marco Correa…you just assumed it like every other woman does." He laughed as though it was their fault.

"Ah, so it's my fault for not figuring it before now. Does Adie Yu know who you really are? Or aren't?" The alcohol began to lose its affect.

"Don't tell her, Talia." His demeanor changed.

By his reaction, Talia could tell he cared about Yulan's cousin which she found most surprising. "I won't because you're going to tell her."

"All right, I will." Marco grew solemn.

"Meanwhile, what's up with the receptionist in your dad's office? She doesn't fit."

"What's your take of her?" Marco asked.

"Sour. How does a man like your father hire someone like Misty to be the receptionist of his elite practice?"

"Long story."

"Shorten it for me." She leaned forward ready to listen.

"Okay, I can do that." Marco winked. "Misty liked me. I liked her. We dated for a bit. I didn't like her. She liked me. When I broke it off, I felt sorry for her with all that crying, so I pressed Dad about it until he found a spot for her. Lots of men go through up here, thought perhaps she'd find one to her liking. It's a veritable undercover matchmaking service."

"And is Misty Trimmings still after you?"

"By now, I'd say she probably has raised her sites to marrying someone with the big greenbacks. I only have shiny dimes. Misty is surely in a good location to find a well-to-do man. I did her a favor."

"I don't understand all the women your dad has working for him."

"They're my exes."

"Whoa. All those women are your former girlfriends?" Talia's mouth dropped open.

"Yup, after I broke it off, Dad gave them a job."

"But there's got to be thirty women up there."

"I'm popular." He grinned, kicking his feet up on his desk and crossing one leg over the other. "Anyway, here I am, master of my own world."

"And what world is that?"

"My, Talia, you sure are spunky today. I've never seen this side of you. Have you always been like this, or do I just bring this fire out in you?"

Talia explained she had to leave. On her way into the parking lot, she nearly missed spotting the driver of the Jag getting into his vehicle. She ducked behind a cement pillar, not wanting him to find her alone in an isolated spot. Watching him carefully, he soon drove his Jag up the ramp and on to the street. He turned right. It seemed as though he were hunting her.

Her legs felt like jelly. Panic made her chest hurt. It was hard to breathe. She closed her eyes and concentrated on calming down. Once she felt more in control, she scampered from her hiding place and pressed the car keypad, popping open the locks. Tossing her pink purse in first, she then leapt into her car, slamming the door closed with fervor. Holding onto the steering wheel, she noticed how badly her hands shook, making it hard to get the key into the ignition. Needing a closer look at what she was doing, she accidentally leaned on the horn. Its sudden blast made her scream and jump all at once. She took deep breaths and then leaned back in the seat to make sure she was sober and ready to drive.

With smoking tires, she peeled out of the parking lot, turning left. Watching for the Jag on all sides of her along the Interstate, she was pleasantly surprised he was totally out of view. A surprise waited on her porch.

Chapter Eighteen

Like rolling stones bound to bump into one another, Luis sat on the porch swing under the shade of the mimosa tree. How fine looking he was in his jeans and T-shirt. Deerskin moccasins clothed his feet, and his hair was carefully slicked back.

Talia opened the car door and sprang forward, nearly falling out. Dancing up the stone walk, she breathlessly expected him to take her into his arms. By the time she stood feet away from him, she gasped with longing. "You look great," she admired, while shaking off her shoes, flinging them one by one at the front door with a thud.

Trepidation and hope bubbled to the surface. "Are you sure you're ill, Luis? Because today you look simply wonderful."

Luis remained motionless. Talia finally gave up her pose and plopped down next to him.

"Talia, why didn't you tell me you met Crystal Favela?"

"Ah oh." She rolled her eyes.

"Yeah, ah oh. Alex Monahan called me from the office first thing this morning."

"How'd he find out?" Talia puzzled.

"Marco Correa went to his office after he learned of her disappearance. He gave full details of your time with them at the museum. Now, back to my question, why didn't you tell me?"

"Oh, that. I just didn't want you to worry." She scrunched her nose. "And you no longer worked there. No biggie."

"Didn't you think anyone in my office would call me even if I no longer work there? My close ties and friends remain."

"Like Jade?" Her jealousy stung.

"I'll give you a pass on that comment." Luis got to his feet and began to pace as Murphy followed along with him, as though he was agitated at her, too.

Talia rose. The wood felt good beneath her feet. It was late-October and promises of a warm fall were stirring.

"Calm down. Let's go inside and talk. I have lots to tell you."

He followed her into the house and sat at the kitchen table with a freshly brewed glass of iced tea; a few smashed raspberries floated at the top for flavor. Talia preheated the oven, thinking this was like old times. Luis waited for her explanation, which Talia knew would never come. After pulling the tray of baked sopapillas from the oven, she rolled them in brown sugar and cinnamon then placed them on a Bateau tray with a doily. Setting down a small pot of honey, she dipped a spoon deep into the sweetness.

"*Estos son los mejores*," Talia declared sliding the plate across the table.

"So you think I'll swallow my concern along with your delicious sopapillas?"

"It's a good place to start, don't you agree?" Looking at him through the top of her lashes, she flirted shamelessly.

Her wit caught him off guard causing him to shoot a quick laugh. Luis poured a bit of honey on top of the dessert. Using his fingers for utensils, he bit into it. "You're right, these are delicious."

"Thanks. By the way, I stopped at Correa Design today to thank Mr. Correa for his generous land donation."

"You actually went to the top floor?" He raised his eyebrows.

"Yes, I did, and a big shocker awaited. I had confused his son with the father. Rather, I met the son first, and he portrayed himself as his father."

"Really?"

"Yes. And I saw his receptionist, Misty. She's…colorful."

"Marco, the son, dated her for a while. All his exes seemed to wind up with a job somewhere in the building."

"And you told me he was married."

"At the time, I was referring to Senior Correa. I should have realized it was his son dating Adie."

"Getting information out of you these days is hard." Talia wiped off the counters with a wet rag. "But then, getting information from you has always been difficult."

"You should really be a P.I. with all you find out, Tee. You've changed a bit these last few months."

"For better or worse?" She stopped to look at him waiting for the answer.

"Just a change is all. You speak your mind. You're more independent. You don't need me so much anymore." Luis finished his sweet Mexican pastry and wiped his fingers, and face with the cloth napkin.

"Maybe I need you in ways you don't know exist," Talia softly answered.

After remaining silent for a few minutes, he asked, "Then tell me what they are."

"I can't. It's something you have to learn yourself." She shook her head.

"Intuition?" Luis asked.

"No. Not that. You have eaten up so much of your life with cases and courtrooms that you forget to look at what is right in front of you. I am not a client, or a judge, or another courtroom person to take your orders. I am a woman who loves you and yearns for you to lean on me." Talia's voice broke.

"Tee, I am a man and cannot do what you ask. I am to be the strong one. Your words frighten me." His eyes filled with tears.

"I'm not frightened." She stepped closer to him, wondering how close she could go before he'd back away.

"There's no more fight left in me, Tee."

"And so, you have also changed. I like it." She came closer.

"Tell me, when you're alone at night, how do you feel? Lonely? Scared?"

"Sometimes both. But, my house is a fortress against any harm that might try to come, especially when it's wired with an alarm, compliments of my ex-fiancé." She leaned across the very short distance of separation and kissed him.

The passion he returned was more than she had hoped. It knocked the breath from her. He wrapped his arms even more tightly around her and pressed his body into hers. Talia felt herself melting into him.

Surrendering to him. She took a step back and slowly unbuttoned her blouse, all the while watching his eyes, noting his reaction. His focus was on the movement of her fingers. Her eyes flitted to the bedroom.

"Talia." He grabbed her hands to stop their work. There was tenderness in his face. "Not now. Not today. I'm not ready."

His words took the breath from her. But she understood. "It's okay, Luis. You leave such fingerprints on my heart whenever you are near."

"Someday, we will finish this conversation, but now, I have a favor."

"Anything." She put her arms around his neck.

"Do you mind me taking Murphy back?"

"When?"

"Today."

She was used to Murphy's company and how nice it was to come home to someone who was always happy to see her. But Luis and Murphy belonged together. "No, not at all. I-I mean I knew you'd take him back with you…eventually. I just didn't expect it to be today."

"I can leave Murph for a little while longer, but since you have an alarm I thought you wouldn't mind."

"No, take him. You're right, and Murph needs to be with you. He belongs to you. I have the alarm to keep me safe." She patted his back on the way to the refrigerator where she stopped, facing the door without opening it.

"Thanks for the dessert. It may be your mama's recipe, but you made it taste even better. Sweeter." Luis slid his large feet back into his moccasins. He walked to the door while Murphy panted and clumsily twirled about, following.

Streetlights were on, up and down the block, baking her porch in long shadows. Luis never looked more handsome, washed in the growing darkness. Talia wanted to run up to him and pull him back to her. What would he do if she tried kissing him again? Back away? Return her kisses? He was about to exit her place, yet so much passion remained. *Turn around, Luis, turn around and see me standing here, wanting you so much.*

As if on cue, Luis turned as his feet touched the prickly brown grass of coming winter. “I nearly forgot. I need for you to sign documents for the museum and then mail them to Marco. Let me get them from my car.”

“Ah, yes, he told me about them today. I’ll follow you.” Barefoot, she shifted uncomfortably from one foot to the other, watching him reach into his sedan. He handed her a large envelope.

“I think Mr. Correa wants you to be the head of the education and acquisitions department, but it’s up to you. I know there are other plans much closer to your heart, far, far from here. If you need help with interpreting any of the legal information, let me know.”

“Thanks for sharing my enthusiasm, Luis. Life is much more fun this way.”

“Wish I had learned that sooner. Things may have turned out differently between us.”

Luis got into his sedan, started the engine, slid it in reverse, and backed out of the drive, turning the headlights on as he started down the narrow street. *Please come back, please let’s start over, please stay the night. Please love me.* An owl hooted somewhere overhead as Talia's face turned glossy with tears. She bit her lip as if swallowing a hard, painful seed. From the corner of her eye, she noticed Luis's car stopped. He turned around, going the wrong way on this street. "What have you forgotten, Luis?"

Just then Murphy nudged her hand. "Oh, no, he forgot to put you in the car. But he's on his way back."

Luis pulled back into the drive, slid the gear into park, and left the motor running as he opened the door and got out. "Forgot something."

"See, told you, Murph," Talia whispered to the dog.

Luis pushed Murphy aside while he took Talia into his arms and kissed her. Their tongues danced together as his hands slid up inside her blouse and touched her skin.

"Our break-up has been a complete failure, Luis." Talia whispered.

Even in the dark she could see him smile.

****

During her lunch hour, Talia drove to Dallas with the contracts, deciding to forgo the view at the top of the Correa building, and leave the fat envelope for security to deliver. With nothing more to prove about heights, she didn't care if she ever saw another view. From here on out, she considered herself a land dweller, not an eagle. Besides, she couldn't stomach another go around with Ms. Trimmings, or her sour lemonade, once she got there—not unless it had three shots of bourbon.

With a single, long, dark braid down her back, she felt absolutely sprightly in cotton slacks and prized flea market find—a silk camellia pinned to the lapel of her blouse. Slung over one shoulder was her pink purse. October be damned. It was still in the 80s.

A bevy of women in scant gray uniforms, trimmed in red, held open the line of doors to the Correa Building. One woman was just as lovely as the next, making them a version of what could be Latino Rockettes. Marco's exes, Talia surmised. Being the noon hour, the lobby was busy with throngs of business people heading out to lunch. Talia worked her way through the oncoming crowd when she spotted Mr. Correa, Sr. Talia frantically waved at him. He was so engaged in a conversation he didn't notice her. Talia continued walking toward the men until she took another look. The man he was speaking with was none other than Baseball Cap man. Goose bumps ran the course of her arms.

Quickly, she darted behind a marble pillar to gather her thoughts. Should she turn and run? No, she needed to get the contracts back to him today. What did Baseball Cap man have to do with Mr. Correa? Spying was not her forte, but as of late, it seemed to have become her favorite activity. Blessedly, the men never noticed her presence. Huddled together near a hefty, potted seven-foot tall palm, thick with foliage, Talia made a wide loop around the lobby and snuck up along the wall, right behind the palm. Pressing down a frond with her hand, she leaned in. Her breath came in shallow, even waves. She needed information about their association. Whispers were low, making it impossible to hear full sentences.

"—told you. Don't let her out of your sight." Mr. Correa's voice came in short, raspy tones. He ran his fingers through his thick, gray hair and licked his lips continually. Clearly, he was troubled. "I can't have scandal. It'll ruin me. It could send my son to prison."

"Hey, I'm a part time cop. You are asking too much."

"Sh…lower your voice."

"If you need a twenty-four-seven man, I can recommend someone." Baseball Cap was adamant. His voice had a nice deep tone. He looked spooky, but sure didn't sound spooky. He sounded reasonable as though he was trying to get from under the older man's influence. If she closed her eyes, she'd imagine him differently, someone who wanted to protect, not harm.

"Just remember your job with me is top priority, I'll pay you anything. Anything!"

"I nearly got caught once. It's hard…discreet and keep—"

"Did she see you?"

"Nah, not then. But I lost her…I think I may have frightened her."

"Well, she's falling all over dead bodies. That wasn't supposed to happen. And what about the pretty little Korean girl…she could be next."

They're taking about me! And Yulan, or is it Adie? She leaned closer to the conversation. Parting the long foliage a bit more, she took out her camera phone. Trying to get the best angle, Talia leaned in a bit too far and lost her balance. Her feet went out from under her and she fell across the potted palm, snapping fronds, legs and head sticking out the ends of the container. The fronds poked her in the nose and eyes as she struggled to climb out as she tried to locate her cell.

"Are you all right, young lady? Oh, my dear, is that you, Ms. Bonilla? What have you done to yourself?"

Mr. Correa pulled Talia from the potted plant.

"Oh, Mr. Correa. There you are." Talia was yanked from the dirt but not before her blouse was smeared with it. Baseball Cap was gone. Good, she could play dumb now. It seemed to be the appropriate moment to do so.

"I came to return these papers when I fell over this thing here. Surprise! And here you are…I found you. Here are the contracts signed. Now where did they go? I just had them in my hand." Talia pulled bits of frond from her hair as she spit out dirt. She glanced about spotting the contracts on the polished floor along with her phone. "Ah, there they are, spread all over the floor right by my purse, how nice." Talia got down on her knees and pushed them all into one pile. She picked them up, jammed them back into the envelope, then held it out to him. "And here you go. Sorry they got so wrinkled."

She slid the cell into her pocket.

Then she glanced at an invisible watch on her wrist. "Well, looks like my lunch hour is nearly over. I cannot be late for my next class. You know what I-35 can be like. Got to run. Bye-bye." She turned about, abruptly heading toward the door.

"Talia? Talia?" Mr. Correa called. "I need a word with you, please. Up in my office?"

Hurrying out the front of the foyer, she headed for the row of glass doors that led onto the street. Would he call security to drag her back? Would he accuse her of stealing something, just to have her taken in the speedy, quick elevator up to his top office, and hold her prisoner with Misty as her guard, plying her with secret recipe lemonade as she bossed her about? Her imagination was running wild, and she was running right along with it, right out the door.

Whatever business the men had, it didn't translate well for her. Maybe it was the real reason she was given the prestigious account. Mr. Correa could really keep tabs on her there. Cameras were all over the place so she'd better watch her back.

Talia slid into her car and angrily aimed it toward the expressway. Streams of traffic ebbed and flowed about her as she headed north on the interstate. Glancing up at the skyline, she shuddered noticing the window washers busy at work at the top of the building. Empathetic terror struck her heart as she watched them dangling there so high above the solid rock cement building.

Fifteen minutes later, clouds split open. Rain arrived, dropping like nails on the windshield, spinning the heretofore invisible dirt into streams of grime. Needing wiper replacements, the old blades streaked the glass making the road harder to see. Talia pressed the fluid button but the container was empty. Finally, a heavy cloudburst rained down clearing it of muck. Turning the wipers on faster, she leaned over the steering column for a better view. It was a relentless downpour. She felt submerged in a sea of water.

By the time Talia reached the turn off for school, the rainstorm had ceased, leaving in its wake drowned lawns and flooded streets, which cars precariously waded through. It looked as though naughty little boys had gotten into a serious water fight with water thundercloud balloons.

Chapter Nineteen

Fall was passing, but it didn't go uncelebrated with Halloween and now Thanksgiving just around the corner. Currently, everyone was speculating about the missing debutantes. Tempers had cooled along with the weather. Even the newspapers admitted the police were being more cautious, that they couldn't afford to make another hasty arrest. Neighbors talked of a botched investigation, called for yet another change in the D.A. office. On the Internet, the theories were wild, revolting. On TV, the families continued to sob, totally distraught over their missing beloved daughters.

Only the police and the D.A.'s office noticed, marking time between missing debutantes. But like the weather, Adie had cooled. Something happened between her and Marco which she refused to discuss. With Marco's architectural business in full swing, thanks to his dad's influence, he had little time to deal with Adie's discontent. Happiest of all was Misty Trimmings for she had just been assigned as Marco's new personal secretary full time and she noticed everything.

Due to budget cuts, and low class loads, Talia worked part-time now at the university. Her primary focus became setting up the educational department for the Latino museum. Its home would be inside the three-story factory building. Working closely with the

Correa's design team, they decided to restore the outside of the building to its original color of deep crimson. Old windows were left, but replaced if they were broken or cracked. The oak wormwood floor was refurbished. The best decision made was to leave a few of the old machinery to add old world effect. A hundred years ago, the factory laborers had been Latino. The museum would be a testimony to this community who had contributed greatly to making the city the diverse Dallas/Fort Worth metropolis it had become.

An eye for restoration, Talia had both eyes on the aged, smaller empty pink sandstone building on the far end of the lot. Mr. Correa initially wanted to tear it down to make way for more parking, but Talia convinced him it could be put to better use. She made her second proposal, which remained top secret to the public, only to be announced at the fundraising kick-off dinner tonight. At the same time, plans for opening the Latino Museum in stages would be explained. This was stage one and it concerned the grand foyer with two main rooms. At least a dozen tables would be laid out with Latino foods, as music played. Five hundred invitations had been mailed a month earlier which included lawmakers and the governor. With so many guests, tents had been erected at the end of the breezeways to accommodate everyone.

The gala coincided with Yulan's twenty-sixth birthday. Unbeknown to both her and her cousin, Adie, Mr. Correa would announce plans for the Asian Museum ground-breaking to begin in three years, right after the completion of the Latino Museum. Talia couldn't wait to see the look on Yulan's face when she heard. This would be the best present she could ever give her dearest friend.

Talia shimmied into her designer dress and felt like someone new. Seeing herself in the mirror gussied up, she was totally happy. Maybe Vera Wang was going to her head, and she was determined to wow Luis tonight. She checked her hair, making sure most of it remained in the French knot. It was held in place with antique Mexican hairpins, hoping none of them popped out. What a shame to lose her mama's heirlooms.

It was time to decide on jewelry. With so many choices, thanks to Luis's generosity over the years, she picked the single strand of sterling Mexican pearls. It was the perfect touch on what she expected to be the perfect evening.

Luis arrived wearing a black tuxedo. "Boy, this thing is uncomfortable," he complained. "Whose idea was it anyway that tonight should be a formal affair?"

"Put that decision squarely on Mr. Correa's shoulders."

"I feel like I did when I went to the prom in high school." Luis kept buttoning and unbuttoning his jacket. "And equally as uncomfortable with the weight I'm regaining."

"I'm glad you are gaining. You should have worn one of your larger suits."

"Still packed."

"You are terribly handsome." Talia walked closer to Luis to kiss his cheek. "You do smell awfully good."

"And you not only smell wonderful, you're gorgeous." He tossed his hand over his heart. "All of Dallas can never compare to you. I'm so proud of you, Talia. You do my heart good."

"I like the sound of that. Does that mean your

checkup went well this afternoon?" Talia could hardly wait for his answer.

"All my heart valves are operating exactly as they should," he told her the good news. "How about we skip tonight and stay here, just us."

"I wish."

"Me, too. But it's your night. You have got to be there. And I wouldn't miss it for the world."

"There's always tomorrow night." She played with the string of pearls along her neckline.

"I love how you think."

Without another thought, she threw her arms about him. "This is a harbinger of miracles to come."

Stepping back, Talia wrapped her shawl around her shoulders and then took Luis's arm. He escorted her to the car, and they drove to the city under a gorgeous sky that belonged to them.

****

Mariachi music played throughout the building. The festivities were so crowded it seemed to Talia as if everyone in Dallas was gathered to celebrate and contribute to the coming Latino Museum. Steeped in rich culture, the Dallas citizens would soon be equally ecstatic to welcome the establishment of an Asian Museum.

Talia hoped Adie would arrive with Yulan soon. She kept glancing nervously at the door. Meanwhile, she watched the social gathering from the balcony above. Back inside her happiness bubble, she thought, *This is my museum and these are my people.* She happily sighed to herself, hugging her evening bag.

Dr. Hancock and June strolled past, deep in conversation after being introduced. Love was in the air. Amanda Pudding was no exception, looking quite adorable in her silk Indigo slack ensemble. Her hair was free flowing about her shoulders. Pitifully, she followed Marco around the room, while he played his finest role of man about town, talking to every unattached female in the room.

The older Correa mingled with the guests. A seasoned man of virtue and style, successful and confident, he moved easily through the crowd of dignitaries, celebrities, and friends. He was a handsome, distinguished silhouette. Then a shock of red blistered across the room as a firecracker. Misty Trimmings was in the room. She arrived alone wearing a scarlet-red dress. Misty's red stilettos slapped her heels as she stumbled about the room like a newborn foal. Her eyes worked the crowd. And plenty of eyes were on her, too.

Talia scanned the crowd noticing scores of society women, a veritable smorgasbord. She couldn't help but wonder if the abductor was in this room tonight. *Who is he anyway?* He had a name, a residence, friends, perhaps a wife and children. Was he one of the guests in this room tonight scoping out his next victim?

There was Luis. He searched faces for her. Hand held up, she waved, calling to him, "Here I am, Luis." But the crowd and music were too loud making it impossible to hear. She reached Luis just as Mr. Correa approached.

"There you are. I've been looking all over for you." Luis kissed her.

"Isn't this just a wonderful turnout? Newspapers from all over Texas and even a few from other states have sent reporters to cover this event," Talia noted.

"Amazing. It's an amazing night," Mr. Correa agreed, and then he addressed Luis. "So, Luis have you been a good patient?"

"I'm fine, sir. In fact, I just got a clean bill of health today. I'm still under doctor's care, and will be for several years, but suddenly, I've a lot to look forward to." He squeezed Talia's hand.

"Luis, that's the best news of the evening. I want you back in the D.A.'s office next election. That Monahan is all over the place with charges and no supporting evidence. He's wielding his authority in that office as if it's still the old West."

"This is Texas, after all. Right now, his style seems to fit in just fine with the political climate," Luis said.

"You know, as well as I do, that the last two cases he brought to the grand jury were both tossed. Talk around town says he's a hot head without any common sense. Before long, Denton County will want you back. Talia, forgive us men for talking politics. I hope you don't think I was ignoring you. And by the way, you look lovely."

"Thank you."

Misty sidled up with a plate of condiments. "Hi, ya'll," she greeted as she dipped a sliced celery stalk into salt.

Everyone cringed. Talia worried aloud, "That's an awful lot of salt, Misty."

"I love salt. It's my favorite spice."

"Although you seem to be the image of healthiness, cutting down on sodium may be a good idea for you," Luis suggested.

Misty crunched her pretzel next. "I balance it out with other things. Like water."

"Luis, did you know Talia's been negotiating with some of the curators at the Mexico galleries and has persuaded them to lend us some of their art for our exhibits for the opening?" Mr. Correa asked as he ignored Misty's smacking.

"Talia, you never said a word." Luis squeezed her.

"She wouldn't." Correa's cell phone rang. After briefly listening to the caller, he spoke, "Excuse me. I, I uh…must see to something." He briskly left.

"I'm thirsty. Where's the punch?" Misty needed to know. "It's time to balance my salt intake."

Talia pointed the way and Misty left. "Luis, where are Adie and Yulan? And what time is it anyway?"

"According to that large clock on the wall, it's about time for the announcement."

The delay made Talia increasingly anxious. The food was quickly disappearing, but Adie and Yulan hadn't arrived. At long last, Adie walked through the door, making her usual grand entrance by gliding into a room like a queen. Her gold gown resembled gold bullion and twirled. Talia didn't waste any time reaching her. "Thank goodness you're finally here. Where's Yulan?"

"Wow, what a great party," Adie blurted out happily. "What's it for anyway?"

"Adie, where's Yulan? I told you to get her here over an hour ago." Talia felt like shaking her.

"I tried but couldn't find her. She didn't answer her door. I figured she might be working late so I waited and waited, but she never showed up at her house. Then I tried her cell phone and no answer. I tried her land line but no answer. I even called the lab, but I was told by one of the nurses, it closed hours ago. Maybe Yulan is celebrating her birthday with friends after work."

"Tell me this isn't happening. Adie, I told you to tell her we were going out for a late supper to celebrate her birthday." Talia groaned. It looked like the surprise was going to be on her.

"Maybe we should stay here instead though, the food looks scrumptious. But tell someone to ditch that happy music. It pinches my ears." Adie covered her ears with her hands.

"Adie, when was the last time you spoke to Yulan? I tried calling her all day yesterday and today, but no answer."

Adie walked to the serving table. "Um, the last time I spoke to Yulan was Wednesday." She sampled a cracker with caviar. "Well at least the food is good. Who's your caterer?"

"Adie, focus. Think, where else could she be?"

"Do you like my diamond earrings?"

"Yes, they're lovely."

"Marco gave them to me." Adie primped her hair in the hand mirror she drew from her gold rhinestone-studded purse.

"Are things back on with you and Marco?"

Adie held up her hand. "Right now, we're on a break. Oh, let me show you what I bought for Yulan's birthday." From her purse, she retrieved a diamond and emerald bracelet. "Nothing's too good for my cousin."

"Oh my…that's the most beautiful bracelet I've ever seen. Yulan's going to love it. It's none of my business about Marco but—"

"You're right, Talia, it *is* none of your business." Adie snapped her purse closed. "It's time for me to mingle." Adie avoided Marco while flashing bright smiles. She even flirted with the Latino male brass band member during a break telling him how inspirational she found his horn blowing. And there was Marco with Amanda. Talia expected Adie would rediscover her jealousy, and put a stop to it, but she seemed to not care. *Odd.*

"I kept the secret from Yulan so well she didn't even show up for her surprise," Talia told Luis.

"You can tell her what a great success it was in the morning." Luis bit into his tamale.

One of the producers of the event motioned for them both to come on the stage. After being introduced, Talia and Mr. Correa would present the high points of the Latino Museum progress and then announce the plans of the future Asian Museum.

"I told the producer to cut out the part about Yulan's birthday." Talia nervously rubbed her hands together. "But I forgot to tell the caterer to ditch the cake."

Just then a chef walked out pushing a five-foot tall birthday cake on a silver cart. The band struck up a lively rendition of Happy Birthday as Adie rushed in front of the cake and blew out the candles. "Thank you all," she gushed.

Mr. Correa stood quietly composing himself and then stepped onto the stage. He spoke glowingly as he introduced Talia, Luis, and then his son, Marco. Speaking in her cultural language, a speaker from the Latino Women's Society served as their interpreter.

As the crowd thinned out an hour later, Luis suggested, "Let's get out of here."

Talia wrapped her shawl tightly around her shoulders and arms so no one would see her goose bumps. Whatever fate had for her she'd accept it. Paris, or no Paris. Luis, or no Luis, children, or no children. Right this very moment, she knew life was good to her, very good. *But where is Yulan?*

They drove slowly past Yulan's place checking for lights. The place was dark. Talia got out to ring the doorbell. She waited several minutes before returning to the car. It was nearly two in the morning by the time Luis took Talia home.

And then she remembered how it used to be. Every time she kissed him, every time he opened his arms, she melted into him. Those moments always felt like a miracle, where she was welcomed, perfectly at home. Talia grabbed him by the lapels on his jacket and kissed him. "I love you, Luis Arroyo." She tucked her head into him. "I don't want to live one moment without you."

"Wait, I seem to remember a little problem." He breathed into her ear.

"Oh? Like what?"

"France." Luis looked her in the eyes.

Talia opened her mouth and closed it again with thoughts whizzing inside of her head like fireflies. "Love is unconditional. I love you no matter what. Will you wait for me?"

Luis spread his arms around her. "I love you too, Talia, and I will wait for you. What you need to hear is I've learned to trust your opinion. What do you think? Is it worth giving me another try?"

Talia didn't answer right away. She tried to collect all her thoughts from the last few months and organize her words into what exactly she wanted to say. "I think our relationship has been rocky, and there has to be mutual respect. But if we're both willing to give it another try, I say let's go for it."

A willing grin spread over his face.

She closed the door behind her and set the alarm. From the front windows, she watched Luis's car pull from the curb and her throat tightened with emotion. Her first thought was to tell Yulan about her reconnection with Luis. But that was the problem; she didn't know where Yulan was. Talia checked her messages. None. She kicked off her shoes, then peeled herself from her gown before sliding into her jammies. Again, she dialed Yulan's home. Still no answer. Trying Yulan's cell phone, it went directly to voice mail. "Yulan, you were to go to dinner with Adie and me for your birthday, remember? Did you get a better offer? Call me. I'm way past worried." Somehow, she knew there would be no call back. Talia fell asleep from sheer exhaustion awakening only hours later after a terrible dream. Climbing out of bed, she picked up the alarm clock, and through sleepy eyes, saw it was only four. She shuffled about the house with her chenille bathrobe pulled about her and no slippers on her feet. She watered, then fed her orchids, did some wash, and cleaned her refrigerator. She always did housework when she had wild imaginations to spar with.

It was now seven in the morning, time to call Yulan to wish her a belated Happy Birthday. She knew Yulan slept late on Saturday when she wasn't at the hospital, but that was tough. If Yulan didn't have the courtesy to call her back, she deserved to be awakened. "This is getting very boring, listening to your phone ringing, and you not picking up!" Talia talked to Yulan's messages once more before pushing the off button. It was the tenth message left in the last twenty-four hours.

Talia dressed for her day in Dallas. She had been so concerned about Yulan, she nearly had forgotten the appointment to meet with the restorer to select the stain colors. But first, she stopped at Parkland Hospital and spoke with Yulan's coworkers. They hadn't seen her since Thursday mid-morning when she left to retrieve something from Adie's boyfriend. *Marco's? Did Yulan go to Marco's?*

Talia thanked them for their information and then tore back to her car. On the freeway, she called the restorer to tell him she was sick and wouldn't be in today. It wasn't a lie. She was terribly sick with worry. Talia punched in Adie's number on her cell. "Adie! I'm on my way over to pick you up. You're going to Yulan's with me. No one has seen or heard from her since Thursday. I have some questions for you."

"Can't this wait? I just started eating my breakfast. I still have to shower and change and do my makeup. Give me three hours, maybe four," she loudly yawned into the phone.

"Fix yourself a food plate, toss on a jacket, and meet me outside your house in fifteen minutes. We're going into Yulan's and I don't want to wait. This is urgent."

"But I don't have a key to her house," Adie protested with a whine.

"I have a key."

"You have a key to Yulan's? Why do you have a key and I don't?"

"This is about her, not you, Adie. Just be ready."

"Should I fix you a plate of toast and melon, too?"

"No, I'm not hungry."

True to her word, Adie stood at the entrance of her long winding driveway waiting with a paper plate in her hand piled with food. Adie slid in the car. She still wore her pajama bottoms with a white pullover top and a gray fleece, zipper sweat jacket as if it made up for the pants. Somehow it worked.

"Maybe she went on vacation." Adie bit into her toast.

"Without telling anyone? I don't think so, Adie. Time to be straight with me. I heard you asked Yulan to do a favor for you."

"Oh yeah, now I remember. I called my cousin and asked her to pick up some of my things from Marco's. I told her we went on break."

"Why didn't you go for your things yourself?"

"Are you kidding? I had a cold sore. There's no way anyone will see me like that. I even called in sick to the modeling agency. Happy for me, my Asian herbs made it go away in two days." Adie chewed her toast.

"Why did you and Marco go on break?"

Adie pressed her lips closed and gazed ahead at the traffic.

"Come on, Adie, this is important." Talia hit the steering wheel with the flat of her hand making the horn blast.

Adie jumped in her seat. "Oh all right. Marco and I got into an argument about shoes. I told him I didn't want to see him anymore."

"You argued over shoes?"

"That's right."

"Okay, you argued over shoes, and then you sent Yulan to his apartment to get something for you?"

“That’s also right.” Adie sucked on the juicy melon while nodding her head. “I had some things at his apartment that I wanted back like my new Blu-Ray, my cashmere throw, and pictures of my cousins who still live in Korea.”

“Did Yulan call you when she left the apartment?”

“Nope.” Adie seemed sure.

“Why didn’t you call her to see if she got your things?”

“I’m a busy girl. I didn’t need those things. I just didn’t want Marco to have them.”

“Adie! You put Yulan in between you and Marco for a few bucks, that you don’t even need, and tons of pride?”

“Stop yelling at me. I told you I didn’t want Marco to have my things.”

Angrily, Talia pulled out her cell phone and tried Yulan’s again. Still there was no answer. With so many messages, there was only a half a ring before the machine picked up and then it just beeped before cutting off completely.

It was an eerie feeling walking into Yulan’s home without her there to greet them. “Try these Asian treats I made for you,” Yulan would say. Her smile would be so broad that it caused her eyes to nearly disappear into her round cheeks. Talia would give a million bucks just to see that grin right now.

As usual, the place was neat as a pin. Nothing was out of place, even her bed was perfectly made. Her toothbrush was dry. Both sinks were dry. Her keys were gone, and so was her purse. Talia trembled. “Things don’t look good.”

The light on her answering machine flashed.

Listening to each one intently, the only messages on it were from Adie, the hospital, and herself. Talia pressed re-dial on the phone and it rang a few times then Marco's voice answered on his machine. She hung up. "So Marco was the last call she made."

"She called to make arrangements to get my things back for me."

"Do you know if she ever got to his place?"

"No, not really. I didn't talk to Marco last night to ask him."

"Why didn't you?"

"For the third time, we're on a break. He was always looking over his shoulder at other women and I got tired of it. I told him it was over, we were finished. Yulan went to get my things back. That's it."

"But you said the argument was over shoes." Talia was confused.

"Yes, we argued over the women who wore the shoes."

"Now we need to find your ex-boyfriend."

****

They drove toward Dallas. Talia used her cell phone trying to locate Marco. They found a downtown parking spot and walked two blocks to the Correa building. Talia pressed the elevator button vowing to take any one that opened first. Her anger outweighed acrophobia any day. In fact, it totally vanished. She could sit on top of the Empire State Building all day if it would bring Yulan home.

Within moments, they hit their fists on Marco Correa's office door. It opened. Marco welcomed them inside with a cheerful greeting, "Hey, ladies. Come on in. Sit down, can I get you something cool to drink? My dad's secretary is around here somewhere. She makes mean lemonade. Want some?"

"No thanks. This is not a social visit," Adie curtly said, trying to cover her pajama bottoms.

"What's up?" He crossed his arms over his chest and sat at the corner of his desk.

"Did Yulan drop by to pick up Adie's belongings?" Talia took out a notebook to take notes.

"She did. Adie left me a message at the office Thursday morning saying she'd be by to pick up her things around noon. Boy was I surprised to see Yulan instead." He laughed as though the joke were on him.

"What time did Yulan leave?"

"What time did she leave?" Marco repeated. "She barely arrived before she left. I deposited all of Adie's things to the backseat of her car."

"Did you watch Yulan drive off?" Talia asked.

"I really don't remember if I did or not. Why? Does it matter?"

"It might. Yulan didn't return to work that day and no one has seen her since." Talia found it nearly impossible to keep from bursting into tears.

"What are you saying?" Marco narrowed his eyes at her.

"Crystal Favela disappeared the day after she met you at the museum. Yulan disappeared the same day she goes to your apartment."

"Ladies, I don't appreciate your insinuations, and now it's time for me to get back to work." He got to his feet and held the door open for them. Talia was the first one through the door and as Adie walked out, Marco whistled. "Cute outfit."

Chapter Twenty

"Hi, I'm Talia Bonilla, may I please see Detective LaRue Jackson? It's an emergency." Talia insisted, standing in the foyer of the town's police department.

"As I told you, when you called on the phone, Miss Bonilla, she's out on a case. Another officer will have to take your information," the receptionist persisted.

"Then I'll wait for Detective Jackson." Talia stood her ground while looking around for a place to sit. There was no chair just a midsized room, obviously not meant for anyone to linger, just state their business and scoot.

"No, you can't wait. That's not how things are done. In order to file a missing person report, you need to speak to one of the officers on duty."

"Talia, you said yourself that time is wasting. Talk to someone!" It was the first time Adie raised her voice that day.

A buzzer sounded and the policewoman opened the door for them. The women were led down a long, narrow, gray corridor into a room with a table and chairs. They sat waiting.

"This is my first experience in a police station," Adie explained looking around.

"Mine, too." Talia felt cold.

"But, Talia, weren't you questioned when you found that body?"

"Yes, I was, but they questioned me at my house."

"It's sure different from T.V."

"Now you sound just like Yulan. Please stop talking, Adie. They could be filming us, or watching from another room." Talia glanced about the walls of the room looking for a camera.

"Who cares? We've got nothing to hide." Digging around in her pajama bottoms pocket, Adie found a gumball and popped it in her mouth. "Sorry not to offer you any, I only had one."

The door opened. A uniformed man with a crew cut walked in and took the seat directly across the table from them, close enough to touch. The hair raised at the back of her neck when she realized it was Baseball Cap without his headgear. Recognizing Talia, he began to act nervous. Talia turned this revelation over in her mind, willing herself to get control over her breathing in order to calm down and act nonchalant. In Talia's estimation, this crime seemed deeply rooted from Marco Correa—both of them—and into the Denton police department.

She raised her eyes to meet his and felt a jolt of electricity all the way down her spine. *So you are as surprised to see me, as I am you. I think I'll play your game.* Relieved her knees were under the table so he couldn't see them knocking together, her heart seemed to catch in her throat. It was as if she had been running a mile; it was hard to breathe. She swallowed but there was no moisture.

"Hello, I'm Talia Bonilla. This is my friend Adie Yu. We've come to file a missing person report." Talia could have been an actress and won an Oscar at that moment. She was playing a game with her part-time stalker whose daytime job was that of a cop. Adie played herself.

"Yes, Ma'am," he responded, sliding a report from his notebook across the table to her, keeping his eyes on hers. Talia kept her composure as she gave a description and the few facts she knew. No longer panicking, she swallowed hard, remembering everything she had to say. It was only when she handed Yulan's picture to him that she couldn't contain herself any longer and broke down in great sobs, shoulders heaving. Adie patted her back gently.

"I'll sleeve this right away."

"Please contact Detective Jackson on the field with this information. Tell her to call me. It's an emergency." Talia was adamant.

"I'll do that."

Talia dried her tears and then read his badge name. "Thank you, Officer Eddie Davila." Saying his name aloud, she realized he was the one who took the phone report about being followed. He also had been at the murder scene at her place; she thought she remembered Jackson saying his name. He seemed to be everywhere from the Jag, to her street, to the restaurant, outside Jupiter House, to the Correa building, even her yard. For the first time, she considered he might be the one who dumped the body in her yard.

After driving Adie home, she returned to her bungalow to wait alone. An hour later, she heard two car doors slam shut. Detectives Jackson and Chavez walked up to her door. Talia pushed open the screen. "I'm so thankful you're here! I've been trying to reach you. My friend Yulan Yu is missing. The last place she was known to go was to Marco Correa's apartment. It's just like Crystal Favela disappearing the day after she met Marco Correa. Someone in the police department is covering for them."

There was something in their manner that said they brought bad news to her door. Talia had to sit from fear and grabbed onto the chair's armrest.

"We've found Yulan's car," Jackson told her.

"You did? Where?" her voice crescendoed.

"In a ditch off Trinity Mills. Inside we found pictures, a Blu -Ray, a few other things. A squad car made the find and called us," Chavez said.

"And Yulan? Was she…" Talia gulped hard before she could begin again. "Was Yulan inside of the car?"

"No one was inside," Jackson said. "Her purse was on the passenger side floor. Inside was makeup, money, driver's license, credit cards."

"What about a tiara? Please tell me," Talia gasped. "If so, it makes the eighth tiara."

"The eighth Tiara? Then you already knew about that?"

Talia nodded at Chavez.

Jackson read her list of the purse's contents. "No whistle but there's mace in her purse."

"Marco Correa took her. I just know it. Arrest him. Make him tell you where she is!"

"Sure, we'll send him up the river. Just give me the name of a witness first. DNA would be helpful, too."

Realizing Jackson was humoring her, Talia answered, "Isn't that your job to get those things?"

The female detective answered quietly and with tenderness. "Look, Talia, I know you're hurting. I want to find Yulan, and the other sweet women whose families are equally as worried as you are. It takes evidence and unless you have something more for me I need to get back to work. Before I go, you mentioned something about someone in our department covering up evidence?"

"Yes. Did you know Officer Davila, in your police unit, has been following me for months? Mr. Correa might be paying him."

"Nonsense," Chavez defended.

"I guess moonlighting's really paying well these days." Talia pouted.

"Accusing a police officer isn't taken lightly."

"That man has been stalking me. Isn't that a crime?" Talia looked from face to face.

"Did you make a report of it?"

"As a matter of fact I did, but Officer Davila took the report himself. Rest assured you'll not find a record of my call."

Jackson turned on her heels and went to her car to look it up on her computer. Talia trailed right behind and waved at June, who was standing on her porch, to join them. She set aside her new binoculars and waited with Talia as the computer keys made quick snapping sounds under the weight and quickness of Jackson's long fingers. The information shot up on the screen. The detective smiled and leaned back in the seat. "Actually, the report is right here."

"Really? Let me see."

Jackson moved back for Talia to look. "At the time, you stated you didn't get the plate number of the vehicle that was following you."

"I didn't have it then, but I gave it to you the day I fell over the body. Remember?"

"Shreds. You gave to me shreds." Jackson rolled

her eyes. "Hello Miss Clover."

"Hello."

"It seems to me that something is amiss here with Mr. Correa, his son, and Officer Davila," Talia plainly said. "I even saw Mr. Correa speaking with Officer Davila. They spoke about me, Yulan, and Adie, I think."

"You think. What did they say?"

"I couldn't hear everything, so I am not sure."

"Eddie Davila is a police officer with an impeccable reputation," Jackson insisted.

"Then you don't know him very well. Just arrest Marco before someone else disappears. If you had done your job, Yulan wouldn't be…missing. Okay, listen, can't you follow the officer?" Talia was nearly accusatory in her approach.

"Whoa…slow down. Take a deep breath. I told you we've got everything under control, and I'm warning you, Talia Bonilla…" The detective remained in the vehicle and pointed her long, bony finger in Talia's face, "Don't even think about trying to play detective yourself."

"If the police can't solve this, then I will," she shot back.

Chavez got into the police car and slammed the door. Jackson leaned out the window and said, "Let us do our job." And with that they drove down the street. Talia wasn't sorry to see them go.

"What was that all about?"

"Yulan is missing."

"Oh no! What happened?" June drew back in horror.

"Follow me into the house, and I'll tell you." After

explaining what happened, Talia turned to the computer. She emailed princess*charming again as June hovered over her shoulder. Within minutes, an answer arrived

*Princess*charming—sorry about not getting back to you sooner. My computer crashed and I lost your email address. Yes, the tiara is definitely one of mine.*

Talia—were any of your shipments to Texas? If so, how many and to whom? This is important.

*Princess*chaming—Yes, I shipped a big order of twenty crowns there nearly ten months ago. It was a business address so I'll need to look it up, if you want it. But I will not give out the address. If you have an address in mind, I will confirm it if it's correct. Give me a day and I'll get back to you.*

Talia's cell rang. She pulled it from her pocket to answer. "June, there's a small problem at the museum with a newly arrived exhibit. I've got to go."

"I'm on duty right here if you need me," June assured her heading back to her porch.

****

Breezing into the museum, half a dozen men were chattering over the broken frame of the religious picture. "It's not as bad as I first thought. This can be fixed since it's wood. I'll find a framer."

Mr. Correa strode into the room brimming with smiles. "How nice to see you taking care of this problem so quickly, Talia."

She spun about to face him. "Tell me about Eddie Davila."

He blanched, stumbling backward. "So, you know. All right, but let's go into your office." He took her by the elbow and ushered her into the office.

First floor office, her name was on the door in black letters. They sat in the only two chairs in the small room.

"So you know about him?" Mr. Correa asked.

"He's hard to miss." Her voice became softer.

Mr. Correa let out a small laugh. "Yes, he is in that Jag he drives."

"Did you hire him to prowl around my house?" Talia felt resentful.

"Yes and no. He's not following you."

Talia sat back in her chair and crossed her arms. "You have to do better than that."

"He's following my son. Anytime my son was around you, so was Eddie."

"He's following your son? Why?" This was a new angle she hadn't ever considered.

"I hired Davila to follow my son and protect the women he dated," he spoke with force.

"Why do Marco's dates need protection?" The hairs on the back of her neck rose.

"You must have heard by now that the common denominator in all the disappearances is my son."

A chill ran over her arms. She had no idea, but quickly recouped to play along as though she had known. "Marco's ex-girlfriends either end up missing, or working in your office."

"Yes, that's a crass way to say that, but none-the-less true." He gave a short chuckle but not in the way a person would when they are happy, only reflective.

"Why protect me? I never dated Marco, and for that matter, neither did Yulan."

"But you're his friend. The police said Yulan was at Marco's apartment."

"The police have talked to you?" This was good news making her sigh with relief.

"Yes, I've been interviewed. You should know Officer Davila was tailing Marco when most of the kidnappings occurred. He has evidence Marco was nowhere near them at the time. He is innocent."

Talia's face fell. This meant Marco had a rock solid alibi for all the women. But perhaps Mr. Correa was being disingenuous. Paying Davila to create a falsified report was another possibility. "And you continue to keep tabs on Marco?"

"I hired the officer to investigate my son, and to protect you. He did watch over you so you can regard him as your guardian angel. As long as he was around, no one would harm you, Talia. I told him to let you know in some way that you had no need to fear."

"Ah, that must have been Davila who left the note on my front door about a guardian angel. I wish I had known this."

That anchovy pizza Marco brought now became highly suspicious. Had he been picking around inside her trash to learn things about her?

Mr. Correa looked to be a man in emotional turmoil. He wrung his hands, his hair was unkempt, and today he seemed older than his years. Feeling unexpected compassion, she hugged his neck. He hugged her back. Just then Luis walked through the door. "Okay, you two break it up," he teased.

"I think Talia and I've bonded. If I had a daughter, my dear, I would hope she'd be as wonderful as you." He smiled as his eyes filled with tears, then walked out, and closed the door quietly behind him.

"What a surprise to see you, Luis. Do we have a

dinner date I've forgotten about?" She hugged his neck. He handed her a folder.

"What's this?" She pulled it from his fingers.

"Autopsy reports on the dead girl found in your garden."

"Where did this come from?"

"Someone in my office delivered it to me…a favor." A cock-eyed smile slid up his face.

Talia realized the enormous chance Luis was taking in letting her see this. She flipped the file open and began to read. "I don't understand what its saying."

"Let me interpret. Traces of poison were found in Salas's tissues. This type of drug paralyzes the victim for several hours. It's usually slipped into a drink to immobilize the victim. There's a possibility this woman isn't related to the other missing women. Until we find another body, we won't know for sure."

"Please, don't talk as if they're all dead. I still have hope and it needs to be kept alive. They were slipped poison in their drinks because that way they wouldn't put up a struggle. That would make sense with Yulan. She's a fighter." She wiped the tears away with the back of her hand, trying to convince herself Yulan was still alive.

"Maybe. Tee, if the police had solid evidence, Marco, Junior, would already be behind bars. You should know that he's been questioned."

"That makes me feel better."

"I'm investigating the case on my own. It began right after my resignation when I went to Miami to talk to a detective working a similar case."

"I thought you were working for Mr. Correa?"

"That's temporary. Mainly checking out properties

he may be interested in acquiring. And I used it as a cover, but I was also investigating." Luis's cell beeped. He read the text message, then said, "I've got to go. See you tonight?"

"Yes." Talia handed the folder back. "Since we're now trading information, I have something you might be interested in."

He turned and looked at her.

"I have a lead on where those tiaras came from. You know the ones left behind during abduction jaunts?"

"How did you find out about that… Never mind, I don't want to know…just tell me," Luis said.

"As soon as it's confirmed, I'll tell you. I just have to be sure first."

She watched Luis leave. Sitting down behind her desk, she decided to scoot out of the place as soon as she found her purse. Talia was glad she hadn't severed her ties with the university. This gig wouldn't last much longer. Working for Mr. Correa became increasingly difficult with the possible implication of Marco.

As Talia reached the door, Adie breezed into the room. A retooled woman stood before her. Adie's hair was brushed flat against her head plus she wore little makeup and no jewelry, not even a pinky ring. For the first time ever, Adie wore faded jeans and a pull-over top. Of course, they were the latest fashion and designer labels, but it was a start. "Adie, is something wrong? Have you heard from Yulan?"

"No, I haven't heard from her. I'm not well. I've gone through half a day of soul searching during my Yoga class."

She looked positively worn out from it.

"Sit down and talk to me." Talia took a seat and patted the chair next to her.

"It's come to my awareness that, at times, I crave attention. Don't say anything to the contrary, it's true." She held up her hand in protest. "Some people might consider my taste for designer labels as materialistic. However, I want to change my false image and be a woman of substance so I've turned over a new leaf even though it's months till January first. My New Year's Resolution comes early this year. I have considered offering prayers in church."

Talia softened toward Adie.

"Yulan is bright and popular. But I'm not Yulan, and I can only be me. Some people say I have been self-absorbed all my life. Maybe they're right, but I really want to change now. I want to focus inward. And I want my life to mean more than wearing the latest Paris fashion. I want to be more like Yulan…not the overweight part with bad taste in clothes. Sorry. I also want to be a charitable person and not pretend I am one for my own convenience."

"Why the change now?"

"You must have observed Yulan is not as pretty as me, not as thin as me, has no style at all. Why are people so worried about her? And then it occurred to me there's much more to Yulan. She is kind, knows how to connect with others, and knows how to love them. She allows the sunshine of her happiness to shine right through her personality."

Talia reached for her hand.

"Let me finish, this is difficult for me. I'm here to fill that empty best friend spot in your life. Now that Yulan is not here, I figured I need a new cousin, and you could use a new best friend. Just for a little while until we find Yulan?" Adie pleaded.

Tears spilled again from Talia's eyes and this time her nose ran. She stood to her feet and took Adie into her arms, hugging her tight. "I think Yulan would love to think we are together looking for her and we won't ever give up."

Chapter Twenty-One

June's face looked through the kitchen window at Talia. "Let me in. I have something pretty to show you."

Talia opened the door and the woman danced into the room.

"How's Luis doing?" June asked.

"Great. He's healing well. Stronger each day."

Then June's left hand shot up in the air showing off the small sparkly ring on her third finger, left hand.

"You're engaged? Your ring is beautiful." Talia jumped up and down, clapping her hands. "I didn't even know you were dating. Who is he?"

"You nearly need a magnifying glass to see the diamond so it's a good thing I just ordered one from Penney's. The UPS man should be bringing it any day now."

"Tell me, who is the lucky guy?"

"Well." June wrung her hands. "He kept coming and coming and coming to my door."

"Who did?" Talia insisted on knowing.

"The UPS man! And he finally asked me out." June danced about. "We're getting married next summer."

"The UPS man?" Talia repeated. How quixotic she found love at her doorstep, and in her later years. Maybe this was a good omen for her as well. "I should have seen it coming."

"I want you to throw me a shower."

"I'd love to."

"We're getting married at sea on a cruise by the ship's captain. We'll then sail all over the Caribbean.

June plopped on a kitchen chair and propped her feet up on another. "I thought my life would never have romance in it again. I resigned myself to a life alone with Lulu. I went to church, sang in the choir, and substitute taught for all the card making classes for years. I expected nothing more. Now I feel windows of happiness have opened. Who would have thought at my age I would find love again?"

"I'm really happy for you." Talia leaned against the counter.

"Any news about our dear Yulan?" Her voice turned sad.

"No. We'll find her." Talia bit her lower lip.

"We'll never give up hope of finding our Yulan along with my favorite beauty pageant judge…oh, and those other women, too. Tell me, where are we on our case?"

"Let's make a list of suspects." Talia grabbed a pad of paper and a pencil then sat down beside June. "Who is our first suspect?"

"I know…the one we suspect the least."

"And who would that be?" Talia wanted to know.

"Luis Arroyo," June said surprising even herself.

"Oh come on…"

"Write it down, please." June pointed at the paper.

Talia wrote in large letters and in black ink everyone they suspected.

1. Name: Luis Arroyo

Connection: Business partner of Correa's.

Motive: unknown

2. Name: Marco Correa, Jr.

Connection: Dated all the women

Motive: Rejection? Basic dislike of women?

3. Name: Marco Correa, Senior

Connection: Knew all the women.

Motive: has them disposed of when they become trouble to preserve good name.

4. Name: Edwardo Davila (a/k/a Baseball Cap Man)

Connection: Hired by Correa, Senior to watch Correa, Junior and me

Motive: Get rid of unacceptable girls for Mr. Correa

Does fit FBI profile but he was hired after killings began.

5. Name: Adie Yu

Connection: none

Motive: none

June read over the notes. "You know the common denominator here is Marco."

Talia pulled out the picture of the tiara. "And here is the picture of the calling card I sent to you. Which reminds me, I need to check my email."

And there it was, her next response from princess*charming, she was thrilled.

*Princess*charming—Attached you'll see the scanned order. Since you seem so sincere and it wasn't delivered to a home address, I decided to give you the address. I sent the package to the Correa Building in Dallas, Texas. Marco Correa signed for it.*

The words made Talia jump in her seat. "There it

is…Marco!"

Talia quickly printed it and then email forwarded all their correspondence to Jackson and Cruz at the precinct. For good measure, she called and told Jackson to check her email.

Up to this moment, she assumed Marco exacted revenge on Yulan for discouraging Adie to date him. But somehow it didn't fit. She was only running an errand. Suddenly, Talia remembered Marco told her Adie had called saying she was coming for her things. Adie was a debutante. Was she the real intended victim, and Yulan just happened to walk into a trap designed for her cousin? If so, that meant Adie was still in danger. Fear leaped through her like lightning. Grabbing her cell, she tried Adie's number. No answer. "I'm getting pretty tired of this."

"Of what?" June asked.

"I need to talk to Adie Yu, Yulan's cousin, right away and I can't reach her. I'm getting a whopper of a headache." Talia reached inside the cupboard for medicine. Her hand struck against the edge of her acceptance to the Sorbonne. Pulling it out of the envelope, she read again. What an honor it was to be accepted. She smiled and ran her fingers over it. Then she tossed it in the garbage.

"Was that a smart move, Talia?"

"For me, it was. Now where should we look for the new Adie Yu?" Talia was fairly sure she would be able to locate the old Adie at Neiman Marcus or Dillard's Department Store, but no telling where this new repentant Adie Yu would be. She wasn't that well acquainted with *her* yet, the one who recently turned over a new leaf.

"Church? Let's see if Adie is at church, shall we?"

"Why don't I drive?" June offered.

As Talia suspected, Adie sat in the front row wrapped in her prayers, hair drawn back into a knot, a long shawl draped over her shoulders, looking quite saintly as if she was born to this role. Talia tip-toed down the center aisle and placed her hand on Adie's shoulder, causing her to jump.

"Oh, Talia, it's you." Her hand flew to her heart. "God and I are becoming better acquainted. It's time."

"I'm sure He's thrilled."

"I feel unworthy."

"You don't look unworthy. You look gorgeous." Talia tried to cheer her.

"Thank you. I want to hurt the person who took Yulan. I want to scratch out his eyes, and pull out his hair, and twist off his arms…and then tear him apart limb by limb." She sighed.

"Adie, I came to warn you about something."

"Warn me about what?"

"I made a list of suspects."

"Very good. I'd like to see that list. Maybe I can help."

"It occurred to me that only one victim didn't fit the mold. Yulan. She never dated Marco but you and the other girls did. She wasn't a debutante, but you were. The only part that doesn't fit is you're Asian."

"You know that's right. I never thought of that," Adie answered with surprise.

"I think you were the intended target, not Yulan, when she went to pick up your belongings from Marco's. Your life might still be in danger."

Adie pitched forward and for a moment, Talia

thought she would be sick. It was too late to get back her words. Finally composing herself, Adie spoke, “If I had gone to Marco’s place instead of sending Yulan, it would’ve been me missing.”

“And we’d be looking just as hard for you,” Talia assured her.

“Really? But it seems my vanity saved me.”

Talia held onto Adie’s hand. “Now we have to figure how we’re going to keep you safe.”

A few minutes passed before Adie answered, “I can move in with you and you can hire me, keeping an eye on me 24/7.”

“Marco works there. Let’s keep thinking.”

“I can go to California and stay with relatives. How I’d hate to give up my receptionist job at the modeling agency, but I can always come back and get another job.”

“California is definitely a safer place for you right now,” Talia agreed.

“I need to go to my apartment and pack my things. Do you think it’s safe?”

“I’ll go with you.”

Adie pulled out her cell phone. “I’ll need to make a plane reservation. I should probably go first class since that would safer, right?”

Yes, a bit of the old Adie still lived and Talia loved her, too.

Chapter Twenty-Two

The stucco walls of the foyer were restored in a creamy mocha color.

A single canister of light from the ceiling enveloped the spot where Talia stood center as she labored over a display exhibit. Her jaw was set. Turning the detailed figure, this way and that she wondered if another smaller piece should be added to the same shelf. Stepping back for a better look, she treaded on someone's foot. With an apology in full bloom on her lips, she turned to see Adie.

"Hey! You're just in time. What do you think of this Latino dancer made of bronze? Isn't she superb? Now my question is this, is she lovely enough to occupy this space alone, or should I place a less important piece on the same level, but further back? Hey…wait…why are you here and not in California? Adie, what's wrong?"

"It's all over the news. Marco Correa was arrested early this morning. The police had a search warrant and found something at his place." Her voice was high-pitched, frenzied. She ran her fingers nervously through her hair.

Suddenly, the form she had been so concerned with lost its appeal. She didn't care if it suddenly fell to the floor, shattering into a million pieces. "Which Marco was arrested?"

"My son." Mr. Correa stepped from the shadows into the spotlight of the statue.

Talia faced him. "If you are waiting for me to say I am sorry, I'm afraid I can't."

"I trusted you. Put you in charge of this museum. All the while, you worked tirelessly on having my son arrested." A mixture of anger and hurt bubbled at the surface.

"And you worked tirelessly at proving his innocence. Surely, you cannot blame me for his arrest?"

He remained silently cold.

"Maybe this is a good time for me to resign due to a conflict of interest."

"I accept your resignation."

****

Once her life had been as falling dominoes; now her life was falling into place. Sam Brimley had been exonerated along with Luis's reputation. Luis's health was holding. Since he no longer scouted properties for the Correa Foundation, Luis became an active member in the ban fracking movement and comfortably lived in the condo. Neither of them discussed their future, but together, Luis and she had weathered the F5 tornado of events. The big dark spot in her life was Yulan and the other women. *Will I ever be the same*, she wondered constantly. Crime changed people. It certainly changed her.

On the first cold night of the season, Talia braided her hair and wore faded jeans with a button-down blouse. She wrapped a sweater about her shoulders. About her neck, she placed her steam punk key necklace, and as always, she wore her fair bracelet with the cage door that opened and closed. Since Luis had a last minute business conference, they decided to meet in front of the Big Tex on the fairway. It was the last weekend of the Texas State Fair and maybe it was time to ride a roller coaster. Certainly, there was one for children she could try.

While searching for the car keys, she noticed her dry hands from gardening. While applying lotion, the cell in her purse rang. Before she could answer, it fell and bounced once on the floor. Checking for damage, Talia noticed the new small crack on the side. Hopefully, it'd still work. She pressed talk.

"Hello?" *Please work,* she rattled it as static sizzled but it couldn't mask the unmistakable deep voice of her Luis.

"Hello, my darling, I'm ru…ing a b…late with …ore contracts at…Correa Build…"

"What are you doing with contracts for him? I thought your business with him was over?" Talia was livid. She wanted nothing more to do with this family.

"You're break…up. Mr. Correa ask…you…meet …here…have a drink…before the fair."

Maddening, the phone was cutting out on her. "Are you sure, Luis? With all we've been through? Yulan and seven other women are still missing because of his son."

"Please?"

"I don't know." Talia never blamed Mr. Correa for wanting her resignation. The man loved his son and nothing was stronger than the bond of family. It was impenetrable. Shoving aside all concern, she decided to please Luis and agreed to meet him there.

"Okay. I'm on my way as soon as I find my keys." Talia pushed the cell phone quickly back into her purse.

On her way out the front door, the heater turned on making a rattling noise. Having set it to automatically kick in when it dropped to sixty degrees, the noise was unsettling. She wanted to turn it off altogether but dreaded coming home to a chilled house. What a noise it kept making. It sounded as if metal on metal was hitting in the vent. Maybe it was something simple like a loose cover.

Getting a screwdriver, she pushed a chair to the wall where she stood to unscrew the bolts holding the plate in place. With a flashlight, she peered around. There was something dangling inside from a small nail that butted out from the wall causing the noise.

What is that? Reaching in, she pulled out a very dirty timepiece covered in dust. Wiping off the dirt it looked familiar. Ah, Luis's lost wristwatch. She laughed. *How did it get in there? The day of the house alarm was put in?*

That's when she saw something troubling. A small motion camera was attached to the inside of the vent. Examining it, she saw it covered the view of the front door as well as the entire room. Printed on the front was written Sony. That didn't come from the alarm company for all their equipment had their own name on it. Then she knew. Luis. He must have put this in himself the day the security people were in her house.

How dare he spy on me! With the evidence in her purse, she planned to confront him with it. How stupid she had been thinking he had changed. *Enough.* She had enough of his controlling nature and would tell him so, the minute they got a chance to speak alone. Something within her tipped and cracked.

The sun was fading fast. Traffic geared up, heading

north as she headed south. Headlights streamed past in the opposite direction. An occasional sprinkle of rain splattered her windshield making her turn on her wipers for only a moment at a time. On and off. On and off. Some streaking occurred so she pushed her windshield fluid button to clean it.

Talia glanced into the rearview mirror as she turned onto I-35, still not completely out of the habit of checking for disaster, or her guardian. All ghosts vanished when Marco was charged and jailed. How nice to listen to the news and hear everyday information. But the case would never go away for her, not until Yulan, and the other women, came back home.

Pressing the knob of the radio, she felt transported back in time, "This just in…another socialite has gone missing. Amanda Pudding of Denton was last seen two days ago as she left for classes."

"Impossible," Talia angrily screamed. The tires of her car slid over the dividing white lines, nearly side swiping the car next to her. He responded to her error with a loud horn and flashing headlights. Talia glanced down at her speed and began frantically checking her mirrors. As a greeting, bright lights flashed behind her as a familiar engine roar filled her ears. It was the Jag. He was back in her rearview mirror. Edwardo Davila was following along, riding shotgun as her angel. He must have heard too. *Bless you Edwardo.*

Obviously more aggressive this time around, he was cocky and showy; revving his engine, talking smack. So unlike him. Puzzled by the change in demeanor, Talia slowed her car and rolled down her window. The Jaguar pulled up beside her and rolled down his. The face in the window made her jump. She accidentally hit her horn and the car veered toward the shoulder spinning her right tires off the edge of the road, shooting debris up into the air.

It wasn't Eddie's face that she saw. It was Marco's. He saluted her then rolled back up his window. She rolled up hers. Panic settled in her bones as raw cold. She nudged the car to the middle of her lane again.

Marco leaned on the horn and yelled something at her. Her heart raced so fast, she couldn't catch her breath. Her stomach lurched and bile stung her throat.

Why isn't he still in jail? Have you come for me now? Well, you won't get me. Where was her cell phone? Grabbing her purse with one hand, she steered with the other looking back and forth from the road to the purse. Finding the cell, she pushed 911.

"911 emergency. How can I help you?"

"I'm on interstate 635 East, no west, no east heading toward Fair Park and a car is following me." She had no idea if he had escaped from jail or if his lawyer did some last minute finagling but the words *escaped convict* sounded right.

"Ma'am, you…break…up. I can…nderstand…ou."

"Someone is following me on the interstate."

"I'm sure…of night…rush hour many cars… appear to be following you."

"Yes, that might be true but only *this* one has an *escapee* in it."

"Yes…location?"

"I told you I'm on the expressway. Do you know Detective LaRue Jackson? Plug me into her." The white line weaved and wavered.

"Plug…in to you? I am sorry ma'am…impossible. Where…you live, Mayberry…in the 50s?" Crackle.

Then dead silence.

"Dallas…hello, hello?" Losing the number, she dialed 911 again. "Please phone, get well." She rattled it in front of her, hoping for it to work again.

This time a man came on the line. "911 emergency …I…you."

Her eyes flitted between the rearview mirror and the road ahead. Marco pulled up next to her again, signaling for her to pull over.

"How can I help you?" the man repeated on the phone. "Ma'am…help you?"

"Sorry, I was preoccupied looking at Amanda Pudding's captor. I'm in Dallas on I-35 East heading toward Dallas. I need help." She watched as the car beside her rolled his window down.

"Who…"

"Marco Correa in the sea-mist green Jaguar. It's a new color. Right there. I'll take a picture of it with my camera phone. Hang on."

As she held up the phone, Marco waved. She waved back. Just as she snapped his picture, he stuck his tongue out. "Now how do I send this?" Her heart hammered her ribs.

"I don't understand. I…exact lo…tion," the operator said.

"If I give you my exact location, I will not be there anymore. My exact location is in flux. How about my destiny? I'm heading toward the Correa building."

Her phone starts to crackle loudly as she hurried to get the words in. "Call LaRue Jackson at the Lewisville Police Department and tell her…"

The phone died.

Pulling off the expressway at her exit, it was

difficult to find a parking spot. Weaving in and out of the few streets that were still accessible to traffic, she finally found a parking lot that was well lit. She parked. Glancing about Marco was nowhere in sight. What a relief. As she hurried toward the Correa building, she viewed it as a beacon of safety with its large towering antenna and a red flashing light on the apex.

Fear had shifted inside of her putting her on a teeter totter of emotional unstableness. One wrong move and she'd go over the edge of rationality.

Mexican music filled the air with joy as blissful people of all races mingled together in merriment. Suddenly, Talia saw Marco at the same time he saw her. Pressing toward her through the crowd in the lit streets, she quickly turned and headed in the opposite direction from where she needed to go.

"Help me, help me," she screamed into approaching faces, but with all the music and commotion from the fair, they couldn't hear her individual words and would either turn away, or smile and vigorously shake her hand in greeting.

Looking up again at the antenna of the building, she plowed her way through the crowd in that direction. Pushing through the double glass doors of Correa Enterprises, she found the lobby empty, not even a watchwoman in attendance. It made an eerie contrast between the entrance and the street.

Pounding on all the ten elevator buttons with her fists, only the elevator that was exclusively for Correa Designs floor shot opened—The Rocket. It waited for her. How she hated it. However, it was the only one unlocked and good to go. Marco charged into the building. He sprinted across the pink Italian marble floor right at her. Talia panicked.

"Wait, I need to talk to you, Talia," he shouted.

"Get away from me." Without further hesitation, she leaped inside the rocket and the doors slid tightly closed just as Marco reached them. Straight into the sky it shot causing her to lose her balance, landing on the floor. She felt woozy. After reaching the top floor, Talia kept one foot in the doorway, as she reached her arm out to grab a rolling office chair. Then she slid it into the doorway to keep Marco from summoning it.

"Luis," she screamed, sprinting down the corridor into the private office of Marco Correa, Senior. Flinging open the door, she saw Mr. Correa and Luis lying on the floor with empty glasses beside them.

"Luis?" Talia dropped to her knees. "What happened?" She felt something wet and sticky on the carpet. She smelled her fingertips. They smelled like…lemons? Talia checked Luis and Mr. Correa and breathed a sigh of relief that they were both still breathing. She tried her cell again. This time, it stayed alive long enough to put in an emergency call. The medics were on their way.

Luis groaned, then tried to move. His eyes blinked open. He looked at her without expression. His mouth opened as though he were trying to speak. Words finally came. "Tee, Marco, not it's…" His eyes closed. He stopped moving.

Talia cradled Luis in her arms and then remembered the emergency personnel had no way of reaching the floor. "Oh no! I've blocked the only working elevator from going back down to the lobby."

Do I dare take a leap of faith to release the elevator? She rubbed her forehead. Jumping onto her feet, she ran out of the private office and back into the reception area. The rolling chair was still lodged between the two doors. Pulling the chair out of the way, she quickly sprinted back. There was a lock on the office door and she used it. That would keep them safe until help arrived. Turning, she saw Misty standing over the two men. She held the eight-inch ice pick in her hand.

"Misty?" Talia wondered if she should be afraid or relieved.

"Oh, Talia, you scared me," Misty spoke with relief.

"What happened here?" Talia breathed a bit easier.

"I have no idea. I served everyone my lemonade and then went down to my office to work. I just got back here."

"From the nineteenth floor?"

"Yes."

"How did you get up here?" Talia asked as prickles of fear spiked at the back of her neck.

"The elevator, why?" She squeezed the ice pick in her right hand.

"That's impossible. Only one elevator is in use tonight..."

"That's right. I came on The Rocket." Misty walked toward Talia.

"You couldn't have. I had it blocked by a chair." Talia backed up until she hit the wall. "Misty, what have you done?"

She dropped her chin and then looked back up, tears streamed down her face. "Everything would've been perfectly fine if Mr. Correa hadn't told me I'd be working out of the secretary's pool from now on. I told him I was Marco's secretary but he told me I wasn't needed any longer in that role. Then he asked me to mix up some lemonade. I hadn't planned on hurting anyone ever again. It just happened. I was squeezing away at the lemons when I saw the knockout drug I used on those other girls to keep them away from Marco. I was just so mad I couldn't stand it any longer."

"It was you, all along. Misty, you've got to tell me where the women are," Talia begged.

"Locked away, safe and sound. I didn't hurt them, honest," she answered in a contrite manner.

Panicked, Talia inched toward the door as Misty prattled on and on.

"None of those women were good enough for Marco. Without them, I knew he'd come back to me. He already has two times before, did you know that? Three's a charm. But I got tired of waiting. At least if Marco was in jail, his opportunities to meet women would drastically be reduced, so I left the drug in his house. I did it to protect him, to protect us, and our love."

"A knockout drug is what you used on Mr. Correa and Luis?"

Misty nodded her head up and down like a yoyo. "But there wasn't that much left. They should be stirring any moment."

"Is Marco in on this with you?" Talia wanted to keep her talking until help arrived.

She looked irritated. "Of course not."

Talia tightened her look on Misty, suddenly too afraid to move even a fingertip. Maybe if she stayed perfectly still, Misty might use the chance to leave. "But the tiaras that were delivered to the Correa

Building were signed for by Marco."

"I ordered them. When they arrived, I pretended to be busy so he signed for them. Marco never knew, or even suspected, what I was up to. I mean, who would even suspect something like this?" she spoke hesitantly. "Not even the police."

"You said they will be stirring soon. Are you sure?"

"They'll be back to normal soon but my, what a headache they'll have. Only now, I better act fast and get rid of all of you." Misty became increasingly agitated and moved erratically about the room.

"Why did you kill Maria Salas?" Talia bit her lip doing her best not to breakdown.

"Maria only has herself to blame. She was greedy and had to have two glasses of my lemonade with the knockout drug when all the others were satisfied with just the one. But I can't be too hard on her, it was a very hot day." Misty's knuckles turned white from making a fist over the ice pick. "You're a very smart woman so you know what I must do."

Talia nodded, and then whispered, "Let's talk first…okay?"

"Okay."

"Why did you drop Maria Salas in my garden? I didn't even know you, or Marco."

"But I knew of you. So did Marco. He made a date to meet some woman at a Denton pizza place, but she never showed. He was just finishing his lunch when Luis arrived and sat facing away from him. You arrived a few minutes later and he overheard your conversation. He already knew Luis, so that was the easy part. Then he learned your first name. Marco said you were so sad that day. 'So lovely. So beautiful'," she mimicked. "He texted me your first name and told me to do a search on Luis Arroyo to find out your last name and address. I knew, just like the others, it was only a matter of time until he contacted you. I dumped Maria in your yard hoping it would scare you so much that you wouldn't talk to strangers—like Marco. Up to that point, I had no idea what to do with her body."

"Since Marco showed interest, why didn't you harm me?"

"I was waiting for my chance and now I have it. Just as Misty lunged for her, Talia sprang toward the lock on the door, twisted it open, and scrambled toward the elevator, but as she suspected, it was long gone. Now she hammered at the button. There wasn't enough time to wait. Talia turned in the opposite direction and raced down the hall, stopping intermittently along the way, trying each of the private office doors. *Locked.* Not one knob turned in her hand.

There was a fire alarm Talia managed to shatter with the heel of her shoe, sending a loud siren into the air. Finally, the last door she tried, opened, and Talia ran through. She faced steps. The steps led up. They led up to the roof. Up to where the antenna beckoned as a place of safety earlier. With no choice but to move forward, Talia started running up.

Chapter Twenty-Three

Flinging open the door at the top of the steps, Talia was assaulted by the full view of the city. Lighted buildings bloomed from the cement below. It was frightening and beautiful all at the same time. The night was colored in slate with pinprick chalk splatter marks of white stars. They sparkled in the heavens as if there were no jealousy among the constellations. Faint sounds of the Texas State Fair wafted up, so far above the fray of the city. The night was absent of the sounds of sirens which was disconcerting. Help wasn't close.

With no time left to waste, Talia desperately searched for something to jack the door closed with but the rooftop was clean of debris. Talia hopped up on the small podium and hid behind the antenna apex.

Suddenly, the roof door flung open, hitting against the wall, and bouncing back, closed again. Expecting to see the five-foot blonde, she was shocked to see Marco. She tucked her head.

"I see you, Miss Talia Bonilla," hollered Marco laughingly. "You can't hide from me. No one is here to protect you, but I certainly won't hurt you, promise."

When she didn't answer, he swaggered in her direction. "Sweet, sweet Talia, don't you know I'll never hurt you? Think about it. All those times alone and nothing bad happened. I may be a liar…okay, I am a liar, but certainly, not a criminal. Think about it. Let's go back down and get help for Luis and my dad."

As Talia got to her feet, she made the mistake of looking over the edge. She froze. Way below car lights appeared as fireflies in the grass. If she took a step, she was certain that part of the building would crumble. The wind was blowing hard. Her throat was dry. She grabbed the antenna and closed her eyes. "No, I can't."

"Talia, come on."

"Can't, I said. I'm too afraid to move." She began weeping.

"Ah, that's right you told me that first day we met that you had acrophobia. And look at you now."

"Yeah, look at me now." Her stomach churned.

"Let me take you downstairs. Don't you want to see your Luis?" He held out his hand.

"Where's Misty? How did you get past her anyway?" Talia opened an eye. No way she trusted Marco.

"Misty? I didn't see Misty anywhere." He sounded sincere.

"Why were you chasing me down the Interstate?" She focused on her feet.

"Chasing? That wasn't chasing. That was playing…having fun. My dad called to say you and Luis were meeting in his office. Thought I'd drop in for a surprise visit. Look, I didn't escape from jail. I was released. That alone should prove my innocence, right?" Now he stood inches away from her, offering his hand again.

Trust was still a huge issue, but she didn't feel there was a choice. She decided to take his hand. Without it, she may not be able to move again. She would know in a moment, or two, if he was sincere.

The only problem was he might kill her, fling her over the side, and say she jumped. But staying here wasn't good either. Maybe she would trust him tonight. One time. Wary, she answered, "Okay, let's go back down."

Talia trained her eyes on Marco. Inching along, Marco encouraged her, holding his arms out. "Come on."

When her feet hit the rooftop, she threw her arms around Marco and held him tightly due to acrophobia. Marco wrapped his arms around her. The door swung open and slammed shut again.

"I knew it! You do love Marco. Nothing showed on the camera I left inside that vent at your house. But now I see you two together with my own eyes. Get away from him." Misty let out one hard, sharp, terrifying bark of a laugh while holding the ice pick in a stabbing position.

"We're not together." Marco released Talia and then shoved her away from him.

"Talia, stay away from my boyfriend," Misty screamed while holding the ice pick in an aggressive pose. Talia slowly stepped further away.

"No, back toward the edge." She directed.

"I-I just cannot. I am too scared," Talia whimpered. "Please Misty."

Misty pulled her by the hair to the edge. "Stay."

Talia braced herself because she knew a few more steps, or a good shove, would put her off the side of the building. Misty walked toward Marco, but suddenly turned about, displaying a devilish smile.

"Bye, bye." Misty gave Talia a slight push. After uncontrolled stumbling, Talia felt herself slide over the edge. Frantically, she grabbed for anything, certain she was plunging to her death, until her feet landed on a twelve-inch ledge. Afraid to look down, she realized it had to be the trim Marco added, years ago. She pressed her face against the cold brick and tried to gouge her fingers into the small spaces between the mortar to keep in place. Flat against the building, there was hardly room left for a breath. She shut her eyes, trying not to be sick. The wind picked up. The only way she could remain steady was if she leaned inward on the toes of the shoes.

From the sounds coming from the rooftop, there was a scuffle. Words were shouted, but it was impossible to make out what was said. Silence followed. Resisting the urge to call out, she waited, not wanting Misty to know she hadn't yet fallen to her death. Then she heard metal on metal banging like that of a door. *Has Misty left*?

"Marco? Are you all right?" she screamed digging her fingertips further into the crumbling rough brick.

"Talia, it's so good to hear your voice. I feared you were dead. Where are you?"

"I'm down here, hanging onto the side of the building. Help me."

She heard him dragging himself toward the edge. The touch of his fingers on her hair help calm her.

"I am right here. Listen to me. Be brave."

"We will both be brave."

"Things didn't go how I intended." His breath was labored.

"Marco, are you all right?" Her words were shallow.

"I'm hurt."

The roof door banged open and then shut. Heavy

footsteps crossed the roof. Talia imagined Misty had returned. Tears streamed down her face. Blood thundered in her ears as she did her best to keep from losing her balance. Her legs hurt. Pieces of the ledge were crumbling. Blood ran from her fingertips and made the brick slick. Panic again rose in her chest. Talia couldn't hold on any longer as her strength gave way. For a moment she considered just relaxing and allow herself to free fall.

"Where's Talia?"

"Luis! I'm down here. On a ledge." A surge of hope enveloped her. She looked up into Luis's face. He seemed to sway, or was she swaying. She felt so dizzy again.

"I'm not feeling well." He coughed hard.

"You've been poisoned. Please be careful."

Luis dropped to his knees and spread out on his belly. He reached for her. "Give me your arm. That's my girl. Hang on, sweetie. I have you." He grabbed her by both wrists.

He tugged and then stopped, breathing laboriously, making her teeter between hope and despair. Then she felt her feet lift in the air. Panic rose in her throat; fearing she would fall, she screamed.

"No, wait. Stop. I can't. I can't do this," Talia insisted.

"Sure you can, Tee. Honey, look at me. We are a team. We can do this together. But I can't bring you up alone. You have to help me."

"Okay." Her weeping became deeper. She released herself from holding onto the brick again and allowed Luis to take complete control. Her feet lifted from the ledge and her shoes fell off. As he pulled, he dragged her over the rough, jagged surface, causing her clothes to tear away and leaving her skin raw, bleeding, and exposed.

Finally, working together, she was back on the roof. They lay on their backs. Bile rose in her throat and flowed from between her lips. She shook as though having convulsions.

Above them, the sky rolled out like a deep black pool of ink, scattered with stars. They were razor sharp tonight, filling the sky with light. Tipping her head back she saw the sky, so huge and dark it could crush her.

Marco whispered, "Where's Misty?"

"Gone." Talia heard Marco's labored breathing. "I think the paramedics are here. I hear sirens below."

Luis pulled Talia to her feet and held her tightly.

"Luis, how are you feeling?" Talia worried.

"My body feels full of pin pricks. But otherwise I'm fine."

"Then you can appreciate how I feel," Marco said, looking down at the silver ice pick sticking out from his chest.

"Oh my gosh, Marco. I had no idea you had been stabbed." Talia sat next to him and held his hand until help arrived.

Within a half an hour, Talia walked between Luis on a stretcher and Marco on another one. She kissed Luis as they loaded him into an ambulance. Once the ambulance pulled out, she hurried to the emergency vehicle where they were working on Marcos.

"I have one question for you, Marco."

He opened his eyes and nodded.

"How come Misty never bothered Juana? How was Juana lucky enough to escape her clutches?"

He smiled wryly and then took a long breath. "I was at the restaurant the day you and Luis broke up. I thought to myself, 'that is the girl for me.' But how could I win your heart?" He stopped speaking to catch his breath, then continued, "Sob stories always get me the girl. Juana was only a way to meet you. I am the deliberate stranger…there never was a Juana."

Chapter Twenty-Four

Talia was taken to the hospital. Her injuries were tended and dressed. She didn't care for the paper clothes they gave her to wear, but there wasn't a choice in the matter since her clothes were shredded. Luis was put on a drip and quickly fell asleep. She waited through Marco's surgery. Once he was in recovery she took a taxi home. Bed never felt so good. Talia pulled the covers over her head. The evening's events from start to finish were so unsettling they made her toss about. It was no use trying to shut off her thoughts. The scare of falling to her death was beyond palatable. The fear of losing Luis was terrifying. The missing debutantes succumbing to Misty's recipe. Misty stabbing Marco, and then his confession about a fictious Juana. All of it was enough fright for a lifetime worth of sleepless nights.

It had been Misty all along, bumping off the women Marco might become, or was, involved with. Remembering the bevy of women working for the Correas, it was obvious she didn't care about the women before her, or there'd be a landfill the size of Austin. Those women were history by the time Misty came on the scene and of no real threat.

Jiggling her feet, which refused to be still, Talia wound her long thin legs around sheets and flipped onto her stomach. Wherever Yulan was, she counted on

Talia to find her. It was as though a movie reel played inside her head with images, sights, and sounds intermixed into a confusing hubbub of emotional traffic. There was the painting by Christina Alvarez at the Dallas Art Museum. She rubbed her eyelids wishing she could remember exactly how it looked. Talia untangled herself from the covers and reached for her iPad. Entering the information, she scrolled through the artist's work and found the painting. It was hard to look at it the first time, but even harder now because it took on new meaning.

Fearing she'd never get to sleep now, she got out of bed and walked into the kitchen. There in a sterile bottle was the single sleeping pill the doctor recommended she take as soon as she got home. Talia turned on the cold water and gazed out the sink window. She envisioned Alvarez's painting again, filled with anguished women's faces with deformed mouths, crying for help, while peering between metal bars of a cage. Pleadingly they reached out. Talia looked closer at every detail. The cage reminded her of the Ferris wheel at Lake Texoma. She ran back to the bedroom and grabbed the charm bracelet off the side table. She searched for a particular charm—spinning the cages on the Ferris wheel. "Oh my gosh!"

Talia quickly dressed and bolted from the house. That had to be it. If Misty were mimicking the painting, that's where the women were held. Marco loved the picture, and Misty loved Marco. In her own sick way, Misty was recreating the image to please him. Kiddie Land had long ago been shut down. Could it still be there tangled in weeds and ivy, or had it been bought out by a contractor who planted fifty cookie-cutter homes on the land? Needing to see for herself, Talia couldn't wait another moment.

Driving northeast at eighty miles an hour, she hoped a policeman would stop her so she'd have help. Not real thrilled to go traipsing into snake territory, especially with Misty running about with her glasses of lemonade, she called both Luis and Jackson leaving messages for them, not sure they went through due to the damage to her cell.

From the Interstate, she turned onto a secondary road, searching for signposts and billboards along the way. It had been twenty years since she was on this road with her mama. In the dark, everything looked the same. Finally, Talia found what might have been the old fair road. The weather-beaten sign was nearly covered with vines. She leaned out the car window and took a picture of it—*Welcome 2 Kiddie Land* on beautiful Lake Texoma. Digging out Detective's Jackson's card from her purse, she emailed it to her and Luis with the subject line of "*Help*." Back in the car, she drove further down the pot-marked road. Coming to a fork in the road, Talia sat for several minutes trying to decide which way to go. It was hard tapping into her childhood memory. Finally, she decided on the right, remembering someone once said parks were set-up to go clockwise. Traveling in and out of ruts at barely ten miles an hour, she drove through the gates, past the sign that said, *Stop Pay Here*. No one to take her money stood there to greet her on this trip.

For another hundred feet, she drove on, her ribs aching. The gravel cracked beneath the tires and the holes in the road rocked her car. Finally, Talia rolled off the edge of the road and onto the hard ground overgrown in tall grasses. It was hard telling if another car had been back here lately. It gave her the willies because there were so many places for reptiles and humans to hide.

Getting out, she grabbed the flashlight from the glove compartment. It served her nicely since the batteries were new. *Thanks, Luis.* The moon was full, but the trees left large sections of darkened areas making it impossible to see very far. An owl hooted overhead adding eeriness to the place. A smiling clown's face had dropped off a billboard inside the park landing perpendicularly on the ground. The wide red painted lips with teeth laughed at her. In the distance, the silenced, rusted, metal skeleton of the Ferris wheel had a few cages that still clung to it. It reminded her of an erector set.

Squeezing the flashlight harder, she walked on slowly, past the sign advertising for five-cent snow cones. About her feet, there were squeaks of small critters; imagining rat-like faces jumping out at her in the darkness she jumped up on a fallen log. *Which way should I go*? There was a noise. *What is that*? *Weeping*? She heard weeping.

Talia cupped her hands around her mouth. "Hello? Is someone there?"

"Yes! Help, help!"

"Where are you?"

"We're in here."

Talia glanced around. Her flashlight hit on a boarded-up building which had long ago given up its fight against the elements of neglect. A weathered sign remained hanging, Gift Shop & Café. She ran to the building, high leaping over the weeds and what might lie below. Talia pulled hard on the door as she wanted to shout out in pain. While the rest of the building looked ready to fall by a sneeze, this side seemed fortified. She pulled again on the door which wouldn't budge and began kicking it.

Those on the other side joined her in banging on the door and trying to open it.

"I'm not sure I can get you out. I can go for help," Talia screamed back.

"Yes, yes, get help. Hurry!"

"How many of you are there?"

"Seven."

"Amanda?"

"Yes?"

"It's me, Ms. Bonilla."

"Oh please help get me out of here."

"Yulan? Yulan," Talia screamed. No sooner had she gotten the name out of her mouth the second time than a whistle began to blow from the direction of the Ferris wheel.

"Yulan…Yulan," Talia screamed louder and louder. The whistle now came in short frantic spurts.

"I'll be right back. Help is on the way." Talia ran through the underbrush until she reached the lake. "Yulan? Where are you?"

"Up here…look up."

Talia shined her flashlight on the old iron Ferris wheel corroded by time and rust. There, in one of the cages was the most beautiful sight she ever hoped to see. "Yulan, I am so thankful you are alive."

"Me, too. Get me out of this thing will you?"

The Ferris wheel began to list toward the water. One of the vertical shafts was badly bent and those remaining had corroded too much to hold the weight. There might not be enough time left to go for help. It was now or never. Talia got to her feet and stepped through the rocky shallows where she ran her flashlight up the contraption.

Although it wasn't that big of a deal to ride, it definitely would be a big deal to climb. Reflectively, she rubbed the blouse covering her hospital bandages. Talia pulled the cell from her pocket to call again for help. But now her battery was totally dead. "I'll go for help. My car is right down the road. I won't be gone long."

"No, don't leave me. I'm afraid to move. This flimsy thing could crash into the water at any time. Besides some crazy woman wearing a tiara is here somewhere. Get me out of here now," Yulan ordered.

"How did you get up there anyway?"

"A cattle prod was applied to my rear, all the way up a ladder."

"A ladder?" Talia looked around hoping to use it. "I don't see it anywhere."

"It's got to be there. Look harder," Yulan implored.

The grass and weeds had grown so tall, it was nearly impossible to see anything. "Have you had anything to eat or drink?"

"Some stale, moldy sandwiches with just a bit of water this whole time. Hey, I think I finally lost some weight. Anyway, remember the saying don't drink the water? I have a new one, don't drink the lemonade! Who'd guess the kidnapper would turn out to be a woman handing out free samples of lemonade? I bet this is a new one for even Nancy Place."

"And you can tell her all about it as soon as I get

you out. I give up. I can't find the darn ladder. I am going to have to climb up to you."

"Be careful!"

Talia set her flashlight at the base of the ride with its light aimed up. It hardly did a thing in illumination, but she needed both hands to climb the metal. Grabbing onto the first vertical steel piece, she pulled herself up and bit back the sharp rib pain. Part of the challenge was choosing the right footing, not to slip, causing a nasty fall. It was a dicey combination of panic and bravery that propelled her to begin to scale the thirty-foot ride. Her hands were cold on the wet, slick steel. Her feet kept slipping. Her ankles were sore. Talia kept moving up, watching her hands, making sure she grabbed onto steel not air. She made sure each foot was planted safely on steel before she put her force of weight on it.

Talia's chest was tight, vision blurred, sick to her stomach, and so dizzy she wanted to release her hands and fall back. Praying she would land on her feather bed at home. Wishing this were nothing but a bad dream and she'd wake up to find none of this had happened and it was actually her wedding day. Her legs began to shake badly again, much as they had on the building, threatening to lose their control so she wrapped her arms about the cold steel. Her brain was frozen without thought, unable to think or reason. Instinct took over.

Spits of more rain began to fall from the sky, making her hands wet and slippery, fearing she'd soon lose her grip. One foot fell out from beneath her causing her to bang her chin and bite her tongue. Talia tasted blood. The wind rattled the metal cage sounding like it would break free at any moment. One side of the metal structure lifted from the ground a bit. Finally, Talia made it to the cage.

"Good to see you again. I'd invite you in but I don't have the key." Yulan smiled until her eyes nearly disappeared in her face.

"Key? Where is the key?" Talia asked frantically.

"The tiara lady keeps it on a chain around her neck."

Quickly, Talia examined the bars. Two were slightly bent. If she pulled them just a little more apart, she'd be able to free Yulan. Grabbing the bars, she pushed with all her might, putting her whole body into it. No matter how hard she worked the metal wouldn't budge. The Ferris wheel creaked, then tilted more toward the water. For a moment she considered climbing down but a noise from below caused Talia to look below. Misty, AKA tiara lady, leaned the ladder against the delicate frame of the ride and quickly started her climb. "Wow, but that woman is strong."

In panic, Talia began to scramble up, but the rungs were so far apart, she kept missing them and slipping. Suddenly, she felt Misty grab her foot. Talia kicked her hard in the mouth, making her scream in pain.

"Son of a bitch! You knocked out my front teeth! I am bleeding!" Misty wailed and started her decent downward. Talia pressed forward again, more determined than ever to reach Yulan, pushing aside her fear and her exhaustion. Daylight peeked over the trees.

The Ferris wheel began to rock and twist. Below, Misty worked at the base using what appeared to be a rod as leverage, doing her best to topple the ride. Just as Talia reached Yulan, the entire contraption swung wildly causing Talia to hit against the metal, which gave a bellowing groan of surrender before listing slowly into the lake. By now, the sun was entirely up. Talia felt thankful the metal hadn't pinned her underwater but saw the cage was submerged. She frantically worked to open the cage door, but the padlock was shut tightly. *Maybe the steampunk key would work.*

Breaking it off the chain, she pushed it into the lock and twisted it, while Yulan's face nearly turned blue with puffed-out cheeks. Her hair floated eerily about like Medusa's. The lock opened, the door swung wide. Yulan swam out. On shore, flashing lights of police cars greeted them. Rescuers were in the water in no time to help carry them to shore. An EMT wrapped them in blankets and walked them toward an awaiting ambulance. Jackson and Chavez sprinted up to Talia. "Lucky for you, I checked my email first thing this morning." Jackson smiled.

"The other women are in the gift shop at the back of the property." Talia pointed in the direction.

"We have them."

"Did you find Misty?"

"Yes. She's in the backseat of the squad."

Chapter Twenty-Five

Winter, two years later

Her shopping bag was wintertime silver.

Talia swung it back and forth as she walked the snowy streets. The bag held a secret that might reverberate like D-Day on the shores of Omaha Beach, and this time it would happen in Denton, Texas. Talia was on her way to share the news with her husband, Luis Arroyo, hoping he would take it well.

The wind was cold and sharp. She pulled the cashmere coat collar closer to her ears as she scanned the sky only to see the thickening white flakes cascading down. Poking its head above the low skyline was the condo, a surprise-wedding gift Luis bought for their first engagement. A couple of yuppies now lived there.

The Arroyos resided in the charming vintage house on Locust Street—the alternative wedding gift they decided on together. Marco Correa, Junior Company restored the place while they spent their honeymoon in Paris. Talia studied painting, and Luis took cooking lessons.

But now they were home. Talia waited at the corner for the crosswalk light to turn green.

A squad car rolled up.

"Talia!" Officer Davila waved. She energetically

returned his greeting by blowing him a kiss.

He tipped his police cap at her and then made a wide turn to the left. The squad disappeared behind the old courthouse.

"You know that hunky cop?" a college girl wearing a heavy university hoodie asked with great interest.

"Know him? I sure do." Talia smiled with tears stinging her eyes. Never would she forget the man who watched over her and kept her safe. "Once upon a time, he was my guardian angel."

Stepping into the warmth of the Mellow Mushroom Restaurant, Talia wondered when to break the D-Day news to Luis, before lunch, or after dessert?

Talia walked casually across the crowded room, biting her lip, as she moved through the clatter of plates and warm conversation.

Luis's mop of black hair was brushed back, but a few maverick curls tugged about the top of his ears. He wore baggy jeans with her favorite deep-gray shirt. Only a glass of water was in front of him. Another bookmarked her place at the table. Ever the gentleman, he had patiently awaited her arrival before ordering anything. She had no doubt he had watched the door for her arrival. His splendid russet eyes sparkled with health and energy. His smile was broad and genuine, showing even teeth.

She felt wired.

Luis pulled out the chair.

She sank down into it. Flipping open the linen napkin, Talia laid it carefully on her lap, then sipped at her water glass, avoiding his eyes. "Thank you, Luis."

Luis let out his breath slowly. His thick eyebrows arched. "What?"

Talia arched her brows.

"I know you. Something is up."

Just as Talia was about to answer, the waiter appeared.

"Hi, guys, I'm your server, Pedro," he greeted.

"What happened to Remi?" Talia asked.

"Rumor has it she fell in love, married, and moved away."

"Interesting, isn't it, Talia?"

Talia shrugged coquettishly. "I will have your raspberry iced tea."

"And I'm fine with this glass of water."

"I'll be back with your drink, and take your order."

Over his menu, Luis asked, "How are things moving along at the museum?"

"Too busy. Too fast paced. I think I'll take a bit of time off."

"Really?" He leaned forward with a look of surprise. "How long?"

"Perhaps, a few years."

"Really?" Luis set aside his menu. "That's so unlike you. After Paris, you couldn't wait to get back and implement all your ideas."

"And they are being implemented and shall continue to be. Work isn't everything, Luis."

"No, but you are everything to me."

"As you are to me." Talia smiled adoringly.

"You followed your dreams, and I followed you. Now, here I am pursuing my own dream of working for an environmental agency specializing in renewable energy."

"I have a feeling this start-up company is going to be popular."

"I believe so. It means everything to have you by my side."

"We are together in this."

"Supporting one another. Taking care of one another. Tee...something has changed. You have me worried."

"Luis, there is something I need to tell you."

"Tee, are you all right?" Worry sounded in his voice.

She breathed in deeply and opened her mouth, only the words weren't coming. Her thoughts were cluttered. So many emotions tumbled inside her stomach. Avoiding his dark eyes was impossible.

Luis reached across the table and took Talia's hands into his. The sparkle of the intertwined engagement and wedding rings caught his attention. Then he looked into her eyes. "I love you. Tell me."

"And I love you." She wiped away a tear. From her bag, she pulled a small box and set it on the table in front of him.

Luis timidly removed the white tissue paper, then the lid from the box. He froze.

"You see? I need you more than ever."

Tears framed his eyes. Stunned, a large smile crowned his face as he removed the pair of baby shoes.

"You see, Luis, our story ends well."

Giggling Talia pulled out the second box.

A word about the author...

Robin Jansen's published works include novels, collections of short stories, and articles. By day, she is involved in the education program at Denton County Juvenile Justice System. By moonlight, she writes desirous romance with a hard twist of mystery.

She has two beloved adult children and cherishes her two Wild Boys, who happen to be her grandsons. The author surrounds herself with beauty, gardens, attends estate sales, sells on etsy, reads, and loves reality TV, but not as much as she loves her three rescue dogs.

Thank you for purchasing
this publication of The Wild Rose Press, Inc.

If you enjoyed the story, we would appreciate your letting others know by leaving a review.

For other wonderful stories,
please visit our on-line bookstore at
www.thewildrosepress.com.

For questions or more information
contact us at
info@thewildrosepress.com.

The Wild Rose Press, Inc.
www.thewildrosepress.com

Stay current with The Wild Rose Press, Inc.

Like us on Facebook

https://www.facebook.com/TheWildRosePress

And Follow us on Twitter
https://twitter.com/WildRosePress

www.ingramcontent.com/pod-product-compliance
Lightning Source LLC
Chambersburg PA
CBHW070835280626
47161CB00015B/669
* 9 7 8 1 5 0 9 2 0 7 1 5 2 *